Air Attack

Air Attack

Claire Davon

Copyright © 2017 by Claire Davon
Print ISBN: 978-1-946621-07-8
Digital ISBN: 978-1-946621-06-1

Cover Design: Kanaxa
Editor: Jennifer Miller
Copy Editor: Kay Copeland
Formatting: Jacob Hammer

Publishing History
First Digital Publication / November, 2017
First Print Publication / November, 2017

Dedication

To the people who helped make the Elementals possible—Stacey Miller, John Foyt, Tim Tobish, Fulvia Tellone, Nancy Van Iderstine, and Kay Copeland, among others—thank you. Without you this series couldn't have happened. To my editor, who has believed in the Elementals since I pitched the concept to her at California Dreamin', thank you, Jennifer Miller! You shape the dream into reality.

A special thank you to all the readers who took a chance on a new series. There's more to come!

Chapter One

She was lying to him.

Griffin pulled the satellite phone receiver away from his ear and glanced at it, the space between his eyes creasing. There was a tinny voice in the distance as the person continued talking.

"Clea is on her way. You owe me," the woman said, her normally lilting soprano voice flat and unwavering. "You will take care of my dcera." Griffin heard the word daughter in Italian, although she spoke the word in the adopted Czech the pantheon now favored.

Stretching out his senses, Griffin verified that the woman was telling the truth, if only about her child. Outside was a sole humanoid form, her vehicle battling the strong winds and steep climb on the road to his secluded Iceland home. This must be the daughter Dodola Perperuna mentioned. The younger woman's rental car sputtered as wind and snow forced its way into the small engine. That the wind may have been aided by him, Griff kept to himself. He didn't like intruders.

"This is not a good time, Dodola," Griff remarked.

"On the contrary." Dodola's tone faltered as if she was not used to opposition. "It's perfect." She paused a moment and then continued in a lower tone. "I had to get her out of the pantheon immediately. You were the first person I thought of."

Griff tried to probe her mind, but Dodola's thoughts slid away from his quick attempt.

"Scusi, but why is the rain goddess sending one of her daughters to me?" His laugh came out harsh. "Did she insult Perun? Miss a step at the Dodole dance?

Develop more powers? Become prettier than you?"

There was a pause on the other end, and he felt in Dodola's mind again. Pain laced through her, but she shielded it too quickly for him to grasp the subtleties.

"None are prettier than I. You will do this," she said icily. "I do not think you would fly so well if it rained, would you? That is child's play for a rain goddess like myself. Don't provoke me. This is necessary. Griffin, I have always known you to be a man who fulfilled his promises."

There was an image of perpetual rain clouds hovering over him, pelting him with thick drops, soaking his wings. Griff flicked it away with the ease of long practice. "I'm not a man," Griff growled. "I'm an Elemental. Challenge is here. I can't have one of Dodola's daughters in the way."

The silence went on for so many beats he glanced at the satellite phone to make sure she hadn't disconnected the call. Griff's mouth turned down in a grimace of both annoyance and acceptance. He sent his answer to Dodola mentally.

"I always honor my debts."

"Děkuji. Thank you. She needs a safe place. Your home is one of the few places Perun won't think of looking." Dodola paused. "I doubt you will need to take care of her the way I took care of you after Challenge, but if need be, you will tend to her wounds, yes? It hasn't been so long since I and my servants saw to you."

Griffin grimaced as the reminder of his helplessness after his last-ditch attempt to strike at his foe had failed. He'd been wounded and the memory raced through his mind as if it had happened yesterday. Yes, he owed Dodola, but what was she saying about her husband, Perun? The ultimate leader of her pantheon and a fearsome thunder god. He was angry with whom? Dodola? Dodola's daughter? Mystery swirled around this seemingly simple request, fraught with layers. "I don't like it, but I will do this," he said. "You have my word."

Again there was silence. When he probed, he felt a smooth patch in Dodola's mind where she was keeping an important something from him.

"See to my daughter. Keep her safe. She needs your help."

"I will." He mentally reached for the small car again and withdrew his weather talent battering the vehicle.

"Miláček, děkuji. I will be in touch."

She hung up, leaving Griffin with a dead phone. Porca miseria! The last thing he needed was an unwanted houseguest. Challenge, that time when he and his fellow Elementals had to face off against their counterparts, the Demonos, was here. Each Elemental stood against their foe in their element; in this case, Griffin would be going up against the air Demonos. It was too soon, though. The last Challenge had been in the middle of the last century, in the event known to humans as World War II. The Elementals should have had several more decades, but there was no denying the stirring inside him that signaled another Challenge. The force, whatever it was, that pushed Elementals and Demonos toward Challenge had come again, and despite the too-few years, it was here. Griff had confirmed with Phoenix, the fire Elemental, that he felt the onset of battle, too. If the Elementals won, humans were safe. If the Demonos won, as they had in the middle of the 20th century, they would be allowed to rampage through the world, sowing death and destruction.

There could be no repeat of that last disaster. Last time one of the Elementals lost—the now deceased water Elemental—forcing all four Elementals into a final Challenge that they had also lost. The catastrophic outcome of that loss—World War II—could not happen again. The stakes were much too high.

Dodola had picked a hell of a time to saddle him with a goddess.

He reached for sweatpants to cover his naked body. His butter-yellow wings stood up halfway away from his body, although he sensed no imminent danger. He scanned out the pane glass windows, searching for the approaching person. Dodola hadn't told him her daughter's name or anything else about the presumed goddess, but it didn't matter. He owed the Slavic pantheon. As he waited, following her progress with his mind, the car sputtered and died. Despite his withdrawal, the weather he'd sent to play havoc with the vehicle had already done its work.

There was something else too, a weakness inside the woman as if she'd been struck. Dodola said that this daughter had been hurt, but what could hurt a goddess? He cursed himself for his stupidity at interfering with the car. Now she had to face the elements.

With a look at the dark grey sky and the snow drifting down, Griffin opened the sliding glass door to the outside and took to the air.

* * * * *

Light snow swirled around her and the wind howled, drowning out other sounds. Clea struggled up the mountain road. The small rental had been defeated by the Icelandic weather a half-mile away, leaving her stranded. Her powers were no good against this sort of manmade machinery, and her body pulsed with the ache of the aftermath of Perun's wrath. Her limbs were heavy, her body slow. She would heal, but not fast enough to face this task. She might have enough air to float off the ground and get to the Elemental's house if she weren't so tired. Her wind powers were solid, but this wind was so wild she didn't think she had the strength to direct it in her current condition. She wasn't properly dressed for the weather in her weakened state. As a goddess, she rarely felt temperatures, but right now everything was a trial. Cold wouldn't kill her. It wouldn't finish the job Perun had started, but it would make her uncomfortable.

She had had to leave immediately, before Perun found her again. That left little time to pack. The suggestion Clea had planted in her mother's mind to send Clea to Griffin had worked. Clea knew Griffin owed their pantheon a debt and had counted on her mental push to get Dodola to send her to the Elemental. She didn't know what it was that Griffin owed her mother, only that it was something that happened after the last Challenge. "You must go to the air Elemental," Dodola had said, to Clea's relief. Her mother told her Griffin would take her in, and Clea would be safe under his protection.

Despite her ice-cold fingers and cheeks, Clea's lips curved up at the memory. She would be a part of this Challenge, one way or the other. Antagonizing Perun had been simple, even if the outcome had been more than she expected. She thought he would flick a few thunderbolts her way and cool down, but his wrath had filled the sky. The thunder god had never liked her, but his enmity had been extreme. As a constant reminder that she was not his, Clea often bore the brunt of Perun's rages. It was one of the reasons she spent little time in the pantheon. That he had actually tried to kill her and might have succeeded if she hadn't nearly burned out her thunder defending herself was something she hadn't anticipated. Still, in a way, it made for a better cover story. She was a woman in danger, and Griffin would protect her.

Hopefully, he will do a better job with you than he did during World War II. Her mother's voice rang through Clea's mind.

The cold may not affect her like a human, but snow clung to her eyelashes and edges of her hair before it melted. The storm churned, touching her exposed face with its icy fingers. Wiping the eddying gusts away from her face, Clea eyed the house perched far away on a rock face, the steep road she'd been following ending at its driveway. Farther down the road were the multicolored smaller houses that made up the bulk of the town. This residence was removed from the rest, isolated and remote. It would be nothing for the winged Elemental to get in and out of the structure, but not so easy for the rest of the world. The road would be difficult for vehicles to navigate, if her little car's failure was any indication. It was a simple way to stop unwanted visitors, most of whom wouldn't be interested in trying.

Without warning, she was lifted from the ground. Hard hands circled her waist and pulled her against a large form. Clea bit off a shriek and kicked reflexively at the unknown person as the land fell away underneath her. She reached for her weakened air powers to create a gust to push the person away. Her nerves, frayed since her mad dash out of the Czech Republic, threatened to snap.

"Calmare," she heard mentally. The roar of the wind made normal speech impossible. "It's Griffin."

Currents of air swirled around them as his heavy wings beat against the storm. Trees and foliage blurred. As Clea relaxed, she had the impression of blond hair and strong features. His butter-yellow wings went in and out of focus as they flew toward the house on the rock face. For better or worse, she was momentarily safe in the wings of the air Elemental. Right where she wanted to be.

* * * * *

A wave of his hand made the door slide open, allowing the Elemental and his passenger access. They landed seconds later in the living room, Griffin touching down onto the hard wood surface. Releasing her, he pushed back, stepping away until he was out of her reach. He folded his arms and flipped his wings over his shoulders until the tips grazed the floor. Tilting his head to one side, his mid-back-length braid falling over his neck and body, Griffin's face settled into harsh lines.

His wings and hair were the same color, a butter yellow with darker yellow hues shading throughout. Clea's gaze slid away from his fiercely blue eyes. She'd heard rumors of how striking he was, how good looking, but those conversations had slid over her uncaring ears. Looks were irrelevant among the gods. A slight hawklike curve to his nose made his features more devastating for their irregularity. He was as handsome as the reports had indicated.

Meh. All gods were exquisite. He wasn't even a god. Model-perfect looks were the standard in pantheons and meant nothing. She had long ago dismissed looks when she chose a lover. Now was not the time to be looking at any man and measuring him for sex. She swayed on her feet as the weakness Perun had inflicted on her made the room tilt.

They had landed in a great room with furniture that smacked of an interior designer. A sleek modular sofa stood between the window and the fireplace on the other side of the room. A flat-screen TV graced the wall in front of the couch, with a computer to the side. Matching tables dotted the room with typical gallery-style framed art set for effect in strategic locations. There were no knick-knacks or mementos, nor any DVDs or CDs. There was a coffee table, in matching black, but all it held was a remote control, a smartphone, and a tablet.

The room was chilly, but Griffin showed no sign that the temperature affected him. Outside, the storm still blew, and snow fell past the large windowpanes. Weather may not bother her like it would a human, but she still felt the cold.

A tingle grew into a roar as a strong probe pressed against her shields. Griffin hadn't moved; his arms were still folded and his face impassive. She blocked his attempt, throwing up her usual well-tended shield, never taking her gaze off him. Her shield, like her body, was weaker than normal, but she could defend herself. He tried for a few minutes before his energy faded.

"My name is Clea." They were was the first words either had spoken out loud.

His brows drew together. He scanned her again but didn't delve deep. At the same time, he lowered his shield, letting her glimpse inside his mind.

Even if he hadn't let her feel his thoughts, she knew what he saw. A medium-tall woman with a lovely face and decent curves, but nothing a man like Griffin hadn't seen hundreds of times. She'd been told something similar often enough throughout the pantheons. She could have changed her looks, but it wouldn't have mattered. Her mother did not tolerate other women outshining her in the Slavic pantheon. By the time Clea had moved on to other parts of the world, keeping her looks the way they were had become a habit. Now it was a source of pride.

"Clea," he repeated. He examined her closer, picking out each feature to memorize before moving on. She stood still, trying not to fidget under his long perusal.

"You don't look like your mother. Dodola is blonde." He pointed to the shining auburn hair on her head. "Why aren't you?"

Clea resisted the urge to run her hand through the shoulder-length red strands and turned what she hoped was an amused glance at the Elemental. She would need to sit down soon.

"I'm a goddess, Griffin. Our looks are flexible. I don't take after the others in the pantheon." Let him make of that what he would. It wasn't hard to figure out she wasn't Perun's. If Griffin kept up on pantheon politics, he would already know that. Perun was a minor god, but still a god. She was not sure if an Elemental was a match for the thunder god. Griffin appeared big and powerful enough to be. It was possible, a hope that had sustained her the entire way to Iceland. A tendril of something long buried curled through her as he studied her. Clea recognized a pulse of desire, even as she dismissed the fleeting emotion. It had no place here.

He inclined his head as if accepting the point, but a lingering beat of curiosity crossed his face. "Now that we've made our introductions, Clea, daughter of Dodola, why did your mother send you here?"

She eyed his black leather sofa. "Can we sit? And get some heat? Not all of us have plumage." Her head spun, and she barely concealed the shaking of her body from Griffin.

Griffin's wing moved, jerking from behind his back and pointing to the couch. He gestured with his hand as well, a slow wave of his limb that showed his reluctance more clearly than words ever could have.

His wings were astonishing. The yellow feathers overlapped to form a continuous drape. They were supported by powerful sinews that ran up the middle until they disappeared into his shoulder blades. There was no mistaking their strength and power; any paranormal could see the danger in him.

With wings like that, moving among mortals would be difficult. Even though his wings couldn't be seen by humans, they carried weight and bulk.

Clea shook her head, fighting back the coil of desire that snaked through her body. He may be the air Elemental, charged with saving the world, but the Elementals had failed in their last Challenge. That battle had cost Clea much. Too much.

She sank into the sofa with a grateful sigh. Griffin took up residence on one of the sections, sprawling his legs wide. She gave him an amused smile, recognizing the aggressive masculine power play. He flipped his wings over the back of the couch and they draped on the floor. The feathers appeared soft to the touch, but the pointed ends reminded her that they could also be lethal.

He said nothing, but a sudden awareness brushing at her skull let her know he was trying to probe her mind again. He gazed at her, and she resisted the urge to flush, focusing on the high beams of his ceiling.

"Dodola told me you knew I was coming. She sent me." Clea shifted in her seat. She wanted to tilt her head back and rest but couldn't afford for him to see the weakness. Instead she inched closer to him but not close enough for their bodies to brush. That Clea had planted the suggestion that Dodola send her to Griffin she kept tightly guarded behind a high mental wall.

"Yes, she did," he said in a flat tone. "Otherwise, you wouldn't have been allowed entry."

Clea opened and closed her mouth, relaxing a little. If he was angry, that was irrelevant. The important thing was that she was where she wanted to be, and she was safe from Perun for now. The question of whether Griffin could—or would—protect her if Perun came thundering down would have to keep for another day. He need not know everything about her situation, now or ever.

"I heard you were charming," she said, forcing a shrug. "Guess not."

He smiled, all white teeth and full lips, the way his namesake might bare its teeth at a quivering mouse before it pounced.

"I am charming to guests and welcome visitors. Not intruders." He seemed to be getting ready to spring on said mouse, and then he pulled back and relaxed. She didn't realize that his wings had been tense until the feathers lay flat and they merged against his shoulders until they could barely be seen. She caught a flash, an image of a bird with talons and a mane, and wondered if he'd been about to change into his griffin form.

"I am sorry, Clea, daughter of Dodola," he said, as if the words cost him dearly. "My manners are appalling. Your mother is a friend of mine. You are welcome here."

He couldn't read her; her shields were too good. Still, Clea buried her thoughts under layers of a current European pop song, just to be sure.

"You know Mother. You don't say no to her. It was prudent that I be away from our home." She hoped her words didn't ring as hollow as they were. As much as she had instigated this, her headlong flight out of the Czech Republic had drained the last of her strength. She needed to rest and determine her next move. She needed to ensure he let her stay.

He smiled again, a brief flash of teeth, before his lips curved down.

"How old are you?"

There was no harm in answering his question. "I'm two hundred and forty-one years old. A baby, by immortal calculations."

"You weren't there when I was with the pantheon before. That explains why I don't recognize you." There was something behind his eyes, a sort of latent pain she couldn't put her finger on. In the span between one second and the next, he regained his charm. His whole face changed, going still before smoothing out into a blank exterior. Then he nodded and gestured with his hand, as well as the tip of his wing, to the gleaming appliances and dark cabinets of the kitchen visible beyond the curve of the open archway. It was a modern plan, out of keeping with Icelandic style, which tended toward the quaint. He didn't seem like the type to bother remodeling, but she didn't know much about the Elementals. Now she wished she did.

"You are right; I am being scortese. Rude." His voice slid over her like chips of ice mixed with frost, his welcome perfunctory. "Would you like something to drink?"

"Coffee, please."

Griff's gaze lingered on her mouth. Desire stirred again. She clamped down that thought behind the song. She hadn't expected Griffin, the air Elemental, to be sex personified. She should have. Nobody got that kind of reputation by accident. Clea cursed herself that she hadn't considered the possibility that she would find him appealing.

It didn't matter. She was around sex all the time in the pantheons. Most gods did not worry about human niceties when it came to sex, and she had seen it in all its forms. She had the experience to handle one Elemental. Even one with wings that begged to be stroked and lips that needed…

There was something in him, a melancholy that leaked out from behind a blank spot. Her mind buzzed again with a probe trying to assault her shields. She wavered under the strong attack and the pop song stuttered. Clea concentrated, focusing on the discordant melody. His probe receded.

"Stop that, Griffin," she demanded, letting some of her anger show. "That's uncouth, and you know it. Has this mountainous retreat of yours made you forget that?"

"Why are you here?" The blue of his eyes was only just visible through narrowed slits.

Maybe truth was the best option. "I had to come, but more than that, I wanted to come," she said. "People die in your Challenges." Griff nodded; an uncertain gesture. "I'm here to see that that doesn't happen again." That was close enough to the truth that he would not be able to see any dissembling if he slipped under her shields.

Griffin's feathers rippled in a wave pattern as if he sensed her conflicting emotions before she cut her mind off from his with the same pop song as before.

It was all suddenly too much for her. Clea's eyes closed, and she surrendered to exhaustion.

* * * * *

She wanted to come? He shook his head at the words. It wasn't the whole truth. She was running from something. Yet her tale wasn't false either. She was a mystery.

He didn't know Dodola's or Clea's true motives, but there was an angle. Griffin limited his interaction with gods for good reason. He probed again and encountered nothing but music. Right before he left her mind, he felt something. Fear. Fear? But she was a goddess. They were immortal. Why would she be afraid?

He turned to ask her the question and was startled to find that she was asleep. Griffin moved to the goddess and crouched down to study her face. Now that she wasn't moving or shielding he could see the dark circles under her eyes and the shadowing across her face and body. If he hadn't known she was a goddess, he might think she was fragile.

He remembered Dodola as a petite, light-haired, light-eyed typical gorgeous deity. This daughter of hers was more pretty than beautiful. Her blunt-cut red hair and clear green eyes capped a heart-shaped face that stopped short of being stunning. In the pantheon of gods she would be considered plain, but there was something about her that made his cock stand up and take notice. The milk white of her skin was dotted by freckles. The pattern would be fun to lick.

Griffin drummed his fingers on the arm of the sofa as he considered the problem. He couldn't throw her out; he had given Dodola his word. He owed the pantheon, and if this Clea was to be the method by which he discharged his debt, cosí sia. So be it.

He waited for three hours before the goddess woke again. She came awake with a start, her chin lifting and the pop song screaming into his thoughts until he wanted to snatch the wretched thing out of her mind and crush it.

"Feeling better?" he asked on a tone dripping with acid.

Clea swallowed and then nodded, her eyes wide with something he would have called fear on anyone but a goddess. He would have thought that after World War II, her pantheon would stay away from Challenges in general and him in particular. His Challenge was here; he could feel it. Obviously the gods had too, although they rarely troubled themselves with Challenges. He hadn't seen Amai-te-rangi lately, but the old demon would be here soon.

His eyes narrowed as he studied the goddess. She had secrets, things unsaid. She had good shields, but he would get past them. He had to. The fate of the world was at stake. If this small pantheon thought they would interfere, they were going to learn otherwise. No red-haired goddess would get in his way.

Clea's body was still but quivered under his gaze. There was something in her, a dishonesty he couldn't put his finger on. It was gone before he could follow it back to its source.

"Yes, thank you," she said, her voice soft. Blinking her eyes as if they were still heavy with sleep, she had an air of vulnerability that made every protective instinct scream to life. "I'm sorry about that. I just…well…thank you."

He would allow this little Slavic pest to stay. He needed time to find out what her real motives were, and what she was hiding. If she was in his way, he would get rid of her. There would be no repeat of the devastation of World War II. Losing his Challenge was not an option.

"You must have been tired." He tried to keep his tone unthreatening. Whatever was going on with this one, Dodola hadn't been lying when she said Clea needed a place to go. No god showed this sort of weakness unless they had been driven to the edge. To his relief, some of the bruised look had faded from her face. Gods, like Elementals, did not take long to heal.

"I was," she affirmed. "It's a long story. Thank you for agreeing to take me in. Perun…I made him mad and had to leave." It was part falsehood, but he couldn't determine how. "I wanted to be here, Griffin. I want to help with Challenge. Can I get something to drink?"

Chapter Two

Griff handed her the mug of steaming coffee. "Kaffi," he said, pronouncing it the Icelandic way.

His voice was too casual. Emotions were riding under his shield, but she couldn't pick out the individual elements. There was something hard under the exterior he was trying to portray that spoke of deep-seated feelings.

Her mother had hastily filled her in on the air Elemental before Clea fled. He was over five hundred years old, three hundred years older than her. His wings were permanent, unlike the fire elemental, Phoenix, whose wings disappeared when not confronting danger. Griffin could change into the half-lion/half-eagle form his name suggested. Air in all its forms was his to command; wind and storms obeyed him. Like all current Elementals, he was one of the heads of Elemental, Inc., the successful company founded by the earth Elementals, Masud and Shani, centuries ago. He had friends and something to call his own.

Unlike Clea. She suppressed a stab of envy. She had been shown from an early age that her non-Slavic blood had made her second best, and Perun never let her forget it. His anger was mercurial but always present. Being so out of favor made it easier to leave, and Clea had done so as soon as she had been permitted to. She roamed the earth, never staying more than twenty years in any one place. She numbered her few friends among those like her. It was safer to keep to those races who knew what she was. Her lovers as well, whether gods or paranormal beings.

Their small pantheon was barely a memory in human minds and didn't hold much power among the gods. The larger pantheons—Egyptian, Greek, Roman—ruled that arena. Her pantheon lived on the fringes, away from humans. One of the few statuses they held was the rain ritual still practiced by some in the Balkans, called the Dodole. Her mother loved the festival, but that too was fading with time and modern ways.

When Clea had learned that Challenge was coming again, she had been determined to act. Maybe if she had been there during the last one she could have done more, saved Patrik from his fate. You weren't there, she reminded herself for the umpteenth time. She hadn't been there, and Patrik had died along with so many others. She'd stayed away from Challenge and lost the one she loved. Nothing would bring Patrik back. Her brother was gone; that could not be changed, but Clea could avenge him. Griffin was still looking at her, his eyebrow arched.

"Do you have any wine?"

His eyebrow rose higher, but she didn't say anything else.

Then he smiled. "I always have wine."

Silence fell in the room, broken only by the pop of the cork and the glug of wine being poured. When he returned, he handed her a delicate stemmed glass and then clinked his against hers.

"Why don't you stop playing games and tell me why you're really here."

She slid her fingers up the long stem, feeling the cool surface. Above the stem was the light red of a high-end Pinot Noir resting in the glass. Clea tipped the bowl, watching the liquid slide.

She met his eyes and their piercing blue caught her again. Tingling started in the pit of her stomach, intense desire stirring to life.

Griffin's reputation was legendary, his appetites indiscriminate. He would take most women who offered to bed, unselective about age or relative beauty. With his blond good looks and Elemental status, women of any race were plentiful. It was widely known that he didn't care about anything other than his partner was warm and female. It would be wise for Clea to run before he could get her scent and pounce.

On the other hand, it would be one way to get into his good graces. As a goddess, she would not be someone he could just discard. She was sure he was good at the art of lovemaking. He'd had centuries to practice. His hands were large, his fingertips ending in blunt nails. She could almost feel the press of those tips against her shoulders, gripping her as he thrust into her, his body hard.

Carefully shielding, she let her thoughts flow. Her last lover, a selkie, had been as treacherous as the legends implied. Even knowing it was foolish, she had still gone with him. It had been fun for a while, until his selkie form reasserted himself and he tried to drown her in the sea. He had known he couldn't, of course, and laughed afterwards at his folly.

It would be as foolish to get involved with Griffin, although he was unlikely to try to take her life when he was through with her.

"Your quiet indicates you're trying to come up with a good cover story." His voice was silk tipped with acid fraying the strands.

Startled, she lost her grip on the wine glass and had to grab it to steady it. She'd lost her way in thoughts about sex, and her cheeks flushed red.

Clearing her throat, Clea tried to present him with a calm exterior. She didn't often dip into the fantastical, even in the privacy of her mind. Having Griffin for a lover was definitely in that realm.

His home did not appear lived in, the lack of personal touches telling her this was a temporary waystation. It had a utilitarian look, as if its highly polished floors and stark black furniture stood waiting for whoever happened to come by. It did not have the charm of normal Icelandic homes with their colorful exteriors and cheery insides.

"I told you. I'm here to help you with your Challenge." The why could be left out for the moment. Griffin was a tool to her end, nothing more.

Movement caught her eye. A large basket made of wood panels with thick hemp ropes attached to each corner descended from the sky above the window. It tilted and then came to rest outside the balcony, bouncing before it stopped.

She couldn't hear any noise. Apart from their voices, there had been silence in the house this entire time. The hush from beyond the panes suggested that the windows were insulated.

"Triple paned. I have protection from the outside world," Griffin said, speaking into her mind for the first time. "You didn't think I'd live up here unguarded?"

She focused on the incongruous sight of a basket, like something you would see attached to a hot air balloon, hovering outside his window. She pointed, her finger shaking a little. Until that moment Clea hadn't allowed herself to admit she was scared.

"What is that?"

Setting his glass down, Griffin rose, his wings rising behind him.

"You don't know much about us, do you, dea? Didn't Dodola tell you anything important before you unwisely came here?"

"She told me what she could."

Griffin followed her pointing finger to the window.

"She didn't tell you enough. That is Amai-te-rangi. My Demonos enemy is paying us a visit."

She followed the ropes until they disappeared beyond the roofline. "A Demonos with a basket," she said slowly. "That's one obscure being." She couldn't recall anyone mentioning a basket, but that part of the story may have been lost in the chaos that followed the Elemental loss of World War II.

Griffin's wings unfurled, and she now understood his need for space. Opened, they must have been ten feet across. The power in the sinew and tendons sang through the room. The butter-yellow feathers seemed to ripple slightly, although there was no wind.

"The Pacific Oceania Islands legends will tell you a little," he said. "Cook Islands. There isn't much, but they will give you what you need." He gestured to the basket. "Amai likes the drama of it. I learned that a long time ago." He held out his hand. "Andiamo."

"Andiamo?" Clea repeated the word, fixing her attention on Griff. "To where?"

Griff grinned, insouciant charm reappearing in the roguish tilt of his smile.

"Why fly when you can ride?"

"Why ride at all?" She pointed to the basket. "This is your Demonos challenger." Griffin nodded and her brows beetled further. "Isn't the idea to fight him? Not have wine with him?"

His smile showed a full set of teeth. There was charisma in the upturn of that smile, but also a hint of menace. It would take only a twist of his lips to turn the grin into a snarl.

He may be a playboy, but he hadn't survived over five hundred years and several Challenges by being easy to kill. She scanned his 6'2" body. He was smooth-skinned, unmarked by scars, but broad and strong enough to take on most comers. His wings would blot out the ceiling when he was hovering over her, their bodies connected at the root.

Ridiculous time to be thinking about sex, she told herself again and cast him a sideways look to see if he had heard. If he had, he made no sign.

"Challenge is here, but Amai and I have done this dance before. For the moment, I believe he wants to talk."

"Okay," she said, knowing her doubt leaked through. She straightened. Never show fear. "Basket it is."

"You are free to go. I would prefer it." He pointed toward the thick front wooden door, painted red on the outside, a nod to Icelandic tradition. "You left your car down the mountain? I'll take you there, jump your car, and then deal with Amai. Go."

He pushed open the plate-glass, his wings grazing the edges of the door. The basket beyond him bounced, as if Amai was tugging on the large hemp ropes.

This was madness. She should drive the rental back to Reykjavik and get away from here. It might be nice to go to Fiji, or somewhere in Oceania. For the heck of it, she could check out what Griffin was talking about regarding Amai. She could leave and let the Challenge play out as it would. If she lived quietly on one of the Pacific islands, Perun may not find her. It was possible she would be safe there.

Then who would avenge Patrik? Nothing could bring Patrik back, but to walk away would be to dishonor his memory. Abandoning her path now would mean her sacrifice was all for naught. She had almost been killed by Perun for exactly this purpose. It would be stupid to leave now when she had achieved the first step toward vengeance.

"I'm not going anywhere but into that basket." She schooled her face and mind to betray nothing of her roiling feelings. Even from that height, hitting the ground was unlikely to kill a goddess, but it would hurt. Her weather gifts were decent, but she'd never attempted to whip up a storm cloud in the middle of the air. She'd never tried to summon enough wind to stop a fall from the clouds. Now wasn't the time to put her weakened powers to the test.

He strode out onto the balcony. On his way, Griff gestured to a throw on the back of the couch.

"Take that," he said. "It's cold where we're going."

Chapter Three

This is a bad idea.

The basket jumped and swayed in the wind, hauled upward by the unseen Demonos. Clea kept a tight grip on the thick rope, focusing on the Elemental next to her. Griff had his head tilted up, as if savoring the wind.

With his eyes closed, she was able to study his classically handsome face. He seemed no more than twenty-five years old. It was only by looking in his eyes that you realized there was no way he could be so young. His blond locks and light skin, coupled with his features, suggested he had Scandinavian or Northern European ancestors, but the Italian he sprinkled through his speech pointed further south. Perhaps Northern Italy, like Milan or Venice. Or he was an ancestor himself? Did Elementals have children? She didn't know enough about Griff or the Elementals and resolved to scour the Internet as soon as she had Wi-Fi and some free time.

The basket continued ascending. She still couldn't see the person who manipulated it on the other end. It was an odd device, archaic and hand-woven, like something pulled from the past.

Clea knew as little about the Demonos as she did about the Elementals. The elders didn't want to remember the war. The pantheon had been wounded, their city destroyed, and that was all she had needed to know. It usually didn't matter to paranormals if the Elementals won or lost. If the Elementals won, then humanity was safe. If they lost, the consequences were only supposed to hurt humankind, but her pantheon had discovered that demigods could be counted among the casualties. She had no idea what Amai-te-rangi was, or what his powers were. She would find out. Her people would not pay the price of another Elemental failure.

Griffin's wing feathers fluttered on a gust of wind. As they continued up, they passed clouds moving in the sky. She wondered how thick the troposphere was in Iceland. In the distance, still far above them, were a few planes flying in the stratosphere, taking advantage of its more stable air.

The clouds thinned until they were wisps of white against an azure sky. She shivered, her body reminding her how cold it was. The air was thinner than anything she'd ever experienced, even in her brief mountain-climbing excursions. Breathing was harder at this height but not impossible. Goosebumps rose on her arms.

Griffin frowned, picked up the throw she'd retrieved from the couch, and put it around her. His warm hands against her chilled skin shot a bolt of sensation through her body, making her knees wobble. The basket began to slow.

"Looks like we'll stay in the troposphere. Sometimes Amai goes to the tropopause, just below the stratosphere. He likes it there." Griff's hands lingered on her shoulders.

"Are you all right?"

The mentally delivered question made her start in surprise. It indicated a concern for her welfare she wouldn't have thought the man would ask.

"Yes, thank you. Cold, and a little out of breath, but I'll be fine."

"We're almost there."

They came to a stop. The planes still flew above them, but they were closer now. The mountains and volcanoes of Iceland were small below them, the buildings mere dots. It was exhilarating as well as scary to be so high. They were high enough to see the curve of the Earth on the horizon.

The ropes grew taut and then began to float down. At first the form above them was indistinct. As it got closer, she saw a giant man with dark chocolate skin. He was wearing only a loincloth, and his body was thick with muscle. The Demonos appeared as if someone torn from the pages of a history book, when the races didn't intermingle. He reminded her of what early sailors might have found when they landed on the islands of Oceania.

Amai-te-rangi jumped into the basket, which rocked at the movement. The ropes vanished into him. By the time he hit the bottom of the weave, there was nothing visible supporting them, only the basket, barely big enough for three, hanging in the troposphere.

They swayed in the higher winds of this layer of the atmosphere. Below them, the ground seemed infinitely far away. The sky seemed to go on forever above and around them.

"Griffin," Amai-te-rangi said. There was a metallic quality to his voice, like small iron shavings had been shoved down his throat and vocal box. Up close, his chest was aggressively muscled and covered in tribal tattoos. She couldn't identify the circles and whorls, but they had to relate to his heritage.

Clea studied Amai's face, committing it to memory. This was her enemy. This was the man, the Demonos, who had killed her brother. This was the man she vowed to destroy.

"Amai." Griffin nodded. It was a formal nod between equals. "Long time." He flipped a hand at the basket. "Still flying coach. Did you get new tattoos, as well?"

Amai loomed like a giant tree, dwarfing even the tall Elemental. His eyes, black against his dark skin, gave nothing away. He did not answer Griffin, instead fixing him with that dark gaze. The silence stretched out for several moments.

"What's with the basket?" Clea said, and then clamped her lips together. She snapped her teeth with a clack, hoping the sound didn't carry.

Amai's slow sweep scanned her, the pace telling Clea the insult was intentional. There was an ancient intelligence in him, speaking of lands long forgotten, of times that existed only in legend.

Then Amai-te-rangi raised a shoulder. "Kia orana. We become what humans expect, over time. The legend the mortals created for me told of my landing in a basket to snatch up unwary humans to eat them. The basket stayed when I became the air Demonos. Do you like it?" He rocked the basket, throwing Clea off balance. She stumbled and slid. Griff's wings half unfurled, hampered by the conveyance. He also started to slide, but reached out and gripped the side, stopping his fall. One wing, free of the basket, fully spread out. The feather tips caught the wind.

Clea tilted as the basket dipped, slipping down. It continued to slant, like a drunk person losing the battle with gravity. Her body slammed against the wood panels, and the hemp ropes creaked. Taking a deep breath, she reached inside, preparing her air powers.

"This is unworthy of you." The edge in Griff's voice was unmistakable. Demonos and Elemental stared at each other, their gazes locked. Before Clea could summon her talent, wind started, a small current out of nowhere, focused in a tight spiral. She felt a shove from below, and the basket once again became level.

"Challenge is here." Amai broke the staring contest and turned his attention to Clea. His eyes were deep and dark, and she couldn't pick out a color. There was something wrong with his face, and it took Clea a minute before she realized he had no hair on it. No eyelashes, no eyebrows, no fine hairs anywhere. "Kairau, leave," he said, with a snarling tone. "This does not concern you."

Griffin's face didn't move, but mottled color bloomed on his cheeks. "Come here," Griffin said, without mentioning her name. He held out his hand to her. She shook her head, pressing her lips together.

"We need to show unity," he said mentally. "He called you a harlot."

"I know." Clea's cheeks grew hot. She moved from the side of the basket she was on to the opposite corner where Griff still stood. He was surefooted and secure in his balance, his wings outspread.

When she reached him, he opened a wing instead of his hand, and draped it over her. His feathers were warm and smooth. She could feel the tendons against her skin, strong and pulsing.

Amai-te-rangi raised an eyebrow. "A new pet, Elemental?"

In the distance a plane soared by, higher than the basket, leaving a small contrail in its wake. She peeked into the minds of the humans and verified that they saw nothing of the scene below them. It always seemed impossible that humans had no clue what went on around them, but the basket, and the people in it, were invisible to human eyes.

"I'm nobody's pet," she spat, grinding her teeth, resisting the urge to lunge at him. This…this creature had killed her beloved brother. He had destroyed Patrik. The demigod could not recover from the grievous wounds Amai had inflicted on him. Patrik was gone in true, permanent death.

Griffin didn't answer. The silence lengthened, words falling flat and thudding on the basket floor.

"Go play elsewhere, wahine." Amai's voice was harsh. "You can't help him win this fight."

"Pantheons paid last time." The words were like acid in her throat. "It's hardly your turn on the chessboard."

Her voice shook, and Clea once again cursed her impulsiveness. Griffin hadn't said her name for a reason. Could Amai tell she was a goddess? If he hadn't known, he did now.

"He aha hoki," Amai said. Clea automatically translated that to "I disagree."

* * * * *

Never before had one Challenge come so quickly after the last. Griff had been looking forward to a century of idleness in Iceland. It was away from the day-to-day press of humans, giving him a measure of peace. If he wanted company, he could fly to civilization, by wing or by metal. Or company came to him when he was so inclined.

Now, instead of indolence and succubi, he had Amai to face. The basket was silly, but lethal. Griff had heard tales of the last Elemental who had dismissed Amai-te-rangi, then new to his Demonos role, as a threat. Griffin had assumed the mantle of the air Elemental after that mistake.

Griffin spared a glance for the goddess. He would have thought Dodola would use the promise of an Elemental on something more substantial than protecting her daughter. There was more here than met the eye. No matter. He would discover the truth before this was through.

The wind he'd summoned continued to hold the basket steady. He could feel the tug on the corners as Amai tried to tip it sideways. He had already turned back to Griff, ignoring Clea. Amai didn't sense the power in her, but Griffin felt it like the eye in the middle of a hurricane. There was more to this minor goddess than was first apparent.

Her back was straight, wind blowing through the red hair that must have come from her father. Perun had blond hair, and Griffin didn't think the leader of the Slavic pantheon had sired this goddess. The blanket he'd settled around her shoulders lifted with the cross currents of his unseen struggle with Amai. Why the hell had Dodola sent her? Why had she come?

"There are reasons."

Griffin cursed at hearing Dodola's mental voice. He raised his shields until his thoughts were secure behind them. He had gotten lazy. Gorging on his own company had made him sloppy. He was going to have to get battle ready, and fast.

Amai's narrowed eyes moved from Griffin to Clea. Now he was sure Amai had gotten more tattoos in the intervening seventy years. They had a fresh look to them, as if he'd them done recently, but Griff didn't know the symbols.

"Never a pet, Demonos." She moved out from the shelter of Griff's wings and to Amai. Not only was her voice steady, but so was her body. She walked across the rocking basket without hesitation. Clearly she had some air strength in her.

Amai snickered. "Griffin and I have a long history, wahine. He doesn't get involved with women. You are wasting your time, goddess. Gods have no part in this battle. Go back to your manna on Olympus."

"Wrong pantheon." Clea was face to face with the much taller and broader Amai. Griff probed and felt fear leaking past her shields, but it didn't show on her face. He stayed motionless, his wings up, poised for action. Stray currents touched his long braid, lifting the strands.

"Prepare, Elemental," Amai said. "Challenge is here." He turned his back on both of them. In retrospect, Griffin should have known what was coming.

"I tire of games," Amai-te-rangi said.

The basket flipped over, tipping out its contents. Then Amai and the basket soared up, too quickly to follow.

Chapter Four

The small mountainado seemed to come from nowhere. The vortex hung vertical, created from sheer winds that hadn't existed a moment ago in this remote alpine pass. The strong gusts would have been damaging if there had been anything other than rocks and scrub trees at the high altitude of the mountain. What little snow there was mixed with the other detritus in a fierce spiral. The wind swelled around the flotsam and jetsam, tightening the coil. The mountainado blew on a downward slope and seemed about to head down, then it winked out and died.

Somewhere in a dark place there was a groan of frustration and anger.

"Try again," a deep voice said. "That pitiful display of power is not nearly enough to convince me you have a role in this battle."

* * * * *

"Father?"

Neit, the war god of the Tuatha Dé Danann, paused in the act of splitting a log and turned to the voice. The pile of wood was twice as high as it had been a short time ago.

"Aye, Cormac." He hefted the axe. Although the tool was heavy, little sweat showed on Neit's face or body. He struggled to contain the irritation still bubbling under the surface. Ever since he'd learned Dodola had sent Clea to the damned Elemental, he had been in a temper. How could she direct Clea to another? Especially in this time of Challenge?

Cormac hesitated, and then stepped into the circle where wood lay around them. "Something in the air isn't right, so it isn't. Is it the Fomorians? Have our ancient enemies returned to these lands to fight?"

Neit shook his head, splitting another log. "There may be a day when we battle the Fomorians again, but it is not this day." He was not sure who his anger was directed at, but at this rate the Irish hills would soon be sparking with thunder and lightning.

Cormac nodded as if Neit's words confirmed something he already knew. "It's Challenge, it is, then," he said.

"Challenge does not concern ye." Even as Neit said it, he wondered if it was true. Clea was with the air Elemental. Strange forces were at work, stirring ancients.

"It may yet, aye." Cormac picked up a log and swung it onto a pile. Dirt clung to the bottom of the log, showing grass roots and a few small bugs. "I am in the way of discovering it…" He trailed off. "I am not yet in the way of pinning this feeling down."

Badb, one of Neit's three wives, entered the clearing in her crow form. She landed, transforming into a woman who appeared to be in her forties, of average height and clad in a simple black dress the same color as the bird. Neit could not tell from the distance what Badb's temperament currently was, but if she had been angry she likely would have transformed into her crone. He breathed a covert sigh of relief. She may be his wife, but even Neit knew better than to anger the Morrigan, one of the most powerful gods in their pantheon. A triad goddess, the Morrigan, or the three Morrigna as his wives were sometimes called, were often associated with fate and influenced the outcome of war. One thing Neit knew for sure: his wives, all three of them, were great warriors in their own right, their worth in the pantheon great. Neit took a look at Badb and knew she had heard about Clea as well. The news had to be the reason for Cormac's visit. Although his son had never met Clea, they were fraternal twins, siblings in the way of gods alike and unalike.

"That's the way of it, then? Not Fomorians, Challenge?" Badb said, her voice harsh, as if some of the crow had lingered. Her laugh echoed of bird, more like a caw than anything human.

"Yea," Neit said.

He eyed the child, big and broad like him, and red-haired, but otherwise their similarity ended. It had been Cormac's choice to look a little rough, like the Celtic warriors of old.

Neit pushed a hand through his fire-red hair.

"What is it you're wanting of me, lad?" He handed Cormac the axe. As Badb watched, the men took turns chopping the wood.

"I don't know," Cormac confessed. "I'm feeling a pull. I do not understand but there is a difference to this Challenge, so there is."

Neit nodded. Although the color had not changed, the sky was darkening with a malevolence he could sense but not yet see. Could one of the true ancients be stirring? Their primary mother goddess Danu had not been sensed in centuries.

"I am after feeling it, too." Neit glanced at Badb, who bobbed her head in a peculiar birdlike way. She did not yet know that Dodola had sent his daughter to the Elemental, but she soon would. He would need the wisdom of the Morrigan before long.

"It's watching we need to do." Cormac's sullen expression told Neit that his answer did not satisfy the boy. "Don't give out about acting." He would have to pay closer attention to Cormac. Neit wondered if he was feeling his sister.

Soon Neit would demand answers from Dodola. His long-ago lover could not put his daughter in danger without answering to him.

* * * * *

As if in slow motion, the wood disappeared and sky emerged. The buildings and landscape were far away, rivers too distant to be seen as anything more than small ribbons snaking through the earth. Even Hallgrimskirkja, the Lutheran church that was currently the tallest building in Reykjavik, was nothing but a dot below them. Clea's body stretched when gravity began to claim her.

Then she was falling much too quickly, the air plunging around her defenseless body. Her skin was pulling back from her face in a parody of the g-forces she had seen in movies where they simulated rocket travel.

She yelped once as she picked up speed. Clea took a deep breath, summoning her wind talents. The power gathered, a buzz starting at her fingertips and spreading to her palm.

"Coming."

Before she could act, there was a whooshing sound, but she couldn't tell if it was the weather or Griffin. Currents swelled up from below, pushing against her, and Clea marveled at the precision it took to form the wind underneath. Then Griffin's hands circled her waist, slowing the downward rush. It was similar to what he had done when he'd plucked her off the path to his mountainside home, but this time thousands of feet in the sky.

Clea's breath rushed out in a sigh of relief at the feel of him. Even in the chill of the troposphere, he was warm, smelling of dew and musk.

"Thank you."

His strong yellow wings flapped, each pull slowing their combined fall further.

She was sure it was only a few seconds, at longest a minute, before the horizon stopped rushing around her body and the wind slowed. To her relief, they now hovered in the air.

Patrik. She was doing this for him. She would have no interest in this Challenge if not for her brother. Otherwise, she would be far away from this battle. Madagascar, perhaps. There was a nice remote resort there where she could have explored the scenery. If not for Patrik, but there was the memory of her foolish brother who had tried to help Challenge and paid the ultimate price. She would fight this Amai, the Demonos with the ridiculous basket. She owed Patrik that.

"Come, let's get back to my place."

Currents of wind blew around and under them. Clea reached out to test the air. There was no need to supplement his gust with her own; he had more than

Claire Davon

enough. She cursed herself, wishing she had used her time to do more research before she had fled to the Elemental. She needed to know what Griffin's strengths, and more importantly, what his weaknesses were. Only then would she know what to focus on and how she could help. She couldn't lose any more family.

Inch by inch, her fear began to leave her as Griff's strong wings beat in the currents. As they grew nearer, Griff again made the same hand motion he had before, and the sliding door pulled back.

"Neat trick."

A rumble of laughter echoed in him.

He deposited her on the floor, landing her gently on her feet. Clea's hands and face lost their chill in the warmth of his remote home. To her dismay, her heart was pounding and when cold left her, beads of fear sweat bloomed on her body. Griffin poured her another glass of wine from the same bottle as before, saying nothing. His wings once again folded against his back.

"That was interesting." Small ripples danced across the red wine as Clea curved her free hand around the stem. In another moment, she would be shaking. Too much had happened too fast. "Why keep the basket?"

"He doesn't need it to maneuver in air, but he likes to let the unwary believe what they will. Don't underestimate Amai," he said, steel in his tone. "The basket may look stupido, but he is ruthless and dangerous. He didn't kill my predecessor by being a fool."

Hoping her voice was level, Clea met Griff's gaze. "I have learned not to misjudge anyone. Danger comes in many packages. Still, you've got to admit, it's ridiculous."

He flashed something that might have been a smile, but it was gone before she could be sure. "That's the point. It's a natural tendency not to take the ridiculous seriously, and he has caught many people by surprise that way. He was made into his current form by the primitive people of Mangaia, and he chooses to keep the trappings of his creation."

Griff didn't move, but he was in her mind, beating at her shields.

"Let's talk, Clea. Who is Patrik?"

She opened her mouth to speak but before she had any words, there was a crack of thunder. It was followed by another one, and another, until their surroundings seemed alive with electricity. Clea's hair floated out and Griffin's feathers stood up. There was a fleeting impression of a hooked nose on his face, like a beak. For an instant, he looked like the half lion/half eagle that was his other form, before it faded to his normal countenance.

Wind kicked up and swirled outside the house, whipping small trees at the bottom until their branches bent close to the ground. It picked up snow, sending it coursing through the air, and bits of debris whirled in the currents. Griffin still hadn't moved, cocking his head to one side.

"Amai's parting shot. He can be a child," he said. "I'll be right back."

Griff's power grew, almost a tangible force in him as he took in a deep breath. When he exhaled, the wind stuttered and then stopped swirling. It began churning in the opposite direction, rising away from the house. Lightning streaked down, but before it could crash to earth, Griffin caught it mentally and sent the electricity back up the path it had followed, lifting his hands as if to direct the path. In the distance, Clea heard a yelp before the storm ended as fast as it had manifested.

The buzz in her body subsided. There was no need for it yet. It may be best to keep her powers hidden until she had need of them. Amai was not the only one people often underestimated.

"Where were we?" Griffin dusted off his shirt, removing a few bits of litter. He smoothed the cloth down, eyeing Clea with an air of expectant waiting. "Ah, sì, Patrik."

"I'd rather talk about my mother. Were you guys a thing? Did you sleep with her?" The best defense...

Griffin raised an eyebrow. "With Dodola? Of course. Your pantheon predates Christianity and doesn't have any so-called modern sensibilities." She could have sworn regret laced his features. "If you think Dodola sent you to me because we are related, that is not so. None of the pantheon can claim me as their father. Elementals rarely have children."

Clea shook her head. "Not that. I know who my father is. I've never met him but I know who he is, and he's not you."

"Ah." Griffin's single word held a wealth of meaning.

Clea swallowed, watching him as he crossed the room towards her. There was menace in his stride, the air of a stalking predator. He moved like the lion half of his Elemental namesake, quick and deadly.

"What are you doing?" she asked as he grew larger.

He was there, big and male, in front of her. The tips of his wings poked out over his shoulders. His blond hair and braid were tossed from the storm. He moved like a jungle cat, every inch of him screaming coiled masculine power.

"What am I doing?" His voice was low, and his blue eyes blazed. "Clea Perperuna, I am going to kiss you."

Clea was no stranger to lovers. Sex was casual in most pantheons, born of time and beauty, as well as immortality. She was not as stunning as most goddesses, but she'd had her share of men.

"I'm not a Perperuna," she murmured. "Even if Perun were my father, we take our names from the matrilineal side. When I need a last name, I use Dodolaka."

"I see," he said, his head drawing closer. She watched him descend until her eyes crossed and his face filled her vision. "I am corrected."

His lips were firm but gentle, gliding across hers and then pressing into them. She tasted the wine he'd sipped. He smelled of wind, and of the clean air after a hard rain. His hands rested on her shoulders, stroking the skin in a back-and-forth motion. He didn't ask and he didn't demand, he just kissed her mouth, over and over, until Clea sighed and opened hers. Then he deepened the kiss, moving to close his arms around the small of her back and pull her against his hard body.

She heard a rumble before she surrendered to the warmth of another person. His tongue swooped into her open mouth to claim it. Clea returned the kiss, playing her tongue over his as a moan built in her throat. It had been too long since she had taken a lover. Twenty years was no more than a heartbeat to an immortal, but her body missed the touch of a man.

She pushed her hands under the massive wings, the feathers tickling her, and curved her fingers around his neck. All the while, his tongue was thrusting into her mouth, seeking and finding her, doing battle before retreating only to come forward again. His breath was coming harder now, his impressive chest rising and falling, and his body stirred to life against hers. Moisture began to seep along her secret places. His length pressed against her belly. Just like the rest of his body, he was strong, hard and long where he needed to be.

It may have been decades, but she wasn't about to let the playboy of the Elementals have her that easily. He went through women like water, slipping from one to another with the ease of the liquid, flowing to the next without any remorse or concern. It would be easy to fall into bed with him, but it was too big a risk. There were depths to him that made the idea too dangerous.

She backed away from his warmth, meeting his crystal blue eyes.

"You live up to your reputation," she said, and was surprised when his face darkened.

Griffin stepped back, separating from her with a rapidity that made her blink. Clea missed him the moment he was gone from her and found herself wishing she hadn't spoken. The sensation dancing along her nerve endings told her that her body wanted something her mind wasn't ready for, and it wanted it from this Elemental. Whatever his reason for kissing her, she doubted it was for simple pleasure.

"Good to know," Griffin said. "You didn't tell me about Patrik. No matter. You will, in time. I will make sure of that."

Chapter Five

The magnificent landscape of Iceland spread out beneath Griffin as he soared in the air, his wings stretched out fully. The birds paid him no attention, going about their business around the Elemental. When he had first arrived in Iceland, they scattered when he came too close, but now they were used to him. The Blue Lagoon, with its deep colored waters and surrounding snow and ice, winked below him to the left. He indulged in the hot springs from time to time, but well after hours, when the press of humanity was gone. He could pass for human, but he kept away from mankind as much as possible. While mortals couldn't see his wings, it was still a task to balance unseen wings when he interacted with them. He preferred his own kind, the other Elementals, and paranormals like him.

Clea Perperuna, or rather Dodolaka, he corrected himself, was an enigma. His familiarity with her pantheon was limited, and after World War II he doubted any of their members wanted to be reminded of Challenge.

The prophecy, one he had long dismissed, now echoed in his mind. "Fire calls to fire. Air will glide with air. Water swims together. Earth is always there." Griff shook his head, dismissing it. It had never proven out in the five hundred years he had been the Elemental Griffin. Just because he had an air goddess of limited power under his protection did not mean the saying, for whatever it was worth, was coming true. Just because it was associated with the Elementals did not make it fact. "Air will glide with air" could mean anything. It did not mean that he had to associate with an air power. He had won plenty of Challenges without outside help.

The last thing he needed was a Slavic goddess bent on—whatever she was after. He rarely had assistance and didn't need the burden of putting anyone else in that pantheon in danger. Still, it was done. He would have to make the best of it.

His red-headed lovers had been rare, and it had been a long time since a woman with pale skin and hair the color of sunset had tempted him. Her curves had called to him, and even now he felt the press of his cock lengthening against his pants.

Griffin banked low, winging down towards one of his favorite places in Iceland, the waterfall Hengifoss near Lagarfljót Lake. The astonishing columns of cooled lava, flow crossed with the sea green and blue of the water tumbling over them, was a scene of true beauty. The pillars rose high, cut through by the lake and reaching all the way down to the bottom. Moss covered the top of the columns, a testament to Nature's enduring strength.

Nature in all her forms was a mystery to him. He had met some minor personifications of the primal earth goddess over the years, but never the one herself. Griff was unsure if she existed. If she did, the entity would be incredible, and terrifying.

He landed on a series of the flatter columns. The rocks were slick and wet. Spray shot off the fall, spattering him with water. Far below his vantage point, lichen and moss clung to the vertical side of the rock, fed by the rushing liquid.

What had driven the Slavic goddess to send Clea, one of her many daughters, to his side? It was not forbidden for the paranormals to aid Elementals, but they often steered clear of choosing sides in their battle. For millennia, the pantheon Clea hailed from had been no different. Dodola and Perun had little power now, their pantheon diminished by Christianity and time, but they still existed. The small ritual performed in the Balkans saved Dodola from irrelevancy, and there were tiny factions of humans that still looked to the old gods, but very few.

Griff idly flipped a loose rock off the pile with his wing, watching it tumble down the giant fall to the quieter waters below. His ears caught a rustling over the roar, a sound like rocks shifting. Griffin extended his wings, letting the movements of the air currents ruffle his feathers.

"Einar, have you decided to come out into the open?"

Griff heard a snort and then a grumble. "I am only hidden to those who will not see."

Griff turned. Floating just over the moss-covered rock was a humanoid-like figure. Griff had become friends with this creature over the fifty years he had lived in Iceland. Einar was ethereally beautiful, with features so perfect that Griffin did not think there would be any way to disguise he was other than human.

Einar was a member of the Huldufólk, the invisible race of humanoid like beings that Icelanders believed in and some called elves. That belief sustained them as it did many pantheons. Their legend was as unique as the land Einar hailed from. The Huldufólk were said to be Adam and Eve's children, but were hidden when God came to look at them. When God discovered the children, he proclaimed that since they had been hidden from him they would be hidden from man from that day forward. Now the Huldufólk could only be seen if they so chose. Just like most legends, the story of the Huldufólk was part oral mythology and part truth. How much truth, Griff didn't know.

There was a rock pile nearby, a place where the Icelandic people thought the hidden people lived. Locals took great care not to disturb the cairns, believing that the Huldufólk would cause harm to those who did. Griffin knew Einar well enough to know he didn't spend time in such ridiculous places. Einar liked waterfalls, though, and when Griff came to this one, he stood a good chance of running into the being.

"Have a seat." Griff patted the rock next to him. When he lifted his hand, it came away wet and slick with lichen. Einar made a negative gesture.

"Not necessary."

Unlike Griff, Einar had no wings, nothing to lift him. And yet he seemed to move through the air as easily as the Elemental. Griff wasn't sure if it was teleportation or something else and had never cared. There were too many supernatural occurrences in the world to concern himself with each one. Einar floated, and that was enough for him.

"You have a visitor, Elemental," Einar said.

Griff nodded. "I do. She is in the way, but I owe her pantheon and I honor my debts. My Challenge is coming."

"Your Challenge is here."

Griff inclined his head, acceding the point. "Our trip to Grimsey will have to wait." He had wanted to see the sparsely populated island that straddled the Arctic Circle north of Iceland, but it hadn't been a priority. He had thought they had time.

"It is of no consequence. There are a lot of islands. After your Challenge, we will visit." Einar glowed a little, his unnaturally perfect features shining in the Icelandic sun.

Griff doubted Einar had ever been human. He looked the part, but did not act like a humanoid. He could be corporeal when it suited him, or more insubstantial. His motives for his actions were always unclear, even to a five-hundred-year-old Elemental. They were friends, although Griff didn't think Einar would think of him for long if he were killed.

"Have you been behaving, Einar? Are you leaving the turisti alone?"

Einar floated up in a graceful movement that made the air dance. "Tourists expect Huldufólk to cause mischief. Sometimes we cooperate. It can be amusing. The woman. Do not discount her. She is more than she appears. This is not random."

Griff nodded. "Things rarely are. I am honor-bound to take her in, but I'll be damned if I know why she wanted to come." *Or why I find this female so compelling.*

The silence was so long that Griff turned to his friend, half expecting him to have vanished. But Einar was still there, his gaze tilted up to the sky. Around them, the waterfall kept pounding against the columns of lava, in a battle of attrition that the water would win, but not for millennia. Griff wondered what a being like Einar had seen in his life. Even measured in the slow progress of the Earth, things changed in thirty thousand years.

"There is a reason for everything." Einar's lichen-colored eyes took in the waterfall. It flowed over the rocks, the sound crashing far below them where it hit the bottom. "What motivates most, even the gods? Power. Wealth. Glory." He waved his hand and the water droplets slowed in the air, surging around him, but never touching him. He moved again and the liquid continued its journey, hurtling toward the landscape below. Einar turned his attention to Griff and Griff saw resignation, or perhaps sadness, in the Huldufólk. "I have enjoyed our travels, Griffin Elemental."

Griff had another name, all the Elementals did, but he rarely used the human name he had been born with. He opened his mouth to ask his friend to call him by that name but then closed it again.

Griff stood, and bits of lichen and damp spots marred his pants. Einar's words had an element of finality, as if he had seen something that would make this the last time they met. Griff reached out to probe, but Einar's shields were smooth and tall, impenetrable.

"Even if we lose, Einar, I will be back."

The Huldufólk slanted a look at him, his body fading. "The future is unknowable. Perhaps we shall meet again, Elemental."

* * * * *

The non-tornadic, or fair-weather, waterspout formed over Luxembourg in the Upper-Sure Lake. The flat-bottomed cumulus clouds hadn't existed the moment before. They hovered over the lake, drawing moisture into them, until a funnel of water mixed with the dark cloud above it. Tourists and locals alike pointed to the rare phenomenon. It moved like a tornado or a landspout would move, rotating in all directions as if alive. There were no weather fronts to account for this; the skies had been clear. People turned to flee from the waterspout, but then it was gone. The clouds vanished and the funnel retreated back into the lake with a splash, disappearing as suddenly as it appeared. People glanced at each other and then wondered if they had imagined the entire thing.

The beings huddled in a location not too far from the area. "That is more like it. Yes. Are there others like you?"

* * * * *

Clea studied the door and the accompanying large glass windows. The glowing red light that signaled that the security system was on, and the readout showing armed. Had Griff locked intruders out, or her in? No matter. She wasn't going anywhere.

The man needed some furniture, and something on the walls. The house looked like it had been staged for sale, and the items never returned. It lacked all the touches that made a house a home; something she was familiar with. Her residences through the years had the same stark quality to them; the same air of impermanence. With no base to call home, Clea had found it useless to get attached to things, just as she refused to get involved with many people. Humans died too quickly, their lifespans too short to make them proper companions.

Now not even her pantheon provided company. She touched the side of her neck, rolling her head from the spot where Perun had struck her. He had wanted her true death, and she had fled. She had wanted to spark his anger, to get to the air Elemental, but she hadn't expected her step-father would try to kill her.

She had underestimated the situation. There was primal power coiled in Amai-te-rangi, and he would be a powerful enemy. Now that she was here, she wasn't sure she was up to the task. It was no wonder her poor demigod of a brother had failed.

Her cellphone rang, a cheerful chirp, startling Clea. She hadn't realized they could get reception up in the glass aerie, but the sound made a lie out of that assumption. Clea reached for the backpack she'd slung into the corner of Griff's house when she'd arrived, and retrieved the phone.

"Ahoj, mother," Clea said. The screen said "private number" but there was no doubt who it was. Dodola liked it when her children sprinkled their speech with Czech words. Clea had never figured out why.

"Dítě," Dodola said, her voice high and light, musical and sweet, like pure mountain air. "Are you there? Are you settled in?"

A quick scan of her mind would have achieved the same result as Dodola's question. Her mother knew the answers to the questions she posed.

"I am here," she affirmed aloud. "Griff isn't."

"He's letting you stay? Protecting you?"

There was an interesting note in Dodola's voice. In someone other than her self-absorbed mother, Clea might have called it concern. No...not concern. Fear. Clea was not sure whether Dodola was worried that Perun would find out she had helped Clea escape, or that she had sent Clea here, to Griffin. An unexpected twist in her gut surged through her at the memory that her perfect, beautiful mother and the Elemental had had an intimate connection.

She peered out the windows to the snow-dusted mountainside. Below her vantage point were the tops of trees and a sky so blue it almost hurt the eyes. Iceland was a riot of blue, green, and white, its topography part icy wilderness and part geological marvel. It lay on the place where two continental plates met, and was subject to constant dramatic changes. Although Clea had no earth power, she felt it in the air, in the shift over the plates. She regretted that she had never visited Iceland before now.

"Yes, Dodola. He is allowing me to stay." Mother was not a word most associated with Dodola. Gods didn't age unless they wanted to, and most of the pantheons chose to appear as if they were in their early twenties. Dodola may be Clea's mother, but in the world of gods, that didn't mean she had been a parent. In her travels, Clea had watched some human families over the years. Her pangs of longing for those same bonds had been fulfilled, for a time, by her half sibling. Now all that was gone.

"Good. Good." Her mother sounded distracted.

"How's Perun?" Her question surprised Clea as soon as it came out of her mouth. A probe pressed against her shields again, but not from Dodola. Perun? The signature was not Griffin's, but the masculine shade was strangely familiar. "Still angry?"

The silence on the other end told her all she needed to know. Clea's thunder powers were bruised and weak, badly damaged by his attack. They were not gone, though. She could feel them, sluggishly moving within her.

Griff should return soon. Other than the fact that he was out in the cold and snow, she could get no sense of where he was. He may be a near stranger, but he was the only person she knew in this land of frost.

"Dcera, stay away." Dodola's words were slow and had lost that crystal-clear lilt that charmed both men and women alike.

A sharp mental foray blasted into Clea's mind. Danger danger. It was tightly focused, aimed only at her.

"I know." Clea paused. "Matka." Mother.

There was nothing but static across the dicey connection.

The probe came again, seeking, but she didn't sense any malice, more a feeling of curiosity. Clea followed the signature back and it vanished, but left behind a clear masculine aura. Had it been triggered by Dodola's call? It wasn't often that she couldn't find an echo of someone, but this time she found no threads to follow the attempt back to its source. All things considered, she should have been alarmed, but something in that mental signature had given her comfort. It had a touch of the known.

Whoever it was, if they came at her again, she would seize the thread and trace it back. If the person could help Griff win, she was all for it, and if they were his enemy, she would do her best to neutralize them. She owed Patrik that much.

Amai was no pushover. Once you looked past the basket, the tall, broad, tattooed Pacific Islander Demonos was formidable. His destruction of Patrik had proven that. It was no small feat to kill demigods, even though they were part mortal. In size alone, Griffin seemed no match for Amai.

"Clea?" Dodola asked, and Clea started out of her wool gathering.

"Sorry, what did you say?"

She heard a light tinkle of laughter, but there was an edge of annoyance in Dodola's voice when she spoke.

Clea wondered, not for the first time, if she should have gone to her father.

She knew little about Neit and the Tuatha Dé Danann and had never cared to find out more. The man had never shown an iota of interest in her. He'd had centuries to seek her out and had never bothered. His was a strong pantheon, though, and Griffin was only one Elemental. But it was Griffin who had access to Amai-te-rangi, and so she was here.

"Be careful, dcera." The sharpness in Dodola's voice was reinforced by her quick mental warning.

"I will." Clea inhaled a deep breath. There was a lingering scent in the room, something wholly masculine, and a small curl of excitement warmed Clea's stomach. "This is something I have to do, matka. You understand."

The silence stretched out for longer than Clea would have expected. She reached out, probing Dodola's mind. Beneath the shields was an emotion that ran deep and strong. It disappeared, leaving Clea wondering what her mother had been thinking.

"I do. See to the Challenge, if you must. He is honor-bound to protect you, and you will be safer under his protection. You are better off in Iceland."

"Thank you," Clea replied. Dodola's signature pressed against her shields, and Clea let it in. A soft caress and a kiss lingered in Clea's mind.

"You're welcome," Dodola said. "Nashledanou."

"Goodbye." Clea hung up and listened to the sounds around her. Had she heard something outside? But there was nothing other than the wind howling around the house. Through the windows was a light dusting of snow swirling, making small eddies before it settled on the ground.

She reached out, gathering her weather gifts to her and directing them out, tasting the storm. It was not going to be a bad one and would only leave behind snow that would not stick. Clea concentrated, and after a moment's pause, directed her senses into the cloud. The snow thickened, becoming wetter and sloppier, dumping thick flakes onto the ground. Clea focused again and the storm vanished. Her ability to manipulate storms and clouds wouldn't have been much use to the water Elemental or the fire Elemental. She shuddered when she thought of the earth Elemental. She had met that entity once, and then only the woman known as Shani, but the ancient awareness blazing out of those dark cat's eyes had unnerved her.

"I am returning."

Relief surged within Clea. Near stranger or not, Griffin was her only port in this storm. He was going to be her weapon, her method of avenging the brother that Amai had so callously killed in the war. This may be his battle, but to her, it was personal.

"I am here."

Chapter Six

"Neit? Father?"

Neit turned at the sound of Cormac's voice. His hair stood out at right angles to his head as if Cormac had been pushing his hands through it.

"Son?"

Few would disturb Neit in this space, this private clearing that was for him alone. Even the Morrigan were judicious about troubling him here. The green and wooded area had a high canopy of trees that blocked the sun, only dappling the leaf- and wood-covered ground below.

Neit stretched out his senses. There was danger on the wind, the beginning of Challenge. His pulse quickened at the thought of a good battle.

The legends had it that he had been killed centuries ago, but like most gods he did not die for long. He wondered if the Morrigan would release the Claíomh Solais, the Sword of Light, if there was fighting in Ireland. Neit's three wives guarded the four Treasures of the Tuatha, rarely revealing them even to the other gods. He could almost feel the weight of the shining sword in his hand, his fingers flexing at the remembered impression of the superb weapon.

"It's worried, I am," Cormac said, echoing their last meeting. If the sword he'd been speculating about had been there, Neit would have snatched it up and parried with the boy. It would have been a good outlet for Cormac's aggressive energy.

"How's the craic? You're recently back from America. How do ye find our lands now?"

Cormac shook his head. "It's a fair place, America, so it is. If I had the doing of it, I'd do it again. But I was always knowing I had to be a man there, never a god, and it got...stifling."

Neit chuckled. He had no need to travel anymore. A human would place him around forty, but the reality of his age was far past that. He'd seen the world when it was sparsely populated by mortals, when the lands were lush and green and unpolluted by the touch of mankind. The only time Neit had visited America was when it had been a place of hills and herds of stampeding animals. Of mountains and great rivers and plains that stretched to the horizon. There had been handfuls of humans back then, small tribes who walked with nature, and not the masses there were today. Everywhere Neit went, humans were changing and molding the land to their needs, their uses, their desires. They may not be immortal, but in many ways humans had overtaken the deities.

"What harm?"

"No harm, aye." Cormac was quiet a moment. "The Slavs. Dodola. I am of that pantheon."

"You are a halfling."

"Aye." Cormac's voice was cool, his flare of pique vanished. "Something is coming. Do you not feel it?"

"I haven't a notion."

Neit stared at Cormac. The boy knew about his sister, but she was not discussed. It had been decided a long time ago that the Tuatha would have one and the Slavs the other. He had always kept track of Clea, although his daughter was unaware of the scrutiny. Now she had become part of Challenge, for reasons unknown to him.

"'Tis the Challenge," Neit began, but Cormac held up his hand. The movement was so peremptory that Neit stopped, focusing on Cormac's hand in surprise.

"'Tis more." Cormac shook his head. "'Tis my sister. I'm after more about her. I'm after talking to Dodola. My mother."

Cormac's voice was firm with conviction. Neit found himself admiring Cormac's single-mindedness. He had never expressed interest in the Slavs up until now.

"Aye. If you's wanting to do this thing, I will permit it," Neit said after a long pause. He did not know why his daughter had not come to him. She would have been welcome. He was honor-bound to leave her alone, but she could have come to Ireland. The Tuatha Dé Danann would have sheltered her. He would have taught her. "I would be glad of it if you did."

"Thank you." Cormac opened his mouth but closed it after a moment. Neit wondered what else the boy wanted to say, but the child didn't speak. Neit felt an impression of confusion, of anger, a desire to act but without a clear direction of what to do.

One of the problems with immortality was that you had to deal with the same people forever. It made a wise person cautious. Grudges could go on for centuries over nothing more than the wrong words.

"It's a dangerous thing, so it is. Be careful, lad."

* * * * *

Thick drops of rain were falling on the roof of the house when Griff returned, their pattering steady. Outside, the precipitation came in strong sheets, the air dark around it, patches of brighter sky visible in the distance.

"What do we do now?" Clea asked. "How do you know what your Challenge is?"

Griff didn't answer for a moment.

"I don't know yet. I know that it is happening, but our Challenges come from unknown sources, between us and our Demonos counterparts. It will be related to my abilities, and Amai's, but we don't know how until it happens. It is something he will cause, or arrange to happen. We have to be diligent."

Clea opened her mouth to speak when her mental senses blared a warning. It was as if a gunshot had been fired through her mind, and her shields came up all at once. Jerking to her feet, her head pounding, she saw that Griff had also risen, his face a mask of concern.

"Already?"

Griff shook his head in the negative.

"Whirlwind, or a land spout." As he spoke, the air behind the paned glass darkened. "It's a preview of Challenge, something unnatural. Much bigger than it should be. It is coming towards us. Amai stole the storm." Griff's wings were spread out, still glistening.

"You can stop it?"

As she spoke, the rain doubled, fierce and heavy. Lightning streaked, and then thunder boomed several seconds later. The storm was still a distance off, but coming fast.

Could Griff fly in this horrid weather? Wouldn't he be knocked around, even with strong wings?

He grinned, and she realized he had heard her thoughts. She must have dropped her shields. Or perhaps she'd wanted him to hear.

"I have other weapons besides flight," he said.

As did she. Clea focused, her skin buzzing as she brought her gifts forward. She had little thunder, but her other gifts were unharmed. Thunder sputtered along her mind, its power dampened like there was a wet towel over it, impossible to reach. Instead she reached for her air senses. Immediately she knew Griff was right. There was something wrong with the storm besides nature and the unstable topography of Iceland. The whirlwind was easy to find in the melee. It was a thick funnel of grey and white, a cloud overhead making it visible, spinning like a top. It twisted madly, shifting in myriad directions.

"Whirlwinds shouldn't exist in the mountains," she said. "The rocks don't allow it. It should have vanished already."

Griff gestured to his wings and back out to the dark grey sky, saying nothing.

Right. Amai-te-rangi. Unnatural. Challenge. Air Elemental.

Before Griff could open the door and plunge out, Clea stopped him.

"Let me help."

Clea put her hand up and concentrated, finding the center of the storm. Griff paused, his hand on the door, and studied her without moving. She stretched out her senses to find the wind and press against it.

Griff studied her for a moment before stepping outside, his wing feathers catching the wind the moment he entered the elements. The storm blew bits of debris inside before he pulled the door closed, leaving Clea inside. Griff's wings were a flash of yellow in the darkness. His air power surged like a living thing as he flew toward the column. Still physically inside the house, Clea added her strength to his, lending him a piece of her air power for his battle. Then he was in the whirlwind, his hands outstretched. Griff used their mingled powers to call to the wind and rain.

"Stay with me. I need everything you have." Griff's mental voice rang in her mind.

As she watched through his eyes, her physical body safe behind his walls, Clea felt Griff create a whirlwind of his own, this one moving counterclockwise to the one threatening the house. She poured more energy into him, and the small storm grew in intensity. Griff flung it toward the storm threatening his house, his arms outstretched as if he had physically hurled it toward the gale. Still it got closer, the air moving toward his vulnerable home. Clea poured more power to him and Griff blasted it toward the storm. To her relief, the winds began to slacken as their combined powers and Griff's anti-whirlwind cut into the tempest. Rain pelted him, and thunder boomed, echoing off the rocks and land. To her dismay, lightning streaked inside the swirling monster as more debris struck the paned windows so near the house her hair crackled.

"Do you need more?"

"Yes. Now."

Crying out, Clea gave him all she could. Her power surged through their link and into Griff. His anti-whirlwind grew and then there was a crash and a boom, the sky lighting up in streaks of white and yellow as if the monster was making one final attempt at them. Several panes of glass curved inward but didn't break. Clea stayed with Griff, who did not pause but continued to beat the whirlwind back, shoving energy at his counter storm until it finally began to lose intensity.

Clea retreated from Griff, severing the energy link. Wisps of the tempest still surged outside even as the force of the storm began dissipating. Griff landed on the balcony, his wings and body drenched with thick rain. His hair was plastered to his head and his clothes were soaked.

He hurled the door open and staggered inside, pain etched on his face, but he never lifted his gaze from hers.

"Well," he said, surprise in his voice. "Perhaps you can be useful."

* * * * *

"Where?" Clea asked.

"Luxembourg," Griffin replied.

They were packing up a car, a sturdy 4x4 Nissan Patrol with huge tires modified for Icelandic needs. The SUV and the house were owned in trust by Elementals, Inc. The company kept the four Elementals, whoever they were, supplied with houses, transportation, whatever else each required. Although it was getting harder to stay hidden in the increasingly electronic and paranoid world, there were still ways of achieving their goals. Many things could be done with money, and when you added the power of the paranormal, much was possible. The company stayed under the radar, just one more old business in the modern world. That was all Clea knew about it, but she imagined she would have to find out more as they went along.

Clea had brushed up on her Elemental history in the past day. The water Elemental was a woman named Ondine, and a recent addition to the group. It would be difficult for Ondine, being new and untested, to face a Challenge this early in her tenure, but that was the nature of their offices. Challenges came when they came, and the Elementals had to be ready.

The fire Elemental, Phoenix, was in the United States, where he had made his home for several years. That Elemental kept to himself and out of the press of paranormal goings-on. He seemed like a loner, but then they all were. It came with the office. They were paranormals who had once been human and didn't fit in anywhere. The other supernatural beings tolerated the Elementals. Some liked them, some did not, the split tending to be along the axis of whether you were a power for good or a power for the dark side. Those paranormals who identified more towards the Demonos side saw the world as a place for their amusement and didn't understand why such lesser creatures as humans should have any sort of consideration in their decisions.

"Why Luxembourg?"

The SUV was loaded with clothes and necessary toiletries for her and the same articles for Griff. He was adding to the pile now, tucking a few personal items into the car.

"Einar said we should go there. He said that there were tunnels below the city, places that we might find what we are looking for. He can't, or perhaps won't, give me answers, but he said that that was where we needed to start."

"Useful guy." Clea picked up her sleek travel bag, one that Griff bought for her. It didn't have a designer's name on it, but the feel of the soft leather told Clea it was expensive and well-made. Any thief with an eye for quiet wealth would pick up on their pricey luggage right away, but the average thief would not. She glanced at her newly-issued passport.

"Clea Dodolaka," she murmured, glad that her given name was the one on the passport. It was always easier when interacting with humans to have as few falsehoods to remember as possible. It was annoying to have to press on a human to do something, whether to let her through or forget, when she did have to deal with border patrols and paperwork. She and Griff could have just slipped over the border, but Griff wanted to do this the proper way.

"Inconvenient that you don't have wings."

"Don't yours get in the way?"

Griff laughed. "They do, sometimes. They often did at first, before I got used to them." He glanced at his passport. "I am Lorenzo Traverso the Fifth, from a long line of Traversos. There is some truth in that. I have some relatives who I can claim as descendants with that nome."

Where was he from, she wondered. Italy, she had assumed from his accent and speech, but where? Clea flushed, and broke off that thinking. Checking her shields, she decided they were adequate, and her wayward thoughts had not slipped out. She had no business speculating about Lorenzo Traverso, no matter how attractive he was.

"Verona," Griff said out loud. When Clea flushed, he chuckled. "Your shields are holding, Clea Dodolaka, but I don't have to be in your mind to see the questions there. You have a very expressive face."

"Verona? Like Romeo and Juliet? Shakespeare?" She cursed herself for being a stupid cliché after she said it. Mortals who believed in reincarnation always thought they were descended from kings instead of peasants. Paranormals sometimes did the same thing, claiming a birthplace or a heritage richer than the actual fact to make themselves seem more important. Just because you were born somewhere didn't mean you knew the luminaries of that time and place. All paranormals born in and around Florence in the 1400s claimed to have known da Vinci. Most mortals wouldn't have resonated in the supernatural world, but even to the paranormals, some, like da Vinci and Shakespeare, were special.

Griff shook his head, his lip tugging up. "No. We existed together, but we never crossed paths. Shakespeare set Romeo and Juliet in Verona, but it wasn't his home. I knew others at the time who claimed they were his friends." His look said he didn't believe those long-dead people any more than she would have.

Griff gets a point for honesty, Clea thought with grudging admiration. Sometimes she felt like a young child among the paranormal. At only two-and-a-half centuries old, she was still considered by many to be a teenager, and not to be taken seriously. Mortals would envy her life, but to the supernatural, she was a mere adolescent. Even Griffin, at over five hundred years old, was barely an adult to immortals. He was a tall, well-built adult, she thought, desire flowing through her blood in liquid need.

His smile tugged at her, making her own lips quirk up. "Good for you for not being personal best friends with Shakespeare. Romeo and Juliet was not my favorite play of his. Too tragic. I prefer his comedies." When Griff's slice of a smile arced his lip upwards, Clea stopped talking.

"Come, Clea, andiamo." He met her eyes for a long moment, an unreadable expression on his face. His shields were so tightly fortified that she had no idea what he was thinking.

Taking her hand and tucking it into his elbow, Griff led Clea down to the car. Heat arced off him, warming her. Clea wanted to lace his long fingers with hers. She wanted to trace his butter-yellow wings and discover what feathers felt like against her skin. She wanted... Clea broke off that line of thinking and focused on...the weather. Nothing but the weather. Clea started humming, retreating to the pop song she had used as white noise to shield the thoughts that had become sexual.

La la la la la la la.

* * * * *

Griff watched his passenger, the inconvenient Clea. She was pretty, but not in that generic way the gods tended to have. She wasn't drop-dead, look-at-me gorgeous like so many chose to be. Among the gods, she might even be considered plain. Red hair had rarely been in style in any pantheon, and the fact that she'd chosen to keep it told him a lot about who Clea Dodolaka was.

Air will glide with air.

His discreet inquiries to Sphynx had only turned up an amused mental face in response. He didn't need to know, not to get his Challenge done, Sphynx had said, and the female part of the duo suggested he ask Clea instead of them. She had shared a little—Griff had learned that Clea had gotten nothing but the most basic of childhoods from the pantheon and had left, or been pushed out, as soon as she was able to function in the world as if she were a normal mortal. She had never pinged on his radar before. Griffin knew a lot about the gods, but he didn't know anything about her. He should have. His failure with this pantheon in particular still rankled. Griff shifted into gear and eased the car down the mountain. The powerful all-wheel drive vehicle took the twisting turns of the road of his former home easily. He didn't look back. He'd lived many places in his life, and would live in many more. Homes could be castles or they could be holes in the ground. In the end, it didn't matter. Dry and comfortable would always be his preference, but unnecessary. Buildings were useful tools, but that was all they were. What was important was what they protected. Not that he would let on about his persistent idealism. That weakness he would keep to himself. Sentimentality was for mortals, and women. Not for air Elementals.

"Luxembourg then," Clea said. The snow and ice gave way to the rocky terrain of Iceland's flatter lands. They would take a private plane to Luxembourg, with all of their belongings, and pick up another SUV in the capital city. "What happens when we get there?"

Griff had no answer for Clea. Einar had been non-specific, only saying Griff's next destination was there, and to check the old Roman tunnels. There was more the Huldufólk wasn't telling, but there was no use pressing the ancient being. He would tell what he would tell, and that would be all Griff could get out of him. Griff hoped to see Einar again, if they survived the Challenge. If he came back, he would have a chance to ask his friend that question. If it still mattered. Once they got through the Challenge, Einar's motives would probably be old news.

The goddess was sitting in the passenger seat of the big car, her face wide open with delight at the scenery beyond them. It was spectacular, Griff had to grant. He had retreated to Iceland after their World War II debacle, needing to get away from things for a while. Even to an Elemental who experienced the short lives of humans again and again, losing eleven million people in concentration camps and eighty million or more in the war weighed on his mind. It was what the Elementals were there to prevent, and they hadn't.

Clea surprised him. She had been useful, redirecting the thunder and the whirlwind. The twister might have scared Clea off, a nice side bonus for his Demonos foe.

But she hadn't fled. She had stayed and fought with him. She had helped quiet the storm, which might have destroyed the mountain retreat.

"You did well back there," he said. "I was…sorpreso."

Clea continued to look out the window. "I'm the daughter of a goddess," she said, as if the powers meant little to her. "Dodola controls the rain and abundance through her clouds. The mortals once labeled her clouds as cows, which is silly of course, but myths often don't have much in common with truth. I have thunder, but not lightning. I can bring rain through the clouds that I control. I also have some air power. The thunder is always unpredictable. Now…" She shrugged, her shoulders twisting. "It can be useful. I hope it returns soon. There are people in my life who needed smiting."

Her sentences were casual, as if the air and weather gifts she had were of little consequence or use. He picked his next words carefully, an idea beginning to form in his head. Griff made sure that that thought was well shielded from the woman.

"That's a great deal of power." To himself he added, too much power.

Clea glanced at him and her eyes were clear. He prodded at her mind and got back nothing but a fortified shield, then wisps of a slow-burning anger. The anger seemed old, and well worn.

"Not as much as you would think, Elemental. My mother and other goddesses control the rain and weather much better than I ever could. When Perun tried to kill me, he burned my thunder, but it will return."

There was so much pain under her simple words that Griff recoiled. It shouldn't matter. Women had been plentiful throughout his years as an Elemental, and he hadn't cared for their feelings. He had learned early on that there were those who were happy to bed the person in the station of the air power. The Elementals held such a strange place in the paranormal world that no self-respecting goddess would be serious about him. Especially not a Slavic goddess.

"Capisco," he said. "I see."

In the rearview mirror, the mountains and glaciers of Iceland began to recede as they neared the airport. He would miss this island nation. He would miss the supernatural folk who had befriended him, the Huldufólk and the elves who had made an Elemental feel welcome. He would miss the spirit of the mortals, the hardy, rugged individualists who lived in a land of ice and fire and embraced it for its dichotomy.

He would miss it, but it wasn't an Elemental's lot to put down roots for long. Whenever there was a Challenge, the Elemental acted and went to face it, no matter where on Earth it was. In a way, he'd been lucky for the last seventy years. Usually there were small skirmishes in between true Challenges, but Amai-te-rangi and the other Demonos had left them alone this entire time.

The interlude was over.

Chapter Seven

They were in the capital city of Luxembourg, in a hotel whose name was as grand as its furnishings. The Sofitel Luxembourg Le Grand Ducal was in the middle of the city. The hotel was spacious and clean despite having been there for hundreds of years.

"Nice place," Clea said to Griff. "Come here often?" They had a giant suite, two bedrooms with a high-ceilinged room in between, with enough space for two or more apartments in a poorer part of town. A fine spread of cheeses, fruit, and a bottle of French wine in a chiller greeted them on entry. Expensive china and glasses stood like sentries on the silver serving tray, waiting for their command. The hotel itself may have been old, but the accommodations were modern. Off-white walls were decorated with circles and high-end bedding matched the wall colors. A sitting area in the corner glowed with indirect light. Plush robes hung on padded hangers in wood-fronted closets, looking as soft as the carpets her feet sank into. She took in the spectacular view of Luxembourg with an appreciative nod.

"A show of wealth makes piccoli funzionari ask fewer questions," Griff said.

Clea had found that she could stay longer somewhere if she kept to herself. She was able to be somewhere for about twenty years before her youth became obvious. Some places she missed, and would consider going back to in a century or more, when all the people who had known her were gone. Others she never wanted to visit again. She had thought she would like the island of St. Martin in the Caribbean, which was famous for being the last residence of an exiled Napoleon. The small population smashed in between high hills and the island's lack of modern amenities seemed as if they would be well suited to her needs, but the rocky hillside that dominated the village was oppressive. She left after only ten years, never to return.

Through her various residences, she'd always kept a low profile. This grand hotel in the center of an old city was the opposite of her lifestyle.

"Really? I thought money would make more people want to get into your business and see if they could get some of that cash for themselves."

He gestured to the wine cooler and cheese tray with the tip of his wing. The porters and room service men had seen nothing strange about the tall blond man. They had been obsequious and overly helpful, but avoided Griffin's personal space. It was as if he had an invisible shield around him, something that told humans to come this close and not a molecule closer. She peeked inside the mind of one of the males and felt his desire to stay away from the Elemental. She judged the perimeter of the man's uneasiness and decided that even though he couldn't see the wings, some primitive part of him could sense them. Griff's station had to be lonely. She knew about loneliness and not fitting in.

"Money makes many paths smooth, including the ability to have people leave you alone if that is your wish. We have layers between us and humankind, trusted employees of the company whose families have been with us for centuries. While they aren't allowed to know all of our affairs, they are tasked with the day-to-day handling of the other members of society."

She wondered if he understood how arrogant he sounded. It was similar to the higher gods in her pantheon, or any of the pantheons she had encountered over the years. The leaders always had a certain bearing, a sense of preeminence born of centuries of being a god.

He smiled, but there was no emotion behind the slight movement of his lips. "Wine? Cheese? You should eat something. Even gods get hungry."

He moved to the old sofa table and removed the bottle. White condensation was visible along the silver holder, level with the line of the ice. Droplets of water fell off the bottom onto the thick Berber carpet below. Griffin's hand was poised over the expensive glasses, his eyebrow lifted.

After a moment she nodded, and with a graceful movement, Griffin poured each of them a generous measure of alcohol.

"I love vino, but no mind-altering intoxicants affect Elementals. Unlike gods," he said with a knowing smile. "As I have seen firsthand. Some gods become silly when plied with alcohol." His expression was neutral, leaving Clea to wonder if Griffin hoped for that effect on her. Griffin handed her a glass and toasted her with it before he took a small sip. She didn't know the vintage or the make, as the label was covered by the wine bucket, but like everything else about this place, it had to be ridiculously expensive. She sipped it, the liquor smooth and easy on her tongue. It tasted fruity with a slight after-effect of something tart. Clea tried to identify the particular vintage. It might be a Sauvignon Blanc, or perhaps...

"Orvieto."

She flushed. She hadn't realized she'd lowered her shields. "Thank you."

He set his wine glass down and picked up the cheese. Gorgonzola, creamy and covered in a white crust, lay in wedges on the tray. There were slices of Gouda as well as grapes and some sort of local pear. He placed a wedge of brie on a small plate and handed it to her.

His presence filled the room, making her shiver. It wasn't just that he was tall and broad, or that his wings could unfurl at any moment, filling the space between them. It wasn't just that he was handsome, with his perfect, unlined features. It wasn't that he was smart and well dressed. It wasn't any of those things, although any one of them would have been enough for most mortals, and many paranormal women. It was that she was attracted to him, but it was more than that. Her body was shivery, silver strands of desire moving up and down her nerve endings. He was lonely, and that tugged at her. She wanted to smooth her hands over his wings and see if he reacted to that. She wanted to kiss him again and watch his blue eyes haze over with desire. She wondered what his body would be like when he was naked, what his penis looked like erect. It had been a long time since she'd sought to touch a man the way she needed to feel this one. She craved him to fill her with his body and feel her legs wrapped around his ass so she could take his thrusts all the way inside her.

If it were just sex, she could cope with that. Sex was easy. She had no fear of unwanted pregnancy, or disease—those were human conditions and not part of her world. Clea had tried to be casual in the past and had failed. She wasn't built that way, to take pleasure from any source and move on when it bored her. Maybe it was a result of who she was. Dodola liked her, but not the way she would love a full pantheon daughter. There had been too many fights with Perun over Clea to make Dodola easy in her presence. She had learned the hard way that she was second best, unworthy of the Slavic pantheon. There had been mortal men who were intrigued by her and her air of mystery, but their thoughts were so easy to read and turned unpleasant when she couldn't be what they wanted her to be. They had no shields and didn't want a woman as unnatural as she was. It had never ended well with humans. She hadn't had much more success in the paranormal world. Not in the way she wanted.

Griffin's eyes had gone dark, blue disappearing to a thin line around his pupils. His cock was hardening visibly against his black designer trousers. Clea snatched the cheese and wine out of his hands.

"Clea." Griff's voice purred, a length of silk with a husky undertone.

She swallowed, her mouth going dry. The sensual threat in his tones matched the desire flooding her body. Her underwear, lacy scraps that someone from Elemental, Inc. had packed, along with a full change of clothes and necessary toiletries, now lay damp against her body. Yesterday she had not thought anything of the luggage, now she wondered why they had fetched her such impractical things.

"Clea," he said again, and she finally managed to look at him. There was no question he was aroused and ready. There was a thin sheen of perspiration on his forehead, and the line of his arousal was apparent. Want and need projected into her, as if he was making a point. His hunger mixed with hers until she was nearly on fire from the lust. She clutched the wineglass and, with one swift motion, downed its entire contents. The delicious cheese followed.

Griff examined her, saying nothing until the edibles were consumed. "We've got nothing to do tonight," he said huskily. "I've arranged for a guide in the morning, but we are free for the moment."

"I… um…" Clea stuttered to a halt. Griff stepped closer to her. She made no move to resist when he plucked the empty wineglass from her nerveless hands and dropped it to the floor. It bounced on the thick carpet but did not break. "I don't think this is a good idea, Elemental. We, I, you, I'm not good with casual sex."

He nodded and then pulled her against him. "And yet you want me. I can feel it. I can hear it. I can smell it. We would be good together, sì? I have had a lot of sex, but trust me, it is never casual." To make his point, he sniffed the air, and she could feel in his mind that he enjoyed the scent of her arousal. He was like a shapeshifter at this moment, an animal side of him scenting a possible mate and staking his claim. She had had a few encounters with monkey and tiger shifters in her time in Africa, but shifters tended to want to stay within their packs when it came to love.

Griffins were part lion and part eagle. How much of his namesake did he manifest?

"Um," she said again, feeling like an idiot. She was no match in age or experience with him, but she still was a goddess. He was right. She wanted him. It had been a long time since she'd had a man, and the last one had been so traumatic it had put her off lovers for a while.

Why couldn't the time to end that self-imposed celibacy be now? Hell with it. She was here in a luxurious hotel room in a gorgeous old city. She was with the Elemental and they had plenty of time tonight. Challenge was here; the outcome uncertain. Griff was handsome, an amazing lover if reports were to be believed, and he was aroused by her. She wouldn't get this chance again any time soon. It would end—he wasn't built for the long haul, but while they were together, there was no reason not to take the pleasure he offered.

Clea nodded. His hands closed on her shoulders as her movement registered, and he drew in a breath.

"Before you begin—" a voice echoed through their minds but also carried on the air, "—I must introduce myself."

* * * * *

Griff whirled, his wings slamming out to their full length. He stepped away from Clea but then pulled her against his torso, protecting her with his body. Clea went pale, and he cursed.

For a moment, he saw nothing. In his mind's eye, he picked out the source of the sound. Then a nebulous form emerged next to the writing table by the window. As they watched, it solidified until it became a man who looked to be in his forties, dressed in clothes that dated him to the eighteenth century. He had a cane, long wig, and hat. Griff felt Clea's shields go up, cutting her off from him and anyone else. Cautiously he reached out, seeking to establish a tendril of mind connection between them alone. To his relief, she opened her shield only enough to let him in, ensuring that Griffin would be the only other person able to access her mind.

"Oh, dear me," the man exclaimed, seeming in genuine distress. "Did I startle you?" He looked behind Griff to his extended wings. "I see I did. I am very sorry."

"Who?" Griff coughed, the man's amused expression angering him. "Who are you?"

The man was solid now, appearing corporeal. Ghosts were common in old buildings, although they did not think of themselves that way. They were an oddity within the paranormal world, beings with one foot in the supernatural world and one in whatever came next. He was not familiar with this ghost, and would make it a point to look up any legends in the morning.

His cock was still hard, but as he studied the man, he began to lose his erection. While he had experimented with sex in the open, he didn't like being spied on.

"I would think that would be obvious. I am the ghost in your hotel." The man tsked, using his cane to point toward them as he came closer. Griff had been looking forward to stripping this goddess naked and laying her back on the high-thread-count cotton sheets to explore her from head to toe. His body mourned the loss, want still pulsing through him. He vowed that he would get Clea in bed, and soon. This woman captured his attention in ways that no other woman had for over a century.

"I see that," Griff said, letting his anger show. "You interrupted. If you're trying to scare us, it's not working."

The apparition did that annoying clicking sound with his tongue again, and Griff wanted to rip the body part from him. If he weren't insubstantial, Griff would be inclined to punch him. He'd dealt with ghosts before and knew that they could not be hurt. It was only when they were ready to go on that the ghosts vanished. This one seemed to be hundreds of years old, and Griff doubted this apparition was in any hurry to transfer to the next plane.

"Oh dear, no," the man said. Up close he was not quite solid, and pieces of the table and windows behind him winked in and out of view. "I simply did not want you to continue whilst I was present. It would be…inconvenient."

He had a British accent, tinged with a hint of French. Griff thought that the man might have been an ambassador to Luxembourg, back in his time, or maybe a wealthy landowner who had met his end in this hotel. There had been a revolution in this country, in the seventeen-hundreds or thereabouts, and that could have been when the ghost died. Apparitions didn't stray far from their last resting place.

The man was still talking, words spilling out of him as if he could not stop them. After a moment Griff realized the ghost was rambling. It must have been a while since he had anyone to talk to. "I am not some common ghost, like the—" the man shuddered, the motion making his body fade for a moment, "—the Stierches-geescht. That ghost will haunt anyone who has had a few too many cordials. I am much more discriminating. And that footbridge. No self-respecting ghoul would be found in something that medieval. He died drunk and I think he is still drunk. Grund is so average. I would never stoop to do something so mundane."

Clea drew in a breath, as if the ghost had startled her. The sound she made confused him for a minute, until Griff identified the noise as giggling. His wings came back to his body until they lay flat, the shirt slits that allowed access covered by the feathers and tendons.

"Hello." She stuck out her hand. The ghost peered through his monocle, studying her hand as if it were a foreign object. It was such a cliché that Griff understood why Clea was amused. He was not, however. He wanted the creature gone and to pick up where he and Clea had left off.

"I do not shake hands. I have seen this custom over the years. Obviously—" he gestured to his form, "—I cannot. Nor would I commit such an act with a lady. I would kiss your hand, if I could."

"No, you would not," Griff growled, pulling her back to his body. He could tell by the quick look Clea gave him that the words surprised her. Griff reached out through their thread and didn't feel any anger, just a satisfied feminine emotion. Women. He was five hundred years old, had been with hundreds of the fairer sex, and did not understand them at all.

The man nodded, as if conceding Griff's claim. "I am William Henry Badsworth the Third."

William, or Henry, Griff hadn't yet determined what he went by, bowed to them with the kind of movement Griff hadn't seen in centuries. It was courtly, with a flourish at the end. He would have wondered how the man died, if he wasn't sure he wouldn't have to wait long to find out.

"Why are you here, William?"

"Henry, please. All my friends call me Henry."

"Henry," Griff corrected, not sure he wanted to call this pompous ghost a "friend", but Elementals didn't always have a lot of choices in their allies. If William Henry Badsworth the Third was, in fact, an ally. Ghosts were part of the paranormal spectrum of good and evil just like anything else.

"He seems harmless."

Griff didn't let any outward emotion show as he waited for Henry to answer. He checked the link and made sure it was still sequestered before replying. Ghosts didn't often have the ability to read minds, but he couldn't discount anything.

"Looks can be deceiving."

Clea pressed against him, a small motion to let him know she understood, and agreed. She stepped away after that, disengaging until their bodies were separated. He slid his left hand over hers, feeling her smooth skin before he interlaced their fingers, tightening his grip. His wings moved out a fraction, alert and ready if needed.

"I am afraid I am but a poor ghost, bereft of true power." Henry's eyes were impossible to see, and Griff couldn't determine what Henry was thinking. "However, my dear man, the reasons for my being here should be clear. I am to help you with your quest."

* * * * *

The local winds spun on the ground, forming into a small whirlwind. The people of the tiny village in France jumped in surprise at the sudden appearance of the windstorm. Dust and dirt came off of it and spiraled upwards, caught in the formation. It did not appear substantial, but the breeze around it was strong. It moved in an erratic motion, going from one side of the road to the other. A car coming up the street didn't see it and without warning ran directly into it. The driver cried out at the gale, and muck scattered across his windshield, marking the glass with fast moving pebbles. Just like that, the force of the whirlwind dissipated, interrupted by the car.

"Better. You can stay. Next?"

* * * * *

A mixture of apprehension and pride warred in Neit's gut as he observed Cormac go down the road. When manifesting as human, the Tuatha Dé Danann lived in a small village, closed to new people, with very few amenities and nothing to recommend it. The roads, such as they were, were pitted and scarred dirt tracks, and it was the rare human who stumbled into their modest main street. More often than not, they were travelers on their way to Drogheda who thought that this quaint little area must be something old and interesting, and they would want to stop at a tavern for a pint and good stories. The Tuatha had learned over the years that it was better to humor such folks than to try to dissuade them. Driving people off only created legends, whereas letting them come into what appeared to be a pitifully poor Irish village and be bored to tears by tales of bad harvests and lazy cows made people go away and never come back.

Sometimes Badb and her crow cronies would follow the travelers out of the area, making sure that they stayed on their way and didn't come back. Nobody did. Their township was not lost to the mists of time so much as it was forgotten. It was easy not to remember something so unremarkable; the tourists had no reason to tell tales of this place when they returned from their vacation.

The small car bumped along the pitted, rough road until it disappeared around the bend that took people out and away from the place. Badb followed, a lone crow high in the air, her black form clear against the rain that pelted down from the sky. Cormac had to know that she was there as well, and Neit imagined the boy shooing off the crow from the safety of the car.

In his guise as local innkeeper, Neit wiped down an already wiped-down table. They didn't keep things precisely clean—not dirty, but not polished. He waited for almost an hour before Badb, now in her woman form, walked into the tavern.

"He's on his way, so he is," she said, the rasp of crow still in her voice. "Does she know he is coming?"

A few Tuatha emerged from their houses, and the settlement transformed into their more familiar pantheon fields and buildings, ancient, solid structures that bore the same outline as the village but were tidy and brightly decorated, with flowers and other feminine things overflowing in the area. It was a far cry from the drab face they presented to the world.

Neit shook his head and then looked over at his wife, this third of the triad goddess Morrigan. Badb, with her round face, pale skin and green eyes looked to the casual observer like any other Irish woman. It was only when a person met her timeless gaze that they saw the power that lurked there. There was love between Neit and Badb, but no longer passion. Both of them took their pleasure among the many willing members of the other sex. She was more like a trusted adviser to him than a sexual being, although they occasionally refamiliarized themselves with each other.

"Sure the Slavs don't need to know he's coming. I am agreeing with you, so I am," he conceded. "I didn't agree to concealment."

"If I had the way of it, I'd teach Clea the doings of a Tuathan," Badb said after a moment's hesitation. "The Morrigan can get after showing her."

"Aye." Neit placed a weary hand on his wife's shoulder. "If I had it to do different, so I would. It is the way of contacting the lass we should."

* * * * *

Clea awoke, startled by something in the night. She used the heavy comforter that matched the thick cotton sheets as cover, ready to duck or roll to one side if there was any imminent threat.

There wasn't. Her room of the suite was quiet and still. There was no thump of footfalls, no sound of voices, nothing obvious in the room that spelled danger.

She listened again, focusing on the rooms beyond her open doorway to the living area, and Griff's room.

Nothing. The room and the air around it were silent. Clea relaxed by inches, her body sinking back into the plush, comfortable bed.

If Henry were lurking around, she might not know it. Clea sighed. Henry the ghost had interrupted something that was about to turn sexual, and more of her was sorry that he had interjected himself than sorry it didn't happen. Griff may be reckless with the opposite sex, but he was also the sexiest being that she'd seen in decades. She'd been with other winged men, like the Japanese god of the wind, Fujin, who could manifest as a demon-like leopard creature when he wanted to terrify people. Usually he preferred to keep his more mild humanoid appearance of a computer programmer in Tokyo. He had showed her his wings a few times when he had shifted into his other form.

His wings had been nothing like Griffin's. They'd been leathery and tough, like a bat's. Griff's were more like the eagle half that made up his archetype. Her hands itched with the desire to touch and caress those feathers. She bet the wings were sensitive. They might unfurl in passion, standing up, rigid and erect, when he lost control. The visual flooded her, making her panties sticky with desire.

Henry told them that he wasn't limited to the hotel, but he faded rapidly if he got more than a block from its walls. He knew other ghosts, he had said, and spirits who could whisper and carry messages. They were strangers to Luxembourg, so if Henry could direct them to the right location, it was worth it to take him up on his offer. She wished he hadn't felt it necessary to extend it right at that moment.

Clea heard a thump and then silence. Then there was another thump; after a moment she identified it as a footfall. Henry wouldn't make noise. An intruder? Clea threw back the covers and leaped to her feet. Her heart stuttered and then began a quick, staccato beat.

"Rilassare. Relax," she received along their private mind link. "It's me. Don't be frightened."

"Sorry," she shot back, hoping her thoughts sounded contrite. "Did I wake you?"

"Yes."

Griff appeared in her doorway, a silhouette of male backlit against the common area light he'd turned on as he moved across the suite. She flipped on the nightstand lamp. He was wearing a pair of cutoff sweats and nothing else. His broad chest, rippled and dusted with hair, was the only sight in her line of vision. His male nipples, flat and darker than the surrounding skin, tempted her with the desire to lick and bite them. His arms were ropy with hard muscle. Griff could probably lift her and carry her above his head without effort.

He leaned against the doorway, his posture seemingly relaxed but his body stiff with tension.

"I couldn't sleep," he said. "Your mind wouldn't let me rest."

"Did you…hear anything?" she asked, still standing next to the bed. Griff didn't move, but his focus shifted to her bare legs. Whoever had packed her suitcase had decided that Clea needed silk pajamas in a fiery red that clashed with her hair, mere wisps of tank top and shorts. Like everything else, they were expensive but impractical. Clea wondered who had given the direction for her wardrobe. Sphynx? Could the ancient duo also be mischievous? Clea couldn't think of a reason to add the items. Her body was covered, but the silk clung to her shape. Goddesses didn't need to worry about their weight. Some, like her mother, had chosen the more generous curves that were attractive when her pantheon came into being. Others chose austerity, with little fat. Clea liked it in between, keeping some curves but preferring a body that was considered "normal" by human standards. It made it easier to fit in, to not be too much of anything, one way or the other.

"Henry non é qui." Griff stepped farther into the room. "He is not around. It's a big hotel. He's got others to haunt."

"I heard something."

She couldn't see his eyes in the dim lamplight, but she could feel desire zinging along their link. He poured his want into her, letting her know that they were alone in a gorgeous hotel, and he coveted her. For the time they were on this Challenge, Clea would be the only stable companion he had. She had no illusions that it would last, that it would be the forever kind of love she'd dreamed about.

"You woke me up," he said. Delineated against his cutoffs was his penis, hard and erect, ready for her. Then he flashed a grin at her and mischief slid down their connection. He wanted to play.

Clea crooked her finger and curled it towards her body. "Come here, Elemental."

Griff closed the space between them and she was in his arms. First he kissed her face, as if tasting her freckles before his lips moved down to hers. He didn't force her mouth open but he demanded a response with his need, his tongue sliding between her teeth. He tugged on her top lip, delving into the small dip there.

Clea moaned, meeting his passion with her own. Griff urged her forward until they reached the edge of the bed. Then they were tumbling onto it together, their bodies tangling in the sheets and each other. His hard heat pressed into her, and Clea drew in his clean masculine scent.

His wings rose above them, a dark shadow in the dim light. They blocked out the room, hovering over them like a canopy. Clea reached up and found one wing whose tip dipped towards her. Griff was still kissing her, their mouths dueling a sensual dance of need. Clea stroked his wings, moving from feather to tendon.

Griff jerked and moaned.

"You like that."

Even through the mind link his reply was ragged. "Sì, sì, sì."

She pulled at the waistband of his shorts, wanting to feel all of his male heat in its naked glory. Griff stilled her with a hand over hers. "I'll do it."

She let her hands fall back to the bed and watched him. Carefully, Griff eased the shorts down and over his thighs and butt until his erect cock pulled free, pointing her direction.

Oh my. He was big and very ready, his cock like steel and tendons instead of flesh. He was impressive, even for a big man. The bed hollowed when he threw himself down, covering her body with his. Part of her wanted to do it now, strip naked and jump on him with no preamble. Griff pushed her back, his hands on her shoulders.

"Naughty naughty," he said with a waggle of his finger. "No need to rush."

He gripped her top, and with a yank, pulled it off her body, exposing her breasts. She wasn't big enough to need a bra and when she wore them it was for fashion and human necessity. The masculine appreciation that screamed down their connection told her everything she needed to know. He kissed each one of her freckles in turn, pressing his lips to her face until he moved lower.

"Mmm," he said. "Mio." He bent down and covered one breast with his teeth, pulling on her nipple. He suckled for long moments, the only joining between them his legs covering hers and his mouth at her breasts. Streamers of want and need surged through her body, jetting to her core. She could feel her body open to his, her lower lips engorged and waiting. Griff switched sides until both breasts were wet, her nipples as erect as his hard flesh. He pressed along her inner thigh and moved. Clea wanted to feel all of him inside her now. She didn't want to play tonight. Her need for Griff was raw and urgent, a primal want.

Griff paused, his avid gaze taking in her body. She undulated against the covers, seeking something she had no words to explain. Her body throbbed. His wings bent down, covering them in a feathered awning. The still-rational part of her thought that he was protecting them just in case the ghost paid a visit. Right now she didn't give a shit about ghosts, or anything else. The entire world could watch, for all she cared.

His face was as set with need as hers. Reaching down, Clea caressed his penis and he jerked.

"I like to go for hours." His voice was strangled. "I like my partners to beg and wait for fulfillment. Tonight, al diavolo." To hell with it. "I want you now."

"Yes. Please."

Taking his cock in his hand, he guided it past her entrance and pushed his tip into her. His head breached her body and then he was slowly filling her, moving inside bit by bit until he was all the way in. He kept his gaze on her the entire time he filled her, growling with satisfaction when he was buried to his root.

He was a living, pulsing part of her. He started thrusting with unhurried strokes, advancing and retreating so just the head of him remained, and then going deep again, an even rhythm that belied the neediness of his words. His hand reached out to stroke her face. Clea nipped at his hand and then, using the tip of her tongue, she licked his fingers all the way to the webbing and back up the other side. Griff shivered and his cock pulsed. Moisture gathered inside her, making his invasion easier. He touched her lips and then urged his fingers into her mouth. She closed around them, suckling on the tips before licking them with her tongue. All the while he was thrusting, seeming in no hurry to reach his peak.

Her eyes fluttered shut. She wanted to feel, to taste, to smell.

"Eyes open," he said. "Look at me."

He moved again, taking her hands and lacing their fingers together. With his eyes on hers, he pinned their joined hands to the bed, holding her exposed to him. He kissed her again, his tongue moving in the same rhythm as his hips. As if her motion had been a signal, he sped up, pounding into her. She thrust up to meet his hips, grinding against him. Clea could feel him adjust his stroke, finding her clitoris and stroking it with his body. Sensation, hard fast and not entirely hers roared through her, and she moaned. It echoed loud in the cavernous room, but she had no time to worry about listeners. Henry could have been standing there right beyond Griffin, but Clea was too far gone to care. His thrusts became harder, more urgent. She stirred against him, his deep penetration sending skyrockets of want echoing through her. Clea continued to look at him. Moving over her, he bit her shoulder. Clea cried out at the unexpected sharp combination of pleasure and pain, twisting against him. His sac was so snug the flesh no longer swung free. He threw his head back, his hands hard on hers, thrusting deep.

"Now, Clea."

Even down their mental pathway his voice was harsh. Ecstasy danced towards him and he gave it all to her, letting her feel his building orgasm. The idea that he was about to lose it sent her over the edge. Pleasure splintered through her, waves of the strongest orgasm she'd ever had thrashing her senses. Griff moaned loudly as he came, drenching her body from the inside.

The table lamp cast eerie shadows on the walls when Clea surfaced out of her stupor. Griff lay heavy and immobile across her, his wings spread down his back, drooping to the floor. His large body was sprawled like a marionette, at odd angles over hers. He'd shifted to relieve her of some of his weight. When she moved he turned his head, tilting it up to look at her. His eyes were unreadable, with only a glint of blue visible in the faint illumination.

"That was..." She trailed off, disengaging her mind from his, needing a small moment of separation. Griff eased out of her.

"Magnifico." He moved to lay his now quiet penis between them. A sticky residue coated her thighs, and Clea welcomed the small wet feeling. Even gods could take lessons from this Elemental. His legendary abilities were not exaggerated.

Be careful, she told herself, making sure he could not hear. Be very careful. You are in more danger with him than you realize. Not all peril is external.

He seemed to realize she had shut him out even though they were still physically entwined. Griff gave her a look that spoke of a strange hurt and then rolled to one side. He propped himself up on one elbow, facing her with no expression on his face.

"Magnificent." She placed her hand on his waist. "Thank you."

He shook his head, and his blond hair, mussed with their lovemaking, flew around. The braid slid over his shoulder and draped between them. Clea caught it in her hand, smoothing the long strands between her fingers.

"Thank you, Clea Dodolaka. It is not often a woman gives herself to me without wanting something in return."

His mind probed hers and she relented, letting down her walls. Griff poured reassurance, gratitude, and something deeper into her mind. Clea wondered what this Elemental really was. He was more than just the playboy air creature she'd been told about—there was something much more substantial.

"What would I want in return?" she asked, trying to lie, but knowing that her mind told the truth. "I think being a great lover and a good protector is more than enough." It was more than she'd had in decades. She walled off the rest of the softer emotions that could put her heart in danger. It had been a long time since she'd wanted to get to know a man who wasn't related to her. In the past, those feelings had always ended in heartbreak. Why she'd chosen a known paranormal Casanova to feel them again was one of the mysteries of her psyche that Clea may never solve.

He grinned, the flash of white visible even in the dim light.

"That will do."

He opened his mouth to say more, but before he could, they heard a noise behind them.

"Oh dear," a voice said, and Clea recognized it as Henry's. "I fear I am interrupting…again."

Chapter Eight

The man handed Griff a sheaf of Euros, which the Elemental slipped into a valise slung over his shoulder. The bag must have been designed for him. It fit around his shoulders and along his chest, resting at the small of his waist. His wings, a shade lighter than the dusky yellow shirt he wore, were free to move.

What did the humans see when they looked at Griff? Clea had wondered it before, when they were packing for the plane ride here, and she pondered it again. Clea opened her senses and felt the human's boredom at the task assigned to him by his boss, a low-level executive at a company affiliated with Elementals, Inc. He didn't seem to think anything about being asked to bring a large sum of Euros to one of the stockholders, or anything beyond which café he was going to eat at when he was done with his task. The bosses had no way of knowing how long the job would take him, the human thought, and he didn't have to hurry back.

There was no sense from the man that he noticed anything strange about Griff. He shouldn't have, of course, but Clea was still surprised that Griff's oddness, the rise of his yellow wings that were such a part of him, could not be recognized by mortals.

"Sensed, perhaps," Griff said, and Clea flushed, realizing she'd been projecting. "They intuit, but don't know. They feel the otherness in both of us," he continued, all the while making small talk with the bored man whose feet were pointing towards the door.

"Is there a café you recommend?" Griff asked.

The man, Pietro, glanced a furtive glance at the room service cart in the middle of the room. The cloches of two plates of breakfast were tilted, and a coffee pot and empty goblet of orange juice were scattered among the towels and utensils.

"Rich people are all alike," the man was thinking, and the emotion was so strong that Clea stepped back. "They think they own you."

She swallowed, and Griff's expression darkened. He turned to the man and stared at him. His wings rose through the slits in his shirt.

"Let it be," Clea urged, shifting her gaze towards the man. "You're scaring him."

"That is my intention."

Griff nodded, and Pietro shook his hand, bobbed at Clea, and fled.

Griff amplified the man's thoughts as he made his quick way to the elevator, tossing them at Clea down their link.

"Something wrong with that guy. I want to punch him. Rich, sleek jerk with all that money. He's just…something wrong with him. Man, I'd love to be him, though. Fancy hotels, wads of cash, that's the life. I wouldn't waste my time with that woman, though. She's not hot enough. I'd have…"

The opinions faded as he went outside, his fantasies about the latest woman on the telly going with him.

"They don't see the wings, I know that. I should be used to it, but it's still shocking to me that what is right in front of them is invisible to them." She watched Griff close the distance between them but didn't move. He put a finger under her chin and raised her head up until their eyes met.

"It is better they can't see." He dropped a kiss on her lips and smiled at her. He gestured at where the man had been standing. "He has no sense of the value of women. Of you."

"Oh, I've been insulted by far better than an ordinary human like him," she retorted. "I spent some time in Albania. Prende, the goddess of love in their pantheon was upset that their leader Tomor took a liking to me. She made her opinion widely known. To her I was nothing special, a minor goddess, and not pretty enough to warrant any male attention. I didn't stay long."

"The Albanian pantheon is no Greek one," he said. "Your Slavic pantheon and Albania are equal in stature. She has no grounds to be superior."

"Have you seen her?" Clea projected a picture of the dark-haired goddess to Griff. She was one of the most beautiful women Clea had ever seen, and could hold her own with the beauties amid any pantheon, even the well-known Aphrodite.

Griff made a seesaw motion with his hand. "She's beautiful, of course. I know dozens of dea like her. It doesn't mean anything to be stunning among the immortals. It takes more courage to be the way you are." He closed his mouth and the mind link shut down as well, as if he'd changed his mind about whatever he'd been going to say next.

He was probably given to empty flattery, but this didn't seem insincere. Griff's reputation as a playboy hadn't prepared her for this real, living, breathing Elemental. After Henry had made a show of shrieking and vanishing last night, Griff had stayed with her, sleeping in her bed, until they made love again this morning. With the sun streaming past the heavy curtains it seemed a little safer from ghostly intrusions, assuming that Henry did not manifest during the day.

"Come," Griff said. "Time to go to the tunnels."

She cocked her head, her gaze going to the large wings on his back.

"I know we have to go, but are you going to fit?"

Griff's expression was pained. "Whether I do or not, it is where we must go."

* * * * *

The Grand Duchy of Luxembourg, as the country was officially called, was landlocked, with no easy access to ocean water. Bordered by France, Germany, and Belgium, it boasted a high standard of living. There was something about the old Roman settlements and tunnels, dating back to the country's strategic location when Rome used it as a fortress and base for their westward expansion into the remainder of Europe, that had made the ancient being tell Griff to go there.

Luxembourg had never interested her. It was one of the smallest countries in Europe but for all its size the languages were varied and rich. She heard English, French, and something unfamiliar, a language that sounded similar to German but with many words she couldn't identify when they were spoken out loud.

"Luxembourgish."

"Why would you need to go to tunnels? You're an air Elemental. Won't your Challenge be related to wind or weather rather than the dank underground?"

They were walking down a broad street heading for the northeast corner of the city and an area called Bock, located in the historical district of Luxembourg City. Bock was surrounded by the river Alzette on three sides and with a rocky cliff face on the fourth. Old fortifications had been built there time and again, and warred over by various countries and populations until the fortress was dismantled in the last century. There was something called "Casemates" there, old tunnels where the bastion had been dug centuries ago. Clea doubted that the Demonos would do anything under the nose of one of Luxembourg's most famous stops, but she didn't know enough about Amai-te-rangi to be sure of anything.

Griffin had foregone the concierge's offer of a taxi. Now that they were on the streets clogged with cars, Clea understood why. Even in a crowd, he had more breathing room on the street than he did cooped up in a tiny vehicle.

"There has to be something to learn in the tunnels or Einar would not have directed me there. I wish to explore."

Griff seemed distant, but a quick check of their link revealed nothing wrong on the surface.

"I don't think Amai's basket will fit," she continued, willing him to smile.

He grunted. She tried to read him, but he was closed off to her. The realization hurt her more than it should have. There was no reason for them to be connected right now. Glorious sex didn't give her additional rights.

"Amai's basket comes and goes, as I have said before. He could be here, he could never have come here, or he could be gone already. I don't know. Einar felt it was important. He has walked the earth since the early days of humans. Einar's lifespan makes mine seem like the blink of an eye. He's my friend and I trust him. We're going to Bock."

Henry had assured them there were no ghosts in the Bock tunnels, although he muttered something about spirits in the nearby remains of the fortress. Clea hoped that Henry was right.

They walked in silence. People gave them a wide berth, few getting close. If pedestrians approached him in the opposite direction, they stepped as far around Griffin as possible, or waited until he passed to continue walking.

"You must trust him to go into tunnels," Clea remarked. "Do you find it hard to be around mortals?"

He raised a wing a fraction and a human near them veered. "I prefer more space," he said. "But we do what we must. What about you? How do you feel about them?"

She pondered his question for a few moments. "They are a necessity even if they would destroy me if they knew what I was. Without them we would cease to exist. It is an odd paradox. I can usually coexist with humans until I fail to age. I travel lightly. There have been times when I've needed to leave a place in haste." Clea checked the mind link and to her relief he had relaxed his block on it. There was still something closed off that she could not see. "You learn not to travel with possessions when you move around." She gestured to the high-end clothing they both wore. "This is nice, and I love the feel of the fabric against my skin, but I am just as happy in cotton."

Slipping his hand into hers, he laced their fingers together and Clea breathed a sigh of relief. Until that moment she hadn't known how badly his dark mood was bothering her. The people continued to ebb around them.

"You are full of surprises, Clea Dodolaka," he murmured. The rock promontory was nearby, and Griff used the tip of one wing to point over his shoulder. Clea giggled, knowing others couldn't see Griff's gesture, but finding it amusing regardless. "We are almost there."

* * * * *

Before they had set out, they had determined that the rock formations on this Bock side of the city were accessible. They had learned from the obsequious concierge that the tunnels on the other side of the city, in Petrusse, required a guided tour, which neither wanted to do. No witnesses. They needed to be alone. Bock it was.

There were plenty of people exploring when they got there, visible in the open breaks that were exposed to the world from collapse and decay. Greenery grew on the shattered remains of the old castle built in the nine-hundreds, and scattered low trees dotted the area.

Clea studied the small openings. There were tunnel entrances of all sizes in the tourist attraction, but some of them narrowed down so even a normal human would have trouble, never mind a broad-shouldered winged man.

Why had Einar sent them there? What had he seen that made him stress so strongly that Griff needed to visit? The first entrance was wide and openmouthed, easily fitting a span of ten people. Two people looked as if they wanted to go in at the same time Griff and Clea did, but hesitated and then backed away.

Guidebooks told them that there were seventeen kilometers of tunnels through the Casemates, tunnels that had been impossible to raze when the castle had been leveled in the eighteen hundreds. The Casemates wound throughout the city and couldn't be taken down without damaging the structures above. So the Casemates stayed and were now a tourist attraction for intrepid travelers.

"I don't understand." She turned to Griff, who looked as puzzled as she did.

"Neither do I." He kept his grip on her hand, his wings raised above his back in readiness. Clea was conscious of the oppression of the rock around them as they went into the rough-hewn stone tunnels. Handrails providing support were cut into the stone. There were people milling in the tunnel, which began to narrow at the point on the opposite side of the entranceway. Stairs led down, and she could see the tunnels begin to branch off.

Clea felt Griff open his senses, letting human thoughts come into his mind. Curious, she followed their link to see the people with him.

"This sucks. I want my tablet." The bored young male was a short distance away with older people who could only be his parents. They were American, speaking loudly in a Southern accent, pointing to the rocks and a guidebook they held in their hands.

"I'd better get laid out of this." Another man, older than the teenager, had two women with him. Either female would do as a bed companion.

"I want to leave. Now." That was from a wild-eyed woman whose stiff body and quick steps toward the top told Clea the human suffered from claustrophobia.

Further on the people were thinning, and Clea allowed Griff to lead her toward that direction. The tunnels branched and went down, with rough stairs carved into the floor, until the handrails ended and the people began to dissipate. There were closed off areas too, those that Luxembourg had been able to seal when they demolished the remainder of the Bock in eighteen seventy-five. Whatever had led Einar to guide them there had to be behind the sealed areas.

"Which way?" Clea asked. Another person dodged around Griff, giving him a wide berth. Griff's grip on Clea was secure as he led them down a sloped set of stairs. The tunnels were narrowing, but still not so narrow as to be uncomfortable. At this width it would be impossible to open his wings. Griff and Clea would be at a disadvantage if anything happened down here.

They kept walking, the tunnels darkening and tapering, until there were no more humans around. Griff looked right, left, and then chose a tunnel that seemed to come to a dead end. They were beneath the city, but she could not determine how far. Light came in through various holes in the distance, filtered through dust, and provided scant illumination. She wished they had thought to bring a flashlight. Then she smiled.

"Flashlight app." Clea nodded to her smartphone. She thumbed through the apps until she pressed one and light sprang from the back of her phone.

"Of course. Grazie."

The door lit by her phone app was obvious to them, but still seeing through Griff's eyes Clea felt no sense that humans had been interested in it. They were deep enough that this tunnel wouldn't have been heavily traveled, but some people should still have seen it. She concentrated and then could sense the spell put over it, an enchantment that made it uninteresting to mortals. When humans beheld the door they saw nothing but solid rock.

There were signs of recent dings on the rock under the door that spoke of some sort of entry. Griff's gaze followed the scrapes from the door to another tunnel, one leading up. The scrapes stopped at one of the open areas to the outside.

It looked as if something huge had been in the vicinity. There were many possibilities. Only one of them was Amai's basket, but whether irrational or not, Clea felt as if that was the object that had caused the scrapes. She had no idea how his basket would have fit down there.

"When you eliminate the impossible, whatever remains, however improbable, must be the truth," Clea said. At Griff's puzzled expression, she made a motion as if turning over book pages. "Sherlock Holmes. I liked mysteries for a while."

"I think we're meant to go inside." He pushed on the door, but it stayed where it was. Griff grunted. "It's not locked, but it's heavy. This was supposed to be sealed off; it appears to be part of the original galleries. It would be a perfect spot to hide something, or someone."

Clea eyed the heavy door. "Something big."

"Yes. Do you sense any humans?" he asked, pushing at the door. "Send a suggestion that any mortals interested in coming this way should try another tunnel."

Clea reached out to the humans in the distant outlying corridors with her mind, sending the thought that other areas were much more interesting than this one. A few who had seemed about to venture down changed direction, heading back the way they had come. She wanted to help him with the door, but Griff's half-unfurled wings blocked the way.

"Let me help," she said, pushing on one wing.

"I can do this alone."

"Whether you can or not, I'm here to help." She slid under the wing to join him by the door. Griff shifted, allowing her access. Together they pressed on the door until it creaked loudly, the rusty iron hinges protesting the shift, and the door began to move. It moved enough to allow them entry. Inside it was pitch black, and then light cut through the dark.

In the middle of the floor, standing with arms folded, was Amai-te-rangi.

Chapter Nine

The distance between Griff and Amai was about eight feet, barely a wingspan if he could find room to unfurl them. The room itself was about fifteen feet across, its tops and sides hewn in rough stone. The only light sources were the doorway, and a torch inserted into a sconce in the wall. The flickering of the flames danced along the walls and ceilings, creating alternate shadows and strips of light. The room had a feeling of abandonment and decay. On the floor in front of them were imprints of shoes and feet, and in the middle of the room where Amai now stood multiple footprints had disturbed the dust. Within the room layers of dirt and grime had been shifted aside, and there were scrapes along the rock.

"Kia orana, old friend," Amai said. "Nice to see you again."

Clea turned the light on Amai and the huge Demonos blinked at the sudden glare in his eyes, but didn't shift position. There was no sign of his basket. Amai had on a simple outfit of cargo shorts and a T-shirt, with sandals on his feet. The whorls of his tattoos could barely be seen in the dim light.

"Do you save the loincloth for special occasions?" Clea asked, standing next to Griff. Her warmth slid over him in the chill air of the room.

"Strange."

"Yes," Griff agreed, not shifting his gaze from Amai. "Be careful."

"Always."

"You make a habit of following me around." Griff stepped farther into the room.

Amai's face remained stoic, but a flicker of annoyance played over the Demonos's features. The glare of the phone flashlight app wavered when Clea's hand shook. Protectiveness surged through him, and he wanted to pull her to him, unfurl his wings, and fly her out of danger.

"We are even," Amai said. "I came to Iceland, you came to Luxembourg." His face settled into harsh lines. "How did you know to come here?"

Without his basket Amai seemed smaller, although his shadow still filled the room.

"I am not without my surprises." Griff unfurled his wings a little, using the movement to inch closer to Amai. Clea stayed with him, aligning their bodies while not seeming to move.

"What of you, wahine?" Amai asked, and Clea gave the Demonos a sharp look. "Woman" was better than "harlot," but Griff could not tolerate Amai, or any man, addressing her in that tone.

"What of me what?" she replied.

"Why are you involved in this?" He pointed to Clea, who studied Amai with a look on her face of such loathing that Griff blinked.

Clea moved forward, leaving his protection. Something surged behind her shields—feelings of anger, hatred, and loss. A face surfaced in her mind, and he frowned. The man was so good-looking he would have rivaled all human models. Primal male jealousy bubbled up inside Griff.

"Why am I doing this?" she repeated and she seemed to grow in size, her presence filling the room. He'd seen the Greek pantheon do the trick, but never one of the Slavs.

"I am from what is now the Czech Republic," she said. Amai's eyes were dark, his expression unchanging. "You remember what happened in the war."

Amai took in a deep breath, his chest expanding and his tattoos rippling. "Your little band who sought to protect the humans did not run fast enough. It matters little. You are gods."

An animalistic wail ripped from Clea, making Griff's wings stand up at full alert. Sorrow pulled her mouth down, and her body jerked as a shudder slid through her.

"Gods rarely die." Her voice was ashes and bile. "Not everyone who opposed you were gods." The image filled her mind again, the perfect features dancing along her memories like a living thing.

"My brother Patrik was a demigod," she said. "You killed him. True death. The kind no god comes back from."

Amai chuckled, his gaze not on Clea but on Griff.

"Wahine, you are on the wrong side."

Oh hell. Her pantheon had taken a severe hit in the war, but he hadn't realized…

A new voice startled both of them. "They sure are on the wrong side, aren't they, Amai, buddy?"

Griffin cursed. They had been so focused on the Demonos that they had failed to search out other minds, relying on the spell over the door to keep their presence shielded.

As one, he and Clea swiveled to face the voice. The man was standing in the doorway, partly shadowed by the room and partly in light. Griff could see he was balanced on the balls of his feet, a battle-ready stance. Clea turned the flashlight app on the man and his face jumped into focus.

The mortal in front of them was familiar, and Griff searched his memory until he came up with it. They had seen him recently. What had been the human's name? The one who had handed them the currency this morning? It had been something simple, it had been…

"Pietro," Clea said.

The former errand boy held a huge gun with a large barrel and a big opening. A bullet was visible in the chamber.

Amai chuckled. Griff didn't spare his counterpart a glance. Did this man think he could harm them? Harm an Elemental with a firearm, no matter the caliber? Even if he got off a shot, the wound would heal within minutes. He glanced at Clea.

"How did I do?" Pietro glanced past them to a motionless Amai. "I followed them just like you said." He sneered at Griff. "You thought you were so clever, but I thought all these thoughts like they taught me and you couldn't pick me out.

You couldn't tell I was following you. Joke's on you."

Griff frowned, trying to ease into Pietro's mind. There was surface chatter, talk of the upcoming elections, his favorite ice cream, a dog he'd had as a child, and the fury and anger about Griff's wealth, all nothing but a mask. It had been cleverly done, far too clever to be Pietro's idea. Griff dug deeper and discovered Pietro thought he was doing work for some Maori tribesman. All he knew was that it was illegal, and the more illegal the better. Amai must have shown him the doorway, removed the misdirection that made the door look like solid rock.

Griff had a choice between facing the Demonos or turning and protecting Clea. If they were shot then they would be slowed down, giving Amai time to make his move. If they left off Amai to engage the man with the gun, his Demonos enemy could act with impunity. Torn between his ancient foe and the human, Griff hesitated.

* * * * *

Clea brought the phone up, the flashlight app still blazing out of the back. Focusing it, she aimed at Pietro's eyes. Pietro let out a loud cry of dismay, and his white noise shield faltered. His fury poured through her when it slipped, inarticulate rage hammering into her consciousness. He hated everything about them. Even though he couldn't see Griff's wings, he knew they were different.

"Damn you!" Pietro threw his free hand up to shield his vision. The heavy gun sagged in his hand but he brought it up again before she could act on the slip.

Griff turned to face Amai. As he glared at the Demonos, he unfurled his wings to their full length. Amai chuckled as if in amusement.

Clea launched herself at Pietro as he aimed the gun. Blinded by the flashlight app, the human's shot was wild, whizzing past her and Griff and making a sharp ping on the other side of the room. The stone echoed with the retort.

"Damn you," Pietro said again, and he put one hand over the other to steady the weapon.

Griff dove at Amai, moving in a rush. Amai stood, arms folded, until Griff was almost on him. Then he stepped aside. He snarled as the Elemental flew past him just as the bullet had sailed past Clea seconds before. Amai's face was reddened and angry and she wondered if he was channeling some of Pietro's anger. Or perhaps he was feeding it to the enraged human?

She had a grip on Pietro. His arm was slick with sweat but surprisingly powerful, and he resisted her grasp. Clea tugged, trying to get a hold on him. Pietro fired.

The bullet pierced her right side, tearing flesh and blood away, before it continued out of her body and fell to the floor.

"Clea!" Griff exclaimed, his dismay pouring through their link. Pietro's eyes were wide in a startled, furious expression.

There was always pain when she was badly hurt. Griff broke off his assault on Amai and the Demonos winked, nodded at Griff, and strode past Pietro and out the half-lit doorway. Griff let him go, running back towards Clea and Pietro.

"First your demigod, and then you, goddess." Amai's mental voice rumbled through her mind.

"Clea!" Griff said again. Pietro turned to run. Pulling him back into the room, Griff wrested the gun from Pietro's hands and hurled it away. The gun went skittering along the stone until it stopped against the far wall, resting on crumbling mortar.

"I showed you," Pietro said, and then he broke off as Griff's wings began thrashing him while his arms held the would-be assassin in an unbreakable grip. Clea watched it as if from a distance, her consciousness fading.

"Clea," Griff said for the third time. "How badly are you hurt?"

Even as her body began to repair itself, Clea focused on the human. It was as if Pietro were getting assaulted by the wind. His smug thought that he had killed Clea had quickly turned to terror. She could see the wings that beat at Pietro, but the man could not. He did not understand what was scoring his shoulders and face. Griff's feathers were lethal weapons, sharp edged and dangerous.

"I'll be fine," she choked out, her voice as thin as her fragile grip on her consciousness.

"Hah," Pietro tried to shout, but Griff's wings muffled his voice. "That's a .44. You're dead."

Griff began slugging the man in the face with his fist, hitting him until Pietro slumped boneless, all fight gone. Even then Griff kept pounding him. He aimed a punch and broke Pietro's nose, sending blood gushing out of his nostrils. Pietro moaned. Griff brought his wing up and using the hook of his talon, dug into Pietro's cheek and slashed it, opening a deep gash along the fleshy area. Pietro cried out in shock, and fainted.

Every time she healed, Clea was fascinated by the process. It was like watching a movie backwards. She made sure Griff was linked in and moved her hand to reveal her wounded side. The wound was wide, skin split open and fat and muscle visible underneath. As they watched, her flesh began to knit together. First the gash was wide, ruined matter leaking out. Then the injury changed color, shifting from red to pink. The tear sealed to a thick line across her skin, the color changing until it matched her normal tone. In a short time, the only visible evidence that she had been shot was her torn shirt and the red that stained it.

"Dio mio. It is amazing to see." Something huge flowed behind his mind, of sorrow and pain and loss. She had felt it before, when she had blurted out the news about Patrik, but the emotion was gone behind high shields before she could follow it.

Clea met Griff's gaze. "I was in an accident once, on Java. I lost control on a dirt path and slid off the road. My car turned over into the woods until it came to a halt in the dense underbrush. Half a dozen bones, including my pelvis, were shattered. I had a deep cut in my thigh, severing the femoral artery." The Elemental studied her, making no secret of his intense interest. "It healed within a few minutes. Once I healed, I pried myself out of the wreckage and walked back to town. I left right away. I didn't think anyone saw, but I couldn't be sure. I don't know if they ever found the car. Lots of things disappear in the forest."

She hooked a thumb at Pietro. "What do we do with him?"

He grinned the pure feral grin of a predator. "Ripping him apart would create unwanted questions. I'll drop him off."

She knew he meant "drop" literally when he flexed his wings and glanced towards the open area to the outside visible from the room.

Clea smiled.

They eased out, Griff slinging the unconscious man on his back. Griff's wings retracted until they once again lay flat across his back. Clea retrieved the gun. He paused after they'd cleared the doorway.

"We need to close it."

Griff dumped the bleeding man onto the floor. Pietro's body made a thump when he landed but neither of them paid him any attention. Together they pushed on the stone door until it disappeared into the recesses. The spell would keep it from human eyes again.

"I thought you were going to drop him," Clea said, pointing to his quiet wings. A bloodthirsty part of her wanted Griff to haul Pietro to a cliff and throw him down. The distance would shatter the little man into nothing but bone and fragments. Clea longed to see his body broken and splintered, all life gone.

When Griff's breath caught, she understood she was feeling his emotions as her own. Wanting to see Pietro scattered against the rocks came from Griff. Some of it.

"He hurt you. He tried to kill you. He would have killed anyone else."

She nodded. Pietro began to stir.

"I wanted vengeance." Griff glanced at the tear in Pietro's cheek, a wound that would leave a fantastic scar. "I still want him dead. If this weren't Challenge, I would take that chance. But there is something else here and he may be more useful to us alive. I'll get an Elementals, Inc. employee to keep an eye on him. I'll dump him for the local Luxembourg police to find, and give them a nudge. Then we need to go."

His gaze went to her now-healed side, where Clea's ruined blouse gaped. "Or I can kill him, if you prefer."

After a moment, Clea shook her head no.

They walked back, out of the Casemates, Griff toting a stirring Pietro until he deemed it a good location. Then they rolled him on the ground. Griff located a police officer mentally and suggested that he might want to come out and arrest the man in the catacomb. Clea dropped the gun beside the moaning man.

"We must go." Griff urged Clea away from the scene and down several corridors towards the wide mouth of the entranceway. They were around humans again, and their low-level mind chatter was distracting.

"Where are we going in such a hurry?" Clea struggled to match Griff's long strides with her shorter steps.

"Out. Away." He seemed distracted and tense, his wings ruffling with his agitation. His big gait ate up the terrain as they walked quickly, covering the area to the hotel within minutes. Humans continued to eddy around them, keeping distance between themselves and the Elemental.

"Where to?"

"We need to pack." He pulled out his cell phone as they walked, talking to the pilot that had flown them from Iceland to Luxembourg, instructing him to have the private jet fueled and standing by.

"We just got here," she protested.

"Sì."

They reached the hotel, and Griff fell silent. His heightened emotions surged along their link. He was angry and frightened and...something else. His face was a mask, his shields impenetrable. He swung the door to their suite shut and turned to Clea, opening his mouth to speak.

"Oh, there you are," Henry said. "I was bored."

There was no mistaking the furious look Griff turned on the transparent man. "Out. Now."

Henry gasped and then winked out of sight with a squeal.

"They tried to kill you." He moved, his hands outstretched, and hauled her into his arms. Leaning forward, he kissed her, dipping his tongue into her mouth and seeking hers. She met his mouth, returning his grip and lashing her tongue over his. He groaned and deepened the kiss, moving their linked hands behind her back. She leaned into him, pressing against his body as fully as she could, joining them from shoulder to calf. Moisture flooded her, and her skin misted with the awareness of his body. Using her hips, she moved over his rising flesh, rubbing back and forth.

He let out his breath in a rush and hauled her closer, his tongue still tangling with hers. His hands pressed into her butt, holding her against his erection. Breaking off, he pulled back to meet her gaze. Clea was caught by the fear and the naked need mapped over his face.

"I'm okay," she said. Hot, deep arousal seared across her nerve endings. He took her hand and placed it against his penis. She gripped him through cloth, tracing his generous length with her thumb and index finger. His breath caught and he groaned, thrusting into her hand. A flush crawled across his face.

Griff palmed the space where her blouse had been shredded. Drying red bloodstains marred the torn edges. "Pietro tried to kill you. If he tries to harm you again, he will die. Get undressed," he said on a labored breath. "I need to feel you."

Together they stripped off their clothes until they were both naked. His erection bobbed. His gaze took in her body, and his wings rose up over them. Then they were airborne, a few feet off the ground. Clea breathed in and summoned her weather gifts to create a small eddy under them. His power joined hers, and it was as if they were standing on a cloud, his wings arched and high. Opening her legs, she exposed her body to him. Something resembling a smile curved his mouth up.

"Mine," he growled. The flap of his wings was the only sound in the room after that. He moved and bent his head to her hard-tipped breasts. Sampling first one, then the other, he played his tongue over her until she cried out and clutched at his head, digging her nails into the smooth skin. With her free hand she touched him, playing over his length until he grew under her palm. Then he moved, kissing her deeply and touching her, opening her to him.

"Now," he said, spikes of desire searing down their connection. His arousal rested outside her lower lips. Hovering with him, Clea opened her legs wider. She panted, her mouth open, needing this, him, right now. He thrust inside her until he was all the way in. She wrapped her legs around his hips and pulled him against her. He found her lips and pierced them with his tongue.

He began a rhythmic movement, pulling his body back before plunging deep inside again. All she could do was moan and claw at him. Feeling his wings above her, she cried out as the orgasm took her, every nerve alive with the piercing sensation.

He groaned and then went still except for his body pulsing inside hers. With a sudden movement, he kissed her again and his hips jerked hard once, twice and then faster. He moaned and gasped and went rigid, his face tight. His essence flooded her insides as his cry echoed in the room, pouring down her and through her.

Chapter Ten

"What is this?" Clea asked.

Griff was talking on his cell phone, but the rising of his wings indicated that he had heard her.

"Uno momento."

After a beat he joined her, and plucked the paper from her hand.

"What is your question?"

The black credit card in the envelope was heavy. She thrust an accusing finger at the plane ticket tucked next to it. "This is an open-ended ticket to anywhere. Why? Where do you think you're going without me? This only lists one passenger."

He pointed to the paper and then to her side where the wound had been. There was no mark and no trace of where the would-be assassin had pierced her skin.

"I have to visit my fire counterpart Phoenix," Griffin said. "Alone. I'll be back in a few days. We are done here." He gestured to the skyline of Luxembourg City behind them. "Whatever Einar saw, and the reasons for him to send us here, are no longer in this city. We must go elsewhere." He pointed to his bedroom where a suitcase lay on the floor. The rest of their items were still strewn around the hotel. "I will meet you in Portugal." He hesitated. Griff took her shoulders and considered her. Concern and something she couldn't identify warred for dominance in his expression. Her careful probe of their link revealed nothing. Awareness beat at the back of his mind, and Clea reached for it, but every time she did, it eluded her.

"Why do you need to go to…where and talk to Phoenix?"

"San Francisco." Griff smiled, but it was just a show of teeth, with no merriment behind his eyes. "He's got a situation on his hands and I should be there. He doesn't know he needs my help, but he does. We've been friends as long as I have been Griffin. I owe him."

Clea nodded, knowing she showed ill grace all over her face. "Fine. Why can't I just stay here?" She caught a whiff of a saying in his mind and pulled the thread forward. Clea frowned. Fire calls to fire. Air will glide with air. Water swims together. Earth is always there. It had the feeling of an old ritual, something that had been around for centuries. She shivered, an icy feeling trickling over her spine, and then focused on Griff again.

He chuckled. "Ostinato. This ticket will take you anywhere. I can tell you don't want to go back to your people. Why, Clea? Why did Dodola send you to me? It's time you told me what happened between you and Perun."

Clea cocked her head at Griff, but he didn't continue. Pursing her lips, she tried to give him a cool look. "That's high-handed of you," she replied.

"Get used to it."

* * * * *

She wanted to protest further, but let the words die unspoken. Clea didn't want to have this conversation, but part of her had expected this moment sooner or later.

She opened her mouth, keeping her mind shielded from him.

"The truth, Clea," he said.

"The truth." The credit card bore her name and a logo she now recognized as the Elementals, Inc. insignia. Cards of that color were only issued to the wealthy, and usually only by special invitation. She did not know if there was a spending limit, but with this card, she could go anywhere, do most anything, and hope that Perun cooled down after a time. She could run. Griffin had handed her the tools. In a remote area like the South Pacific, she could hide out for decades until

Perun cooled off. If not for Patrik, she might have. She hadn't been there when he needed her and now he was dead. Clea would help with Challenge and make sure Amai got what was due to him. Nothing would stop her.

"The truth," she repeated. She sighed, flicking a corner of the card with her thumbnail. Clea relaxed her shields enough to let him see Patrik.

Griff made a sound. His lips pulled back, revealing teeth in what she could only call a snarl. "This Patrik you keep in your mind, he was your brother?"

She nodded and he made that sound again. The half eagle/half lion overlaid his features and his eyes began to change to gold.

"I do not understand your kinship. How was he your brother?" Griff said, and a ripple moved under her skin. It may have been phrased as a question, but there was no doubt that he expected to be told. Now.

There were many ways she could answer but in the end there was only one.

"He was Perun's son by a human lover. Not technically a brother by blood, but a brother in every way that mattered."

She turned her face to him, moisture gathering in the corners of her eyes.

"He tried to fight during the last Challenge when the battle reached our area. He identified with his human side. He gathered a group of humans and went to war." Tears ran down her cheeks. Griff stood motionless, his wings rippling as if there were a breeze, but there was nothing in the room but the two of them, and memories. "Amai killed him."

"How did it happen? He was a god."

"Demigod," she corrected, her voice harsh. She had cried so many tears, but more slid over her cheeks. Griff remained motionless. He turned away from her and went to the window. His wings slumped until the bottom feathers dragged on the floor. "Nobody is sure what happened, but we all felt his life force go out. One moment he was there and the next he was erased from the earth as if he had never existed.

Griff's mind was turbulent, unreadable. Many of her pantheon still blamed the Elementals for the war and its aftermath, but Clea knew where the blame lay.

"I wanted vengeance, and I pushed Perun to let me act. I kept at him, and he refused time and again until one day he turned on me and struck at me. The skies opened up. I've never seen him so angry. He shouted at me that I should have left it alone. His thunder rumbled with his rage, and he threw lightning at me again and again. I barely dodged it. He just kept shouting, the words and his mind inarticulate. He would have killed me, I think. He tried. His lightning was nothing like I'd ever seen. It crackled with energy, scoring the earth to black where it struck. He created cloud-to-cloud lightning, using Mother's clouds to strengthen the effect, and hurling the whole thing at me when they built up enough charge to satisfy him. If not for Mother, he would have struck at me until I was nothing but ash. He was so angry. I had to get away. I don't understand his anger. He has no love for Amai. The Demonos killed his son, perhaps only a demigod, but Patrik was much loved in our pantheon. We mourned when he died." She studied Griff's back, his peculiar slumped posture tugging at her.

He said nothing. His wings fluttered, the feathers moving in a small motion as Griff heaved his chest.

"I know Mother called in a favor, and thank you for taking me in. I don't know what would have happened if she hadn't gotten me out of there. But it doesn't matter. It served its purpose. Patrik deserves vengeance. Amai will pay for destroying my brother, Lorenzo Griffin Traverso."

He said nothing for long moments, and then Griff nodded. "I see."

She took a deep, ragged breath. "I will have a reckoning. You of all people should understand. Aren't you running off to check up on your fire Elemental? Isn't he the closest thing you have to a brother?"

Griffin faced her. His eyes were in shadow as he stepped forward. Griff took the plane ticket from her hands and placed it on the table. It didn't surprise her that he would use paper tickets in this electronic age.

"Sì. I have to go to him," Griff said. "I want you to consider what you do next, Clea Dodolaka. This card will take you anywhere and sustain you for as long as you need. There is no limit on it. You should leave here and go someplace far away from Challenge. Argentina is beautiful this time of year."

It would be so easy. Part of her was tempted. Nothing would bring Patrik back. "No." She gripped the black plastic. "I am not going to run. Amai has to pay. I am not going to let Perun stop me. I want to see Mother. I need answers, ones only she can provide."

Griff's look showed concern and something she didn't understand.

"Before I do anything else, I need more information. Mother won't lie to me if I confront her directly. I'll stay away from Perun. I will ask her to come here. Griffin, if you have Elemental business, you need to do it. I'll talk to Mother. But make no mistake, my brother will be avenged."

Again an odd look passed over his face, as if someone had walked over his grave, if Elementals had graves. He opened his mouth but then closed it.

"I will tell the hotel that the room is yours until you have no further need of it. Clea, if anything goes wrong, you reach out to me immediately. Perun may be a god but he won't want to tangle with an Elemental."

* * * * *

"Miláčku." Darling, Clea translated. "You look marvelous."

Clea stepped back from the doorframe, allowing Dodola entry. Her mother swept into the grand hotel room as if she belonged there.

Dodola had a headband and fringed gold dress on her body, a long cigarette holder in her elegant left hand completing the nineteen-twenties flapper look. Her blonde hair was cut pixie short, and framed her perfect heart-shaped face. Even humans who looked upon her would not have been surprised to know she was a goddess of fertility.

Henry the ghost appeared as if summoned, peering through his monocle at the new arrival before he was fully formed.

Dodola turned to him, a bright smile on her face. "Oh my dear, you have a ghost! How wonderful." She strode to Henry, who straightened and then bowed, his air of exaggerated civility amusing in context.

"My lady, you are stunning." He reached out as if he wanted to kiss her hand.

His hand passed through hers and a look of mournful regret crossed his face. He faded out for a moment and then returned.

She cooed at him, turning sideways to favor Henry with a coquettish glance. "Oh how charming you are, ghost. Now run along if you would. My daughter and I have business to discuss."

Henry poofed as if he had never been there. Clea eyed the spot where he had been. She had to learn the trick of that.

"Why did you summon me?" Dodola asked the moment Henry was gone. Her face was hard and set, and all trace of levity gone from her voice. "You need to stay away from Perun. He will be angry for decades. You're a fool to come even this close."

"So much for small talk," Clea projected to her mother's tight shield. Immediately she felt like the imperfect god-child she had been two-and-a-half centuries ago. She was once again the one who was cast out and told that she was not, and would never be, good enough to have a place in the pantheon.

"Griff had to run an errand." She didn't understand why it was so important for him to fly off to the United States to chat with his fire counterpart, but he'd blazed out of town in a big hurry. He had promised to be back in a few days and meet her in Comporta, Portugal. Maybe he would show up. Time would tell.

"Griff was supposed to take care of you," Dodola said, and there was no easy smile to charm her daughter, no honeyed words to make the message easier to tolerate. "Does he understand you are in more danger with us than with him?"

She nodded. "He knows. I told him why I wanted to fight Amai, too."

Dodola reached out a hand and touched Clea's face.

Straightening, Clea drew her shoulders back and looked her mother in the eye. Dodola was a goddess, and unaccustomed to direct visual contact. Most in the pantheon averted their eyes at the sight of their leaders.

Dodola didn't blink, but she paled and sent out a mental probe. Clea envisioned a thorny wall, and Dodola's foray subsided.

"Prosim, Clea, you are rash. Isn't it enough Perun damaged your thunder?" Dodola let out a breath. "I thought sending you to the Elemental would be enough. I assumed seeing Amai in person would show you what a foolish thing it was to think you could avenge Patrik. He made his choice. Nobody made him fight."

"What happened?" Clea asked, and was surprised to see Dodola recoil. She studied her gorgeous mother. A tendril of fear flickered behind her shield, but was quickly gone.

Dodola let out a breath, examining her fingernails instead of meeting Clea's gaze. Clea waited, trying to conceal her impatience, until Dodola raised her wide, cornflower-blue eyes to her daughter. Her innocent, wounded expression would have charmed men. Human and god would rush to her side, but it had no effect on Clea. Dodola was no Helen of Troy. The actual Helen had died a long time ago, long before Clea had been born, and was a subject of jealousy among the pantheons for a time, but like all humans, she existed today only in memory.

"He went to fight, even though Perun forbad us from taking sides. Patrik wanted to make a difference in the war. He joined with a band of humans to fight," she said, waving a hand. "The details are unimportant. He was killed along with his mortals. It was a slaughter. We all felt it."

Clea nodded. "I did, as well. It was like he was sucked into a vortex and vanished. My dinner companions were terrified when I screamed."

Dodola made a pained sound, her shoulders hunched. "I have never understood why the two of you bonded like that. You were not siblings. You did not share blood."

"He befriended me when the rest of the pantheon only showed me their backs. Maybe it had something to do with him being only half of our blood, as I was," Clea said. "He took care of me. Now I will take care of him. We were siblings in all the ways that mattered. I will pay Amai back. I vow it."

Dodola made a tsking sound. "Vengeance is not for us, miláčku. It is done and cannot be changed." She paused. "It is better you are here, while Perun cools down. The Elemental can protect you in ways I cannot. Perun is furious. Leave it alone. In time, Perun will forget, but if you persist in this path he may never take you back."

Clea brought the heel of her hand down on the table in the sitting area, making the silverware dance.

"I don't give a shit about Perun. Amai took away the brother who loved me."

Dodola's eyes widened to look like a giant doll. "I suppose it is good you have another brother."

Clea made a noise. All Clea's efforts to get information from the pantheon about Patrik led to evasions and dissembling. No more.

"I have lots of other brothers, Mother," Clea said. "Sisters too, for all that they can't stand me."

Dodola clucked her tongue. "I don't mean one of those. Perun's children will never like you. I mean a brother. My son with the same father as you."

Clea gasped, her mind whirling. "Brother? A full-blown brother? One of you and Neit, like me?"

Dodola nodded. "It was our agreement. One for each pantheon. I've never met Cormac as Neit has never met you. It was the deal. You would be raised in the Czech Republic and him in Ireland. I named you Clea for camouflage. It's Greek, as you know."

"Greek, as in Zeus? You wanted people to think he was my father? Did you ever…?"

Dodola's ripple of distaste was pronounced. "Oh, nebesa no, not that man. He thinks he's so much better than the other gods. He has attempted it, of course, as he does with all the maidens. He would have tried to get you into bed too, if you had come to his attention for long." She gave Clea a sidelong look. "The name was a good way to keep the other gods guessing, though, wasn't it? They were never quite sure if your father was that man and it made them wary of interfering with you."

"If that was the only way…I guess so. What about my brother? His name is Cormac?"

Dodola let out an exaggerated sigh. "It was a great love affair with Neit for a little while." Clea had heard such things before from her fickle mother. Each new lover was the best ever for a while. It was the way of things with many pantheons.

Lovers came and went, but Perun and Dodola were constant with each other in their way. Clea had found over the years that despite being Dodola's daughter she wasn't built for casual affairs.

Clea knew little about the Tuatha Dé Danann, the pantheon her father came from. He had never expressed interest in meeting her and she had never reached out. Neit was a war god, and the legends would have had him die in some battle, but that was human mythology. He had a wife, or wives, the Morrigan, if she remembered her pantheon correctly. She understood that the three women making up that fierce goddess weren't females you wanted to mess with.

Clea raised an eyebrow. "That's interesting."

"Don't be judgmental. It would never have lasted, of course, but it was good for a while. That is why I chose to have children with him. I wanted something to remember him by."

"Perun was jealous? Is that why he is so furious now?"

Dodola nodded. "He was enraged. He thought that I loved Neit better than him." A private smile made her lips turn upward. "It was true for a time, and he could never forgive you for it. It is hard for him to look at you, the reminder that my heart was another man's for a little while." She paused. "Your thunder powers remind him of Neit every day."

"But…the Morrigan." Clea tried to think of their individual names. Badb, maybe, and…she would have to search the Tuatha Dé Danann when she got access to a computer.

"Oh, he had no reason to be worried," Dodola said with a flip of her hand. "It was just a brief liaison, and it was never going to last. The Morrigan understood, Macha especially. Those women are quite wise about these things, wiser than my ridiculous husband." Dodola's voice was edged with sorrow. "It was dangerous of you to ask me to come to you."

"I'm with an Elemental. Perun will think twice."

There was something sharp in Dodola's expression. "The Elementals, ano. The Elementals failed last time. They cannot fail again."

Again, a wave, a dismissive gesture. Clea was fascinated by the perfect gleaming polish of Dodola's blue nails. They weren't too long, just long enough to let the observer know that this was not a woman who did manual labor. For a brief moment, Clea wondered what humans saw when they were allowed to gaze upon Dodola.

"A beautiful woman, one they can covet but can never have."

Clea flushed, realizing she'd let her shields slip too far. "That makes sense."

"Griffin is a proud, stubborn loner of an Elemental. He walks in and out of people's lives, always friendly and easy to talk to, but never serious."

"Kind of like you," Clea thought. "What about my father? What about Neit?"

The look Dodola gave Clea was deep and full of meaning. "He would be pleased that you've turned out as you have. As pleased as I am."

Clea flushed. Maybe she would go to the Tuatha Dé Danann. It would be good to belong somewhere.

"I want to meet my brother."

"That is arranged." Dodola concentrated for a moment. There was a knock on the door.

There was a mind signature of another god on the other side of the door, one she had never encountered before.

"It is your brother, dcela. Open the door."

A man stood in the doorframe when she strode on the plush carpet to open the door. He was big, probably 6'4", broad-shouldered and blue-eyed, every inch a warrior. She scrutinized him, knowing who it had to be. Clea looked for resemblances, and found few. "Who are you?"

"Maithrin didn't have the doing of it, I see. I'm Cormac."

Out of the corner of her eye, Clea saw Dodola glance around the room, as if trying to disappear. After a moment Henry appeared again, his body solidifying until he could have been mistaken for someone still living.

"My lady, if it would suit you, there is a park nearby and it would be my pleasure to take a turn around the common with you." Henry spared a glance at Clea and her new brother before turning his attention back to Dodola. The Slavic goddess smiled in relief and placed her hand just above Henry's still insubstantial arm.

"What a lovely idea, you marvelous ghost," Dodola said. "Can you leave this place? You're not...bound here?"

Henry made a dismissive gesture with his hand. "I am not entirely stuck in this dreary hotel. I can travel to limited places."

Dodola's face was wreathed in a smile that seemed tinged with relief. Searching her mind, Clea felt that emotion behind Dodola's shields. She spared a glance for Henry. Ghosts were good for some things.

They watched as their mother and the eighteenth-century ghost left the sumptuous room. Clea turned back to Cormac.

"You're the brother I didn't know I had until a few minutes ago?" Clea asked.

Cormac nodded, his wide face open and encouraging. After a moment, Clea smiled and walked into his arms, which opened for her as soon as she moved, and then closed around her gently. His embrace was both comforting and familiar for all that he'd been unknown to her ten minutes ago.

"'Twas a deal it was, that I stay with the Tuatha," he said, his words muffled in her hair. "That was the way of it when we were bairns."

Clea pulled away and then stepped back. She studied Cormac again. A brother, with the same blood she carried in her veins. Clea hadn't understood until that moment how much the thought meant to her. He had the same shape of eyes and mouth as she did. They could have chosen to resemble each other, and likely would have, if they'd grown up together.

"Why are you here? Did you always know about me, about Dodola?"

So many questions. He had just met her and she was pouncing on him for information, all eagerness and nervousness. Clea straightened her back. She deserved answers. She was a goddess, a worthy member of two pantheons.

"'Tis never been secret among my clan, nay, it has not," Cormac said. "It was come I had to. You're with that fellow, that Elemental. Perun has it in for you, we heard that. You need protecting. I'm after wondering where the Elemental has gone round to?"

She shook her head. "He had something to do." She studied her brother again, committing his features to memory. His accent would take getting used to, but she understood him perfectly in her mind.

"Aye?" Cormac's voice was dark with displeasure. He held out his hand. "Come, deirfiúr. There is much to discuss, so there is."

* * * * *

He was fucked. Cazzo.

Griffin accepted another glass of wine from the first-class flight attendant. It wouldn't get him drunk, of course, but if he were thought to be smashed then people would let down their guard.

On the way back from San Francisco he had picked up a tail. The man had started following him in New York before the flight continued to Europe.

The man wasn't subtle. His nervousness was easy to spot to anyone with an ounce of sensitivity. Griff could sense him in coach, sweating and shifting around, making his seatmates angry. Griff found one thread amusing. The woman behind Joey, the ineffective tail, wanted to push her knees into his seat "accidentally" and make the squirming man jump.

After another sip of his delicious wine, Griff sent a suggestion that the woman act on her wish.

The wine made him momentarily lightheaded before his metabolism burned off the alcohol, leaving him with nothing but the faint memory of a good vintage. Why was he being followed? And by whom?

He had told Clea he had gone to San Francisco to see Phoenix, and to see for himself what Phoenix had brought into his life. His fire comrade was powerful but held himself away from others and had no idea what the woman was. Griffin had to ensure that Phoenix wasn't being drawn into a trap. He'd had no real business checking up on his friend, but he'd done it anyway. He'd needed to get away, to absorb what Clea had told him and figure out what the hell he did next.

For the first time in Griff's memory, they had companions at Challenge time. It was unlikely, but not unheard of, that more than one of them would be coupled when faced with their battles.

The old Hippocampus had had a same-sex partner, a man who had vanished into humanity's midst after Hip died. If the man knew what Hip had been, he had made no reference to it at the wake. As the man was human, Griffin doubted that he had any idea what Hippocampus really was. Likely he accepted that his lover was a wealthy man with secrets. If the water Elemental hadn't been killed, it wouldn't have been long before Hip would have had to explain, or move on. Elementals usually chose the latter.

Fluffy clouds floated outside his window. Griff wanted to launch outside and feel them against his wings. When he was uneasy or restless, he would take to the clouds and float there, unseen by any except birds, until his mind calmed. He had met Amai up there once or twice, when Challenges weren't on the table, and they had had conversations. It was an odd thing to run into your enemy in times of peace, but Griffin and Amai had an unspoken understanding during those years, and they let each other alone.

Peace was out the window. Griff was dealing with a bloodthirsty goddess with vengeance for her brother on her mind. Oh yeah, he was definitely screwed. He coughed and the flight attendant hurried over. Her mind showed pleasure at helping the handsome blond gentleman, and desire to add him to her list of partners in her mile-high club.

Griff waved the woman away. He was still absorbing the bombshell Clea had dropped on him. In addition to the humans, good paranormals had been lost in that war. She blamed Amai.

She shouldn't.

Not knowing that she'd lost a beloved brother didn't excuse him. It just laid one more layer of guilt onto the heavy weight he had carried since the war. He would never be able to repay Clea what she had lost.

Cazzo. So fucked.

If he could have sent her away, he would have. He had tried, but she was still meeting him in Portugal. He would do as he had promised, knowing that when Clea found out the truth about Patrik she would go from hating Amai to hating him. There was nothing he could do about it.

Right now, he had an unwanted tail at thirty thousand feet. Griff sought the man's thoughts again. It was no pleasant task. His tail's mind was dark, a miasma of depravity and ugliness. It showed a series of petty thefts and casual violence that regularly landed him in and out of jail. The nature of his crimes ensured he never spent long in the overcrowded jail system, and the man stayed under the radar enough to ensure he didn't graduate to the tougher prison structure. He had been paid to follow Griff as long as he could. His name was Joey, but everyone called him Bubba. He had a handful of prison pals, more partners in petty crime than friends, and one of them had tossed this job his way. He was big, sweaty, and obvious, and an odd choice for a tail. Joey's mind showed that he knew the person hiring him didn't expect much, but a free trip was a free trip, and he could use the Eurail pass and fake passport to cause some havoc in Europe before he had to get back to Jersey. He'd been hired for expedience, not capability.

Still, it was strange. This guy was as ineffective as a slobbery dog. Whoever was working with Amai had talent and skill and this man had neither.

A female thought traveled along a strange connection, breaking into his confused thoughts. Griff turned in surprise.

"It's the wrong question ye be asking."

* * * * *

Clea toyed with the remains of their breakfast that was not yet cleared away. She had hung a "do not disturb" sign on the door. Her brother was seated in one of the guest chairs, his big frame spilling out of the fabric.

"You...how did you get here?" It was not what she really wanted to ask, but the question would do for starters.

"The human way," he said and smiled. "Marvelous invention, planes." His eyes, a light-brown shade that reminded Clea of autumn leaves, sparkled. "'Tis not that far from Ireland. It was questions I wanted to ask of our maithrin."

"Did you get answers?" Clea asked. This big man was nothing like the godlets that dotted their pantheon. He appeared to be a child of the earth, solid and large, more like her unmet father than their willowy mother. Curiosity now burned inside her about her unknown kin. She wanted, she needed to understand the Tuatha Dé Danann.

"Some," he said. "It was come I had to. Something is on the wind, I feel it in the ground. Do ye not feel it, deirfiúr? This Challenge, 'tis bigger than us, bigger than the Elementals. It is danger I feel, if they do not succeed."

Clea studied him for a moment. "There is always danger when there is Challenge. Millions of humans die if they fail."

"Aye," he said. "I am aware, so I am. We are not so far removed in Ireland that we do not feel the ripples. I am not speaking of that, no I am not. I would have come to you anyway, sister, but I was compelled. Neutral Ireland and the Tuatha Dé Danann were during that war the humans called World War II, but neutral I fear we cannot be in this one. We are part of this, you and I. Do ye not feel it?"

Slowly, Clea nodded. Plucking at a thread on the purple sofa, she studied Cormac.

"I do feel it, brother," she said. Emotion she couldn't name filled her and then rumbled through her as if it wasn't her own. It shot through Cormac as well, filling them with power before it receded.

Cormac's eyes widened, matching the stunned look on Clea's face. She wanted to ask him what had just happened but could tell by his mind signature that he was as uncertain as she was. It had been a sort of approval, but from nothing she'd ever felt before. It was unlike any power she had ever experienced. She reached for the force, but it was gone. Shaking her head, Clea turned her attention back to Cormac.

Cormac went to her and knelt before her on the carpet. Clea put her hands on his shoulders. He felt warm and earthy, like the land after a good tilling. He was her brother. He was the only full-blood brother she would ever have. It would take time to get to know this man, and she looked forward to it.

"You are my sister and I am glad of it. I am after protecting you while I get to know you. I am also after helping your Elemental with Challenge. Where do we begin?"

* * * * *

Griff regarded the first-class passenger on the other side of the aisle. To humans, she would have seemed like an unkempt middle-aged woman with flyaway hair and clothes that had seen several years of use.

He'd known that Macha, a third of the trio of women making up the Irish goddess the Morrigan was there with him, travelling to England before going back to Ireland. They had exchanged pleasantries and then he had forgotten her. Although she was a powerful Irish deity, she was the last thing on his mind. The idea to forget her had been skillfully done. He frowned. It was rare that someone got the better of him. Up until now he had very little interaction with the Tuatha Dé Danann, and now he not only was involved with one of their daughters but one of their powerful goddesses was with him. Griffin did not believe in coincidences.

Griff checked his shields and was relieved to find they were strong. It was enough that some silly human thought he could tail Griff, and now this one. Macha was far too clever to put him at ease.

The woman had piercing hazel eyes behind her glasses. Anyone with any sensitivity would see that she was more than she appeared. The glasses gave a momentary affectation of weakness, but only for an instant.

Now that she had reminded him she was there, he should be polite. He didn't want to be. He could usually muster up charm, drag out an old-fashioned kiss on the hand and some flattering words to any woman. Today he couldn't find it within him to flirt. He was ragged, out of sorts, and jealous of the emotions that shone in Rachel for Phoenix. The woman was into his fire Elemental friend and had made it clear. There would be no such happiness for Griffin.

The silence had gone on too long. Macha was still eyeing him with an expectant air, a glass of wine in her left hand. Wine should affect her as it did most gods, and she'd had two or perhaps three. Maybe it had loosened her tongue and prodded her to speak.

"What is the right question?" He discovered he was growling and his wings started to rise. Griff willed them back down. Even in first class they would pierce the bulkhead if unfurled.

"Ooh." She peered over the bifocals to the wings behind him. Her voice held no terror. She sounded more like an amused teacher with a recalcitrant student. She left her recliner seat and came over to his area, taking up residence in the side of the flat fold-out bed that he wasn't using. Griff shifted aside to allow her space. There was something coiled in Macha, this third of the Morrigan, that made him blink.

She tapped the wine glass and looked back beyond the curtain covering the opening between the first class and coach.

"He is not important. You will lose him in customs, my lad, if it be after taking you that long."

He tried to probe her mind, but she batted it away, as if his questing were nothing more than a troublesome insect.

"You'll not have the doing of that, Elemental," she said with no anger in her tone.

"I don't give a damn if I have a tail," he said. "Once we get to England, it will be quicker for me to use my wings. He can't follow me that way."

She nodded. "Gods above, he's obvious, that one. It's missing something you are, Griffin."

He shook his head, frustrated by her superior tone. She appeared to be laughing at him, smug in her superior knowledge.

"It's the blanks you are after looking for, Elemental. It's the blanks."

Chapter Eleven

He stared at her, trying to make sense of her words.

"This man here is a decoy, so he is. Ye be looking for another."

Macha gave him a sharp glance, her gaze saying that he should have known it all along.

"Perche?"

She smiled. The flight attendant came to see if they needed more wine, and both nodded.

"We are not after caring about your Challenges, Elemental." She took a sip of the new beverage and smacked her lips in appreciation.

"I have rare tasted finer. This would be helping fertility, so it would." She winked, and Griffin fixed her with his gaze. She wasn't flirting with him, was she?

"I lost my place, so I did. Oh, yes, your Challenge. We are not after getting involved in such things, in normal times. The times are not normal that are coming now." She studied Griffin, and her look was so serious that unease curled through him.

"We care not for your Challenge, or you, so it is. We care about Clea. It's she you be after minding, or you will have the Tuatha Dé Danann nipping at your heels. 'Tis not a thing you should want."

"Why do you care about Clea?"

Macha pushed her glasses back up onto the bridge of her nose.

"Ye have been told she is Neit's, yes?"

Griffin nodded.

"We protect our own, Elemental. Ye need to watch yourself, aye you do. It be protecting her we will."

* * * * *

Griffin ground his teeth in frustration as he waited in the slow customs line. If there had been another way, he would have taken it but he'd had no option but to go see Phoenix. He owed his longtime friend that. The half-Ifrit woman who had so suspiciously entered Phoenix's life seemed genuine, but Griffin hadn't known that for sure until he got there. She may even be an asset in Phoenix's Challenge, but that remained to be seen. In addition, it was a good opportunity to spend a few days away from Clea, to give himself a chance to think.

Her brother. He knew the leader of the unfortunate band of fighters had been a demigod, but it wasn't something the Slavic pantheon spoke about. Nothing could remove his guilt, or bring the man back. He and Dodola didn't discuss it. It was his cross to bear, but he had thought that was all. He had waited for Dodola's marker to be called in and had prepared for it. He hadn't known the man was dead until he had been nursed back to health by the man's stepmother, his promise of an Elemental's assistance to the pantheon granted as the price for that boon. He would have healed eventually, but Dodola's skills hastened his return to health. At that time he hadn't been sure if Amai would strike again and was grateful for Dodola's ministrations. It was thought among the pantheon that Amai had been the one to destroy the pantheon's much beloved demigod, and Dodola and Perun—and Griffin—were the only ones who knew the truth. Griffin had never been sure why Dodola and Perun chose to keep that secret.

Never would he have expected that the luckless man, the one caught at the wrong place at the wrong time, had a sister who would want to avenge him. Nor that the sister would be the far-too-appealing Clea.

Macha had refused to answer any more questions, leaving Griffin to puzzle over the fragments of clues while they landed.

We care about Clea.

Focus, Griffin, he told himself. There is more at stake than one dea.

He reached out down their mind link and found Clea asleep. She was like a drug and he the addict. Not wanting to wake her, he sent soothing thoughts to her and retreated.

Griff walked through the terminal, his mind elsewhere. He wished Macha had been willing to tell him more but few paranormals made the Elemental job easier. She had told him what she was going to and the rest was for him to piece together. As usual, humans eddied around him, keeping as much distance as they could in the crowded area.

Remembering Macha's words, Griffin opened his mind to the human hubbub. Joey, his tail, was caught in the customs line, cursing and fidgeting, seeing his prey elude him. Griffin "suggested" to the woman agent that the man three people back might need extra checking. That ought to slow him down.

But he was not the real concern. Griff continued to reach out, feeling the paranormal and human minds each in turn. Griffin cursed. There was nothing here, no…

Wait.

There was a blank mind space, a hollow echo where a person should be. The crowd was dense and thick, hurrying to baggage claim, and the spot moved with it.

This supernatural being had one of best shields he had ever seen. Griff used the throng to track the blank space, moving quickly toward it. He would lose them if they got into an open area with no other minds, but for now, he could trail the man.

Griff's wings poked up, at medium alert.

With the negative space in front of him, Griff touched the minds of the humans surrounding the space. They seemed to be shying away from the blank zone, as they similarly gave Griff a wide berth.

Joey, still being held at customs, swore as Griff disappeared. Griff pressed on the customs agent again, and two police officers with bomb-sniffing dogs descended on Joey.

Griff took advantage of the human reluctance to be in his personal space to clear a path. He drew closer to the blank as they moved down the long hallway towards baggage claim, pursued and pursuer.

"Humans are lazy."

Griff started, feeling the unfamiliar mind shoot him the message. It was tinged with amusement and contempt. It also had the unmistakable feel of the female.

A woman, then. Not a man.

"Who are you? What do you want?"

There was a light chuckle, and the link vanished. He could wait. They wouldn't have set the sweaty man on him, they wouldn't have ridden on the same flight as him, they wouldn't be leading him on this merry chase of "who are you" if they didn't want to talk to him. It had all been too obvious. His wings tugged at his back, wanting to rise.

He pushed through the thick doors of baggage claim and saw his prey.

A tall, broadly built woman was in front of him, with dark curly hair and a tilt to her eyes. She was dressed in layers of clothing that evoked what humans called a "gypsy" now.

Griff searched his mind as he hurried toward her.

A Vântoase. A Romanian weather spirit. They did not like to leave their country, preferring to travel by wagon and stick to forests and lakes. At least, that was the folklore. In truth, the Vântoase were like all the other beings in legends—part of what was said about them was true, but more was nonsense steeped in time and superstition. Like most paranormals, the Vântoase stayed in the shadows and interacted with mortals as little as possible. They could cause dust storms and powerful winds, that much of their lore was accurate, but they didn't attack children and there was no mysterious "grass of the winds" that would shield humans from them. The Vântoase were minor malevolent beings and liked to stir up trouble for the sake of it.

Another weather being. Too many coincidences. He caught up to her, or she stopped moving long enough to be caught. To his dismay, Griff still couldn't sense her.

Her mind, rich with contempt for people, sprang into his consciousness. Griff sent up a quick shield, reducing her blast. Around them was the buzz and hum of humanity's mental noise, something Griff paid as little attention to as their physical beings swirling around him.

He reached the woman, who smelled of cloves and looked of Romani. Her neck and arms were thick with chunky pendants and her fingers dripping with rings. She watched him steadily, never taking her gaze off him. Her unblinking gaze might have been disconcerting to a lesser being.

"Come si chiama?" He didn't think she would tell him her name, but it was worth a try.

She licked her lips, making no answer. Rain, wind, and giant storms buffeted his consciousness. It brought to mind the recent tsunami in Indonesia, a natural occurrence but one that had caused much devastation. He saw huge category-five hurricanes, swirling for hundreds of miles, their clouds thick, and their eyes huge.

"You are getting drunk with cold water, Griffin," she said.

After a moment's confusion, he translated the idiom to something to the effect that he was kidding himself. "Why are you here?"

Griff itched to unfurl his wings, grab her, and soar into the air. It would be fantastic to snatch her out of the building and scare the crap out of her. If he dropped her, she would die. Vântoase were not immortal.

"Naughty." She flipped a hand as if his thoughts were of no concern, but a worried look crossed her face. "Don't stare like the crow at the bone, Elemental. Your Challenge has begun. You have been slow, and humans are useful. Find the answer, and we will show you our power. Dă-i din bascheți." "Move faster."

Griffin took a breath and pressed thoughts of wind currents, being in the stratosphere, carrying her helpless body across his back as he flew upwards. He pictured being level with planes and then dropping her, her robes flapping as she fell, shrieking, to her death.

It would be so satisfying.

Griff felt her heart quicken and her mind cloud with fear she struggled to keep away from him. Good. He had achieved his goal.

The Vântoase stared at him for a moment, her throat working. Then she stepped into the crowd and Griff let her go. She wasn't his Demonos challenger. At best she was a servant of Amai, sent to bring Griffin that message. There was more, though, buried under her shields. He sensed a deeper ruse, connected to her but yet not related. Challenge was here, but he hadn't detected any disruptions in the earth's air patterns to suggest anomalies. There was nothing on human radar. He had checked. It was too quiet. He was missing something.

Although part of him wanted to go and rip the Vântoase apart, she was right. His Challenge had begun. He had to discover the trap before the world went to hell.

* * * * *

Clea had to admit that travelling by eight-passenger luxury jet was preferable to the methods she'd used in the past. Sometimes there had been pack animals and a couple of times, a camel. Clea had always taken the position that since she didn't need to hurry, she could enjoy the journey as much as the destination. Humans missed much rushing from place to place in search of the next tourist spot. Nevertheless, this was a comfortable way to travel.

Comporta, Portugal was a quiet beach community on the west coast of Portugal. Clea wasn't sure why they were going to a place with so little to recommend it except canals and rice paddies. They were flying to the nearest local airport, called Sines Airport, and then would head to the town about thirty miles away.

She watched the azure sky float by as the jet soared from Luxembourg to Portugal.

She didn't know much about the Tuatha Dé Danann. Neit, her father, was a thunder god in the manner of Zeus, but not as well known. Cormac had filled her in as much as he could, but there was no doubt he'd left out a lot. Once this was over, she was going to pay them a visit and learn. She wanted to know more about her brother, her actual brother, someone to call her sister without irony or rancor. There was a lot to be explored once the Challenge was over and she'd avenged Patrik.

Cormac and Dodola had stayed behind in Luxembourg. Clea would let him know where she and Griffin ended up, but her brother rightly guessed that she wanted to spend time with the Elemental alone. Their parting had been warm, the promise of meeting up again soon extracted. They would. She was going to hold her brother to his vow of assistance in Challenge. As much as he didn't want to admit it, Griffin needed all the help he could get.

Clea was absorbing all of this as she flew to Portugal in the Elementals, Inc. plane. Was this notion of avenging Patrik mere foolishness? It suddenly seemed like a futile quest. Patrik would stay dead no matter what she did. Angering Perun to the point of bloodlust had done nothing more than lead her here.

It had led her to Griffin, the Elemental. He had taken her in without hesitation when it hadn't been safe for him to do so, when he was in Challenge. He'd become so much more to her than she expected. Yet what future could there be for them? There would be little for a goddess and an Elemental to talk about when Challenge was done.

"To your left."

Startled, Clea broke from her reverie as they slowed in preparation for landing. Below her the landscape was growing larger as buildings and streets took shape.

Griffin was gliding alongside the slowing plane. He matched the pilot's speed, hovering outside her window. He smiled and winked at her. His blond hair was streaming behind him, the braid bobbing in a draft she couldn't see. Similar wind rippled his jeans and close-fitting shirt. Clea wondered if he got cold.

"You can warm me up."

A rush of happiness suffused her, an emotion she buried deep within her shields. She would see the Elemental again in a matter of minutes, and feel his body pressed to hers. For the duration, this man and this mission were also hers.

As hers was his. He hadn't specifically said he would help her avenge Patrik, but he hadn't said he wouldn't. Defeating Amai-te-rangi would go a long way to settling that score.

Suddenly there was a crash, as a huge thunderclap boom shook the sky. Then there was a streak of lightning. Clea registered the out of order events right before a giant storm opened up above the plane, drenching both the craft and Griffin with huge raindrops. One moment the skies were clear, with no threatening clouds. They had been decelerating as expected, anticipating an easy landing into Sines Airport. The next moment there were huge drops of rain and kroupy, as her mother called hail. Griff dipped, his body sagging at the unexpected torrent. Excited chatter came from the cockpit as the pilots tried to cope with this bizarre turn of events, fighting the controls against the sudden precipitation.

Thunder cracked again, and lightning, out of order, and the flash of white against the sky revealed a wet, struggling Griffin, buffeted by heavy winds, fighting to regain his altitude in the storm. The lightning streaked past him, almost hitting him. It was near enough that it lit him up for a moment, and his hair and wings glowed with static electricity and flame.

"Griff!"

"Non molto. It's nothing. Just caught off guard." He sounded pleased. "I like lightning."

Clea reached out with her weather senses but couldn't find the center of the storm. Griff's mind joined hers and together they focused. All they could see were black clouds hovering above them. It was like they had been manifested from nothing, and aimed at the plane.

Thunder and lightning struck, almost on top of them.

Griff banked in, using the bulk of the aircraft as shelter. Relief took her. His attacks on the storm were weakened by the kroupy he was fighting. A little hail wouldn't slow him down for long. The plane dipped at another crack of thunder, and lightning streaked. The ping of small pellets of hail resounded through the jet. Clea threw her talents against the storm, willing winds to scatter the dark rain and blow the drops out to sea. She saw the spot where the vortex coalesced, thick with heavy rain. There was something artificial within the storm. Griff's confusion at the unnatural nature of the storm's desire to push its advantage, like a living thing, matched hers. The resistance came from a place outside of this area. The clouds gathered again. Clea combined her efforts with Griff, and they braced their power at the unseen force driving the tempest. Together, they shoved, pushing the storm away, using their combined talents to drive the clouds back. The gale gave reluctantly, inch by inch. After long minutes they backed away from the plane and began to dissipate. Clea let out a sigh of relief. The pilots whooped and cheered as they worked their controls, leveling the craft. There were bursts of chatter from the tower traffic control and the pilots answering back.

Clea reached out with her mind when Griff was nowhere to be seen, her heart pounding.

"Below you. Taking a short break. That was nice work."

There was an image of the landing gear and Clea realized Griffin was underneath them.

"What are you doing?"

"I'm hovering." The lights of the runway came toward them. Clea breathed a sigh of relief. That had been a bad moment when the lightning had struck so close to Griff. Elementals were hard to kill, but not impossible.

"You could get tangled up in the gear," she protested.

"I'm not breakable."

"Senhorita?" the pilot called. "We'll be landing soon."

Chapter Twelve

The pilots made no outward look of surprise when a dripping-wet Griffin emerged from the small terminal building, although Clea heard their speculation at his appearance. She let it go. Let them have their private thoughts, as long as they didn't disturb her or Griff. The men loaded the luggage into a large town car with rectangular white plates with black lettering and a blue stripe on the side saying "P" for Portugal. Griff wiped his face and body down with a fluffy towel. Clea's mouth went dry at the idea of licking each individual raindrop off Griff's chest. Or she could rub him dry with her body, pretending to be the towel. His braid, tufts escaping from the plait, hung down the front of his chest. His blond hair was plastered to his head, and he ruffled it to get the worst of the water out.

"Are you okay?"

She wanted to run to him, to check him over for singe marks or other after-effects of his wild flight. Clea knew enough about alpha males to know that he wouldn't want to be fussed over. Licked, though. He liked being licked.

"That was an unexpected storm," the pilot said with an apologetic tone. "We weren't tracking any weather."

Griff didn't take his gaze off Clea.

"She's safe, that is the only thing that matters." He turned to the employees, who saluted. "We will be a week or so. I will summon you when we are ready to go."

"You know something more," Clea said.

Griff nodded, and if he appeared to be nodding at nothing, the Elementals, Inc. pilots had long experience with the eccentricities of the people in charge. Their carefully schooled faces revealed no sign of curiosity, but their brains buzzed with speculation.

"Merda, to be rich." She smiled at the wayward thought and flicked a glance at the man it had come from. The driver's face was carefully neutral, betraying nothing of his feelings.

Their luggage secured, Griff and Clea got into the car. She was unsure why they were making an unrelated trip to this place.

They headed toward the water to the small town of Comporta. Clea couldn't see or smell the water yet, but at the speed the driver was going, they would shortly.

"Ondine is meeting me here," Griff said when they were alone in the car. It seemed like a non-sequitur for a minute. Griff projected the ocean, sea life, and mammals until Clea realized he was talking about the water Elemental.

"I heard that the Elementals had had a change in their water Elemental. I hadn't expected a woman. Why did you choose her?" Jealousy spiked her tone, despite her attempts to keep her voice level.

Griff burst out laughing. He projected an image to her of an average human female, with short, dark hair, a slender shape and a face that seemed bland. Sharp claws of possessiveness dug at Clea, and she fought to keep them from showing. Ondine was nowhere near as beautiful as a goddess, but she was an Elemental. Clea had never thought she would feel inferior to anyone other than a goddess, but Ondine understood Griff in a way that Clea never could.

Clea shut Griff out, creating a wall so high that nothing could go in or out. Jealousy was new to her. The gods could be petty and many battles raged over objects of desire, but those periodic skirmishes were born out of boredom. There was a lot of time to fill when you were immortal.

He chuckled. "You've met Shani, who would resent your thoughts, but the idea might make Masud laugh. Ten years ago, Hippocampus was killed by sharks, in a way that even a strong Elemental couldn't survive. We wondered if it hadn't been an accident; sometimes Elementals can will themselves not to live. When Hip died, Lara was chosen. She'd been an ocean scientist of a sort. I don't know the details. She's been learning her role, and spends most of her days near water.

She is so new…a Challenge coming so soon after the last one is bad timing, but we have no control over that. Our last Challenge had only been sixty years before Hip died, and we weren't due for one for some decades yet, so we thought we had time. Her Challenge is on hand as well. Her Demonos foe is…" he held out his hands and spread them wide, doing the same with his wings in the limited space of the car, "…gigante. She needs advice."

"Why do you want to meet her?"

"I don't know. This Challenge feels different, and it's not that Ondine is new to us, it…." He broke off, and paused. "It feels like we are fighting for more this time."

"What do you think about what happened out there?" Clea let down her wall a little, sensing Griff had no interest in the unseen water Elemental. Still, she was going to look this woman up and down when they met.

"There was a woman at the airport. A Vântoase. She was taunting me, but she also gave me valuable information. There is a group of people helping Amai, and they are near completing their task. It relates to Challenge. It feels…important to find out who his helpers are."

Clea put aside thoughts of water Elementals and focused on what had happened outside of the plane. The storm had an unnatural feel to it, as if it had been spurred by something besides nature. She thought about the disturbed dust in the tunnels in Luxembourg. So many clues, and the answer dancing out of reach. "It's only a trap if it springs."

* * * * *

Badb, Macha, and Nemain shifted into human form and sat down in the green grass.

"Well?" Badb demanded.

Macha took up a piece of wood she had been carving before she left and studied it. It was formless, although a masculine shape was starting to emerge.

"I expected him, so I did," she said, and the others nodded. "He will do. He may be after handling the task. It is not yet in the way of our knowing this."

"Is he after protecting our kin?"

"I believe so. He'd best be. Else he will answer to the Morrigan."

Macha turned the wood over in her hands. She was feeling the shape begin to form in the lines of the former oak, and knew what she would be carving shortly.

Nemain looked beyond the clearing as if expecting someone. "It's been keeping to ourselves and Eire the Tuatha Dé Danann have nigh these long centuries. We don't need to be after interfering yet. She is kin, but not blood."

"She be Neit's blood, and Cormac's sister," Macha protested. "She be ours. Aren't you in the way of seeing war in it, sisters? It is coming."

Badb pressed her hands together as if delighted. "Aye, I do. This is not the small wars of our country. I can feel its grandeur. The Morrigan has not taken up arms in so long. We could ride again to battle." Her expression showed how much she appreciated that idea.

"We must be careful." Nemain focused on the entrance to the clearing. "I feel a stirring in it, a power I have rarely felt before. We must be after getting ready, but we must not be hasty. We will prepare the sword and the spear, so we will. 'Tis need of them I believe we will have."

Neit strode toward them, his big boots kicking up dust along the path. He appeared cheerful, ruddy and smiling, as if he had consumed a few tankards of ale in the recent past.

"Wives," he bellowed, clearly in good cheer. "What word have we?"

* * * * *

Comporta, on Portugal's Tróia peninsula, was quiet with an air of elegance without the normal tourist buildup. The rented villa was a short distance from the beach of Carvalhal, behind one of a multitude of sand dunes. The sand was a faint yellow that echoed the color of Griffin's wings. No ghosts showed themselves here, which was more of a relief than she'd anticipated. Although she was almost sure that Henry the ghost hadn't stuck around to watch them make love after Griffin had banished him, she couldn't be a hundred percent sure. This was much better.

The Elemental was on the deck of the villa, naked to the waist, his wings spread as if taking in the sunshine. She admired the strong muscles of his back, the heavy lats and shoulders that helped support the infrastructure of his enormous wings. His feathers ruffled in the wind, blowing gently. She liked running her hand over that plumage, enjoying the small danger of the sharp tips.

Her hand itched to pet him right now. She didn't care about the water Elemental they were supposed to meet in this exotic location. It would be more fun to make love here, in this hotel, with the windows open to the sand dunes, and dare the rich who frequented the place to peek in.

Air will glide with air. She wanted to glide with him. Right now. Fly with him into the clouds and make love there. She did not want to go to the water and meet the water Elemental. Water swims together. Water could swim together all it wanted, as long as it left air alone.

"Tell me again why you are meeting Ondine?"

Griffin turned to her, and the sun streamed in past his wings and hair, lighting him with its glow. He seemed otherworldly, more godlike than any of the pantheons.

"Ondine was compelled this way. So it goes with Challenge. Perhaps the Iku-Turso, her Demonos foe, has lured her to this ocean. Ondine wants to talk, and I want to help her if I can. I wish we still had our Hippocampus. The old Hip would have known that this Challenge is bigger."

"Hmm. You sound a little sexist there, Mr. Air Elemental. Don't think a woman is up to the task?"

"I'm a realist. Our Hippocampus was the second oldest, after Sphynx. He'd been through many Challenges and he knew how to battle. Lara—Ondine—she is untested and still learning. It's a hell of a time for a Challenge."

"Sexist. Women are stronger than you know."

"Realist. Women are carino, and I adore them, but they're not as strong as men. They need us to protect them. I would feel better about our chances if Hip were here."

"I've been on my own for a long time. I haven't needed anyone's protection." Or been offered it.

He cocked an eyebrow at her, and his feathers ruffled. It was fascinating to watch them move in a synchronized fashion, as if dancing.

"You're a goddess. Tell me about your meeting with Dodola."

Clea sighed, knowing this was the wrong time for the conversation, but she supposed there would never be a right time. She reviewed what Dodola had told her, picking out the relevant parts to speed the telling.

Clea paused. "I have a Tuathan brother. When we were born, he stayed with his pantheon and she took me home. He was raised among the Tuatha Dé Danann."

"Neit," Griffin said, respect in his tone. "Did you meet your father?"

His wings were now sloped down, no longer perpendicular to his body. A quick check of their link told her he was listening, rapt in the story. There was no hint of censure in his mind.

"No." Clea shook her head. "Cormac assured me I'd be welcome but Neit was not there." It stung more than she had known at the time. Perun had never been her father, and Clea hadn't thought she missed having one until a red-haired man with her eyes showed up. What would it have been like to have been welcomed, as Cormac was, into a community? From all accounts, the Tuatha Dé Danann were close knit.

But then, if she had been with the Tuatha, she never would have known Patrik. As painful as it had been to lose her adopted brother, she wouldn't have missed knowing him for anything.

Griff studied her, his blue eyes fixed on hers. "Neit can protect you, can he not?"

"I didn't ask. It is too dangerous for me to go to the Tuatha right now. I can't put them at risk. They don't know me, and it's not fair to ask them to get involved in a pantheon-to-pantheon conflict over me. It's why Mother sent me to you. You are an Elemental, removed from pantheon politics. Perun will think twice before taking you on."

She thought he would press the subject, but to her surprise he dropped it. "Didn't the Tuatha object when you came here? They are protective of their own." He smiled with a glint of mischief. "Macha's presence on the plane makes sense now. She was checking up on me, and making sure that Neit's bambina was in good hands."

"I don't know. Dodola didn't say. You know Mother, she is unpredictable and vain. She came to Luxembourg and that was more than I expected. I met my brother. He's very unlike me. Maybe I would be welcome in Neit's pantheon, but I can't ask the Tuatha Dé Danann to take risks for me."

"I am glad that you have somewhere to go," Griff said.

"In case we fail," she said.

"We won't fail." Striding all the way across the sun-dappled room to her, Griff swung her into his arms. His wings also wrapped around her. She was safe in a cocoon of skin and warm feathers.

"However," Griff said, and she heard the desire in his voice, "we should always make sure to take pleasure when we can."

* * * * *

Griff rented a small boat at the dock, and they set out, navigating the distance on the sea until they had the area to themselves. On either side of the narrow strip of sand, there was a gentle slope, with scrub trees standing out at forty-five degree angles to the water above the sheen of bare rock. Griff navigated their boat close to shore and then cut the engine. With a wave of his hand, he pointed to the coastline and back to their boat. They would swim the short distance to land.

There was a woman sitting alone on the shoreline, the waves lapping at her feet. Sand surrounded her, with small rocks and some strands of seaweed breaking up an otherwise deserted piece of land. She appeared to be wearing a wetsuit, and her hair was damp. Behind his boat, in deeper water, were forms that Griff thought were dolphins. One in particular separated from the pod and was making no secret of the fact that he was watching them. Griff reached out and touched the creature's mind. Intelligence streaked across his vision, human yet different. A dolphin shapeshifter, one who preferred the ocean over land. There was a shark as well, and Griff recognized the mental signature instantly. That surprised him. It didn't seem possible that Ondine would fraternize with a shark who may have had a hand in killing Hippocampus, but there was no question it was Sullivan, the powerful shark king. He also seemed to be taking a keen interest in their newest Elemental. Griff hoped he concealed his surprise, but Clea gave him a sharp look that told him he'd failed.

The cove Ondine had chosen was off the path of the beachgoers. They shouldn't be disturbed here, but just in case, Griff sent up a psychic wall of potential danger around the area cove to deter tourists.

He turned to Ondine. He had not known her when she'd been mortal. She still liked to be called Lara, her former human name. It showed her lack of preparedness for this role. Ondine. Water Elemental. Untried recent human and the weakest link of their quartet.

"Sexist." Clea's censure rang in his mind.

Clea turned a bright smile on the water Elemental, who rose from the grainy sand. Clea seemed different than she had been before the visit with her mother. She caught and held his eye but he couldn't tell what the difference was. Perhaps it was a trick of the light. Nothing had changed about Clea, except everything.

Insecurity was new to Griffin. Since he had become an Elemental, he had played hard among the supernatural beings, but had never been serious about one for long. Women went through his hands like water, cherished and needed, but transitory. He kept his emotions locked away, preferring to be alone. His playboy reputation had been a careful mask, one he wore to keep others from seeing who he was.

Now there was Clea. Real, flawed, fascinating Clea. A goddess with little experience with her true powers. He wanted to scoop her up and carry her back to Iceland. He wanted her. He…needed her. He'd been with goddesses before. Granddaughters of granddaughters of granddaughters of gods, minor deities with bloodlines so diluted that they were no longer immortal. They were usually simpering hangers-on, females whose beauty and long life were the only thing that recommended them, serving little function other than decoration. He had thought that was what he liked, until Clea arrived and reached into places he hadn't known could be touched.

Ondine got to her feet, her skin gleaming in the midday sun. He'd taken it upon himself to be available to the water Elemental, and she came to trust him. He'd reached out to her first after the Elemental strength had transitioned from a shredded Hippocampus to her. "Now you are Hippocampus," he had told her, and she shook her head. She said nothing for a long time, her mind whirling with all the new sensations. She was vulnerable, and he would have done what was essential for the good of the Elementals if the wrong person had been chosen. After her long silence, the former Lara turned her attention to Griff, her mind muddy but one thought clear.

"I don't want to be called Hippocampus," she told him, as though in a trance. "Ondine. It works out to more or less the same meaning." She hadn't wanted to know anything else that day. Griff had watched her transform, struggling with it a little, but managing, and dive into the cold, choppy water. He had tracked her mentally and seen that she was with a pod of dolphins who had surrounded her the minute she entered the water. Both of the Sphynx pair had come into his mind. The three of them agreed they should let Ondine alone for a while to come to terms with the ramifications of her new station. They thought there had been time.

"Hello." Clea held out her hand to the smaller woman. Again there was that sense of royalty, as if Clea had become something different after her visit with her mother. A curl of something unfamiliar lodged in Griff's belly. "I'm Clea. What should I call you?"

Ondine didn't look waterlogged, other than the fact that her hair was damp. Her skin wasn't puckered from the water; it was smooth and unmarred. After long exposure to Hippocampus and other shifters, Griffin was used to the idea that their skin didn't behave like humans', and Ondine was another kind of shifter. He knew from past experience that the sea shifters maintained an illusion of modern wetsuits when they emerged from the water, so they did not appear naked. Ondine hesitated, and glanced at Griffin. "Ondine. Nice to meet you."

Her accent was American, from the East Coast somewhere. Maine maybe, or Baltimore. It didn't matter.

"Nice to meet you," Clea returned. Her gaze flicked to him.

Griff had learned to trust his compulsions when they came over him, as this one had. It had seemed important to meet the water Elemental. Although he was the one she most trusted among the Elementals, they were still figuring out how to interact.

Griff's wings unfurled until they were standing at medium expansion, more a show of power than a sign of danger.

Clea and Ondine glanced at him and then back at each other.

"Does he always do that?" Ondine seemed more amused than intimidated by his wings.

"He's showing off."

To his surprise, the women laughed. They covered their mouths as if they were schoolgirls giggling at a boy. Griff shifted, annoyance surging in his veins, hissing like water that hit lava.

He sensed three other shapeshifters in her group in addition to the males who had caught his attention. A powerful ancient whale god and some other creatures were close by as well, not all aquatic beasts. Good. They would help keep Lara safe.

"Have you determined your Challenge yet?" Griff strode into the middle of the female conclave and directed his attention to Ondine. He felt the masculine presence inside her mind. Shifter. Shark. Intimate. The shark king had gotten a foothold.

"We have some ideas. The Iku-Turso is…" Ondine pulled her hands apart in a gesture similar to Griffin's earlier. "Big. You? Any thought about your Challenge?"

"Many. We have a great deal of weather anomalies these days. The trial is finding the right one."

Clea looked at Ondine closer and then turned to him in surprise. "She doesn't have gills, or a tail. I thought she'd look more…obvious. Like you. You always have your wings."

At that Ondine laughed. "They come and go. When I swim, I can breathe underwater and have gills and modified flippers. I can go to depths you would not believe. Maybe all the way to the bottom, although I haven't tried that. On land I look human. I always feel like people can tell I'm part fish."

"You look human now. That must make it easier. Mortals can't see Griff's wings but they are always dodging around him like they sense them."

He could feel the questions beating against Clea's skull, but she refrained from asking them for the moment. She gave him a questioning look.

"Più tardi." Later.

Whatever they were going to say next was interrupted. Cold, blustery wind swirled around them. The sky darkened as if the sun had been eclipsed. Rain started, heavy and fierce, an echo of the storm that had surrounded them on the plane. Griff saw ripples in the water, frothing at the surface that told him the sea creatures were agitated.

The drops of rain were thick and wet, drenching them within seconds. Ondine's attention went to the water. The boat bobbed there, dipping on the swells that had also cropped up as if pulled from the air.

"This is not natural," Griff called, the wind threatening to suck his words away. His wings stood out parallel to the ground, and the specially designed shirt whipped around his body. His feathers were already damp. He focused on the women, measuring the distance to safety. Ondine could dive underwater and escape, but Clea had no gills or wings, only her air power in a sky gone mad.

Before he could scoop her up, a flash in the sky caught his eye. Griffin knew what he would see when he turned his head to focus on the thing.

Above them, descending past the thick black clouds, coming into view one foot of hemp rope at a time, was a basket.

Chapter Thirteen

"Amai," Griff shouted, pointing upwards.

Clea followed his finger. The wind tugged at her, threatening to knock her off balance. She reached out with her air power to create a small area of calm around her. Thunder boomed and lightning struck, almost simultaneously, signaling that the storm was right there.

A form emerged from the water, changing from shark to human as they watched, and held out his hand to Ondine. He was a huge man, bigger than Griffin, dark skinned and dark eyed, with a look at the water Elemental that told Clea she had nothing to fear from Ondine. His nudity was covered by the wetsuit that was their convention. If she chose to, Clea could see beyond the illusion. She did not so choose.

"Go, Ondine," Griff urged. "This is my fight." He watched as the basket came into view. The tops of the ropes were still out of sight. "My Demonos awaits."

Ondine's eyes grew big. "Is it your Challenge? Aren't they all supposed to happen at the same time? Is that now?" Her head swiveled from side to side as if searching for an enemy.

Clea wondered if Ondine knew who her Challenger was before remembering the Elemental had said the name. Iku-Turso, but Clea had no idea who or what that was. She plucked an image from Ondine's mind of something like an octopus, but far bigger.

"It's all part of Challenge, but there is more to come. This is one more contesta. You and your friend should go where it's safe." He said the word friend with pointed significance, his gaze hard on the other man.

As if summoned, small waterspouts started, little funnels bobbing randomly like malevolent sprites. One wound toward them. The man made a gesture with his head and the surface of the water rippled again as bodies, barely visible under the blue/green of the sea, headed to the spout.

"Nice to meet you," Clea said to Ondine, her eyes on Griff.

"Bye."

As Clea watched, Ondine shifted. Gills formed at her neck, and her feet, while they didn't fuse, became more tail-like. Her skin changed to something more like the dolphin's had been, a hide that protected her body. Her hands grew webbing, and in seconds, she was ready for the water. She raised one webbed hand as her shapeshifter friend's face began elongating. Rows of razor-sharp teeth emerged, as well as grey and yellow/white hide. Together they dove into the sea and were gone. The other bodies circling the waterspout broke off and the group moved out to safer water.

Rain pelted them, soaking both of the people left standing. Clea's windbreaker was no match for the driving shower. Water sleeted down her shoulders and seeped past the cuffs.

"How much air power do you have?" Griff asked. His dilemma surged through her as if it were her own. He couldn't leave her there but couldn't take her with him and fight Amai. He would break off, get her safe, carry her back to the hotel, and deposit her in their room before trying to engage Amai.

"Not on your life. I'm in this with you." She shot him an image of dead weight, and then of a struggling, wriggling person, what she would be if he made any attempt to take her away from danger.

Griff's rain-wet eyebrows rose, but his mouth tugged in a grin.

"I will get to those rocks." She pointed to an outcropping a short distance away. "I've got my air power to keep me safe. Go get him. Let's have some fun. I'll see if I can do something with my thunder." She mentally crossed her fingers.

Griff picked her up, his wings flapping hard in the strong wind. Wrapping his arms around her waist, he half flew and half ran her to the rocks she had pointed toward. Once there he pushed her to a place where there was some natural shelter.

Griff kissed her, kicked his shoes off, and with one powerful sweep of his wings, took to the air.

Amai was now visible, descending the ropes like a sailor climbing down the rigging of a ship. The rain was around him but did not seem to be affecting him. His basket descended with the smooth trajectory of an object that had no weather to concern itself with.

Far off she heard voices and then shrieks of terrified humans. Griff faltered in his climb to Amai. She couldn't make out what was going on in the rolling, boiling sea. Reaching out with her mind, she found a ship made for pleasure excursions and not furious water, caught in the pitching and dipping of the large waves.

"I got this," she assured Griff. Before she could ask, he reached out for Ondine and she followed his thread, touching the awareness of his fellow Elemental.

Above her, Griff circled the basket, taunting Amai with flicks of his wings as he passed. The Demonos lunged at him, grabbing for his wings. The basket rocked each time but never seemed in danger of going over.

A streak of lightning, so close electricity would have lifted her hair if it were dry, brightened the sky. At that moment Clea saw the small craft that was in danger. There were fish bodies around it, steadying it. Thunder boomed, deafening her. Griff circled Amai. "Not natural."

Clea nodded. The wind shifted, and a heavy bout of rain broke her cover and soaked her right side. Shivers ran up her at the icy droplets.

Amai jumped onto the lip of the basket and reached out, almost closing his fists on one of Griff's arms. At the last moment, the air Elemental spun away. He fell for a brief second and then caught the wind and headed back up.

Clea's heart thumped in her chest before she saw his form darting away. She concentrated on the ship again. She wasn't sure what use her thunder could be, but she pulled it forward, feeling the buzz in her hand. Focusing, she shot her hand up and aimed over the basket. A small boom crashed overhead, inadequate to her ears, but Amai flinched. She hadn't thought it was possible for such a big Demonos to wince, but she seemed to have caught him off guard. A gust of gale-force wind unrelated to the storm swirled around Amai and knocked him back. The Demonos fell into the basket, sending it lurching away from Griff. With a roar, Amai jumped to his feet, and the basket steadied. Griff flattened his wings behind his back and shot straight at his enemy like he was a human-sized, winged arrow.

"Clea."

The voice was female, and had to have come from Ondine. Clea turned her attention back to the boat and saw through Ondine's eyes that despite the sharks and dolphins, it was taking on water and in danger of capsizing. She couldn't make out the individual faces, but she could feel the human terror. Not all of them were wearing lifejackets. Fools.

Clea pulled all of her skills to her and focused. The water smoothed; it had to be Ondine's work. Clea raised her hands to her waist and pushed them forward, the power singeing her nerve endings. She reached out and sent her influence into the storm. It resisted her, swirling harder for a moment, but she kept the pressure on, and it gave. The wind slowed and then stilled. Clea opened a small window of calm air. She found the captain and gave him a mental push to try to start the engine. The shore was only a few hundred feet away but impossible for humans to reach in the choppy waters. The ship began to glide forward, into the safe water. Clea kept the wind at bay even as it fought her like a thing possessed. Ondine continued to soothe the sea. After some tense moments, the ship glided into the harbor and landed.

"Thank you." Ondine's response was a wave of her hand/flipper, and then the pod went into deeper water and was gone.

"Griff." Clea tilted her head to the sky where she'd last felt him.

She found him grappling in hand-to-hand combat with Amai-te-rangi. Through Griff's eyes she saw that Amai's face was mottled red with anger, and his heavy muscles bunched with each furious blow aimed at Griff. Griff's power beat at Amai's basket, creating counter currents to the storm. Thunder and lightning boomed together, and the sky lit up in vivid yellow and blue. A tendril of yellow reached out and touched the basket and both of the men's bodies became unnaturally bright. Griff's hair lifted. Amai laughed and drew back, then without warning rushed forward, shoving Griff, a movement that sent him tumbling backwards, his arms pinwheeling.

"Not yet, Elemental."

Griff hit the edge of the basket and went over. His wings unfurled. Rain and wind caught him before they were fully extended, sending him landward. Clea shot a different air current toward Griff, pushing against the forces above him. His downward plunge halted. He turned his body back as soon as he regained control and went in the direction of Amai, ready to strike again.

All of it, the wind, the rain, the gale, stopped as suddenly as they had started. The skies cleared as the storm clouds broke up like they had never existed. Griff began to double back but Amai raised a hand. For a moment she thought he was going to send another strike Griff's way. Clea pulled her power to her, getting ready to counter that blow as well. Then Amai and his basket made a rapid ascent upwards.

Griff's wings beat, carrying him back up, but Amai's basket gathered unnatural speed. As they watched, Amai became a small dot and then vanished.

"Mannaggia tua. I hate when he does that."

A dripping-wet Griff landed in front of her. His shirt lay in ragged strips across his muscled chest. His jeans had survived intact but were so filthy they looked brown. She went to him and held his shoulders. Griff gripped her and in a swift move, kissed her hard.

Pulling back, he smoothed his hand over his hair and shook the water out of it. "Amai has more than his own considerable air strength in this battle. There are other weather talents helping as well."

* * * * *

"Dodola." Neit tried to control his surprise at her use of the landline phone. "'Tis unexpected, this is."

There was a pause on the other end, and then Dodola began.

"Did you know?" she demanded, and there was accusation in her tone. "Did you know that the Demonos had help? Who dares assist Amai-te-rangi?"

The Morrigan were nowhere in sight in the village. Neit was glad about that. His wives could be difficult at the best of times and while they never got angry about other women, there was no need for their knowledge of this call. Likely that that was why Dodola had called on the landline.

"Nay, not humans. Weather folk," he said. "I wasn't after being sure before. It seemed like natural storms, so it did. Now 'tis obvious. They are in the way of showing their hand." He thought about the fight over Comporta. "It's interfering you are after, Dodola, and I can't see that that is smart, so I can't."

There was a long pause on the other end before Dodola spoke. Neit realized she was speaking to herself. "Samozřejmě. Of course." Her voice was soft. He couldn't tell if what she was feeling was anger, disappointment, or both.

"Dodola?" he asked. Waves of conflicting emotion were rippling through her.

"It's Perun," Dodola said after another pause. "Neit, you have to help her." Her tone was almost frantic. "Perun is part of this. He has to be. It's the only thing that makes sense. Now his anger is understandable. Clea's thunder isn't as good as Perun's but you are a thunder god."

Neit shook his head, knowing that she could not see him. To be sure, he sent a link down a thin mental line. He could visualize Dodola reacting to his negative response with one of her own.

"It is Tuatha we are, so she is. Clea has a home in Eire any time she is after it, but we do not go about meddling with Challenge. 'Tis bad enough our son has done so. I am wondering why are you asking." He was repeating himself, but this was very out of character for the selfish woman. He had enjoyed his time with her and was glad two rare and special godlings had come out of their coupling, but he had no illusions about who she was.

"She…" Dodola paused. "Perun. Clea is in danger," she said again.

"It's surprised I am that your husband would help the Demonos." Neit let the anger coursing through his body feed into his voice. He chose his next words carefully. There was a strangeness here, a piece that didn't fit neatly into place. He didn't have a name for it, but a strange emotion crawled down his spine, a thing he hadn't felt in centuries.

"We lost much in the last war. He blames the Elementals," she said, and there was no mistaking her despair. It was in her voice as well as down their link.

"That is the business of your pantheon, so it is, not the Tuatha." He hoped Dodola could not sense the lie. He would not have agreed to let one of his wives go to meet Griffin if he didn't feel as if the Tuatha were linked to this Challenge. He would not have given Cormac his permission to seek Clea out if he did not feel the connection. Mayhap it was through Clea; time would tell. If Perun was indeed part of this, it wouldn't do to tip their hand. He sent a caution to her and felt her assent.

"It is our business." Dodola's tone was almost frantic. "Our daughter wants to avenge her brother. Not Cormac," she said. "One of our pantheon. A man who was her brother in every way but blood."

"Ah. You are not in the way of altruism. You were after a token and our daughter was it," Neit said. "She could be spared, so she could. You were in the way of getting rid of her centuries ago. Perun made you choose, and he was your choice. You had the power to make him change his mind, so you did, but you didn't."

"You don't understand. You never did. Neit, you have to help her."

He searched around mentally for a sign that others were listening. After a long moment, he found it. They had a lurker. It was not unexpected.

"Goodbye, Dodola." Neit hung up on a still-speaking Slavic goddess. Would it be enough to throw off Perun? Dodola was an excellent actress.

"Neit?"

It was Badb, in woman form. He hadn't heard her approach. A few feathers dotted the ground, evidence she had just shifted from crow. There was a subtle echo to her face, something that still spoke of bird, in beak and forehead. Macha was in the distance, and Neit knew Nemain couldn't be far behind.

The village was quiet as the other members of their small pantheon were going about their daily routines.

"It is tired I get sometimes," he said, and Badb's expression softened.

"Aye, husband. Life is long, and immortality is not always a gift. I am wanting to talk about Clea." He didn't need to go into Badb's mind to know that she had overheard part of his conversation. "I am after knowing how we can help your daughter."

Neit motioned without direction. "Ye are knowing what must be done." They hadn't used the great Tuatha Dé Danann Treasures in centuries, since they came to terms with the Fomorians. Neit had showed Cormac the sword, of course, but all four of the Treasures had use. The stone and cauldron may not serve much function in this battle, but the spear could be a tool in Clea's hands. His war wives had preferred the edged weapons, and the bloodthirsty warrior in him cheered.

"Aye," Macha agreed when she arrived, sharing a look with Badb. "It is time, so it is. We must be after summoning the others. If we be raising the Treasures, we need the gods united."

* * * * *

Off the coast of Africa, a wind formation started, too small to cause concern. Normally the winds wouldn't come together, but these were forced to grow. A pressure system pushed them into a grouping, forming a small tropical wave. It would continue to become better organized, and within a few days, would be tracked on radar and weather instruments as a tropical depression. It would first be noticed west-northwest of the Cape Verde islands off Africa and the monitoring would begin there. It would go from a tropical depression to a tropical storm. By the time the storm hit the tracking devices, it would be too late. It wasn't yet time for the anti-cyclone that would aid its formation, but the sea temperatures were warm enough to facilitate the gale as well, courtesy of a few well-paid shifters. Those assisting the Demonos only used creatures who could not be heard by

Ondine and the powerful whales. Within another day, an eye would form, and the storm would be upgraded to a hurricane. Humans would be slow to recognize the danger, thinking that a storm could not strike the way this one would. Even if it became a hurricane, it couldn't do serious damage.

But this was no ordinary storm. Fed by weather powers that channeled their energy together, this would become a storm of legend. Mortals would not understand how it could do what it was about to do, and when the carnage had retreated, would speculate for decades about how this storm had happened. They would never have an answer, the few that survived it. Conditions never existed for any huge storm to strike Europe the way the ones did off the coast of the Americas and in the Pacific.

That was the human belief. They were wrong.

* * * * *

"Weather powers?" Clea's voice was thick, dread crawling up her spine. "He has enough strength of his own. Why would they help? Who would help Amai?"

Griff shook his head. "This storm has the signature of paranormal, but the others helping him are good. We didn't feel it, and you and I are both tuned to air. It could be human." He went to his laptop, a sleek black box of powerful machinery that had just been released by the manufacturer. Only the best and the newest for Lorenzo Griffin Traverso.

"I've been investigating patterns. I knew there were anomalies but I haven't been able to find the right ones. That was my fault. I should have been more attento."

He booted up the laptop and frowned.

"We're in a bad area for Wi-Fi. These coastlines are charming, but they're rough on modern technology. I need more than mental energy. Come, we need to get to a city. Let's go to Lisbon. We can take the town car."

Griff took charge, loading their scant luggage and Clea into the car and asking the driver to take them to a hotel—it didn't matter which one—as long as the amenities were five star. All for Wi-Fi.

Travel time between the charming seaside town and the large city was a little over an hour and a half. The town car ate up the road efficiently. Lisbon was Portugal's capital city, with the Tagus estuary protecting it from being right on the ocean. It was hilly, and Clea wondered if that might be part of the reason Griffin wanted to come here. There would be more protection in this strip of land than directly on the Atlantic like Comporta was. Comporta had been a way station, nothing more, a place to meet Ondine. Why they couldn't have met in Lisbon, Clea wasn't sure, but she did not understand the ways of Elementals.

As the driver wove through the dense traffic, Clea's gaze took in the city. The people in Lisbon seemed to know that their metropolis was older than Rome. She had been here before, over a century ago, and enjoyed her time. She enjoyed the view of the long Vasco da Gama Bridge that spanned the Tagus River before the river emptied into the Atlantic Ocean not far away. The Padrão dos Descobrimentos and the Torre de Belém were just a few of the many welcome remembered sights of this global city. It had changed much since her last visit, and yet much also remained the same. One thing that had exploded was the population, both in humans and in vehicles. The persistent babble of unshielded minds made her want to clap her hands over her ears. Humans universally had the same problems. There was always the sense of being outdone, of not wanting their neighbors to have more than them. She touched the thoughts of thieves and con artists, looking for their next victim.

All this for Wi-Fi?

"Not just Wi-Fi, dea," Griff said. "We need to be somewhere cosmopolitan, where I can take a moment and figure out what our next step is. We were too exposed in that small town, charming though it was. We were there to see Ondine. I'm glad we did." He frowned. "It's important."

"Why?"

"Non lo so. Because it is."

The town car driver's blank expression revealed nothing. He had no opinions about his charges—to him they were just one ride and one fare closer to being off for the night. Currently, he was trying to decide which of his mistresses he would call tonight. He had decided on the dark-haired older one—she was always so eager to please—but after seeing Clea, he was thinking that his red-haired mistress would be better.

Clea frowned and shot him a look that would have frozen giants in their tracks. "Maybe you should go home to your wife."

Although the dividing panel was pulled across, separating the back half from the front, the driver shook his head as if he heard a fly.

Griff laughed, long and slow. "I didn't think you were *tradizionale*." He gestured with his head to the driver, whose thought patterns were now muddled. "Considering who your parents are."

Clea turned his words over in her mind. She had never thought of herself as conventional, but for the first time since she'd left the pantheon, she didn't want to continue roving. When this was over she would go stay with the Tuatha for a century or two and find out what it was like to put down roots. She looked forward to Ireland, the Tuatha Dé Danann, and her brother. Once this was finished, that was where she would go.

"I'm not conservative," she said. "But he's lying to several women and that's not right." Griff's wings caught her attention as they rested along the back of the seat. "Why does Ondine become indistinguishable from human when she's not in the water, yet you always have your wings?" Clea gestured to the butter-yellow appendages in question.

"What Elemental am I?" he asked.

"Air," she said, not understanding his line of questioning. "And Ondine is water," she continued, as if rattling off a school lesson. "But..."

Griff's wings unfurled just a little, peeking out over his shoulders.

"Water isn't everywhere. Air is all around us." He gestured out the window, pointing to the azure blue of the Lisbon sky. A soothing touch traveled down their mind link. It was like being stroked mentally.

"That is what we have determined. We don't know. Sphynx and I have permanent manifestations of our stations, but Phoenix and Ondine's come and go. Ondine manifests gills and fins when she is in water, and Phoenix's wings appear when he needs them. There have been many times when he's cursed me for always having mine while his are capriccioso."

She reached over and stroked the length of one feathered section. How would that gesture look to the driver taking them to the hotel if he could see them?

"Which is better?" Clea flashed on the memory of Ondine's gills manifesting. "Humans can't see your Elemental side either way, so which makes your jobs simpler?"

"Both have their advantages. Phoenix can blend in easier without his wings when he has to move among humans. You've seen how mortals give me a wide berth. It's rare to have a place I feel comfortable."

"Is there nowhere you can claim as home? Iceland? Verona?"

He shook his head. "Verona is where I'm from, not where I am." Both his mind and his face were clouded. "I like Iceland, but no, I have no place like that. Io sono nomade. It's part of the job."

"I think it's funny that you, the air Elemental, make liberal use of a company jet. Shouldn't you fly under your own power?"

He coughed, his lips tilted up as if covering a laugh. "It's faster," he said. "I like to fly, but I can't match the speed of modern jets. Ondine doesn't need the jet. As befits the water Elemental, she prefers to be on her yacht. Phoenix stays in one place unless he has to go somewhere. He's a homebody, that one, despite the fact that he's the second oldest of us now. Sphynx, they're remarkable. I don't know how they move through the earth. They use it somehow and rarely need alternate transportation unless they are traveling between continents. They cannot use their powers to cross the ocean. We have more than one plane, if we need them."

"Do you all change? I've never seen you be anything but human."

"I have the ability to change into a griffin, but I don't often need to. Phoenix can shift into his namesake, but like me he rarely does, although his fire Phoenix is terrible. Our powers manifest whether we are man or shapeshifter, and the advantage comes down on the side of human. We are faster in our other forms, but we're not as smart. I did it quite a bit when I was younger. It's fun to sneak up on people as a griffin and surprise them, but I'm older now."

Shielding her thoughts from Griffin, Clea wondered what it would be like to build a life with someone. Other than her mother and Patrik she was not well-loved in the pantheon, and it had never felt like home. Why else had she wandered, if not in search of some place—or someone—she could call home? Now she had found that, in an Elemental. Life was funny that way. It never took anyone, even a goddess, where they expected to go.

If the Elementals won these Challenges, Griff would be free to relax for a time, until the next Challenge. He would have a century or so of peace, and he could be…what?

What, Clea? What could he be? A boyfriend? A husband? What can a goddess and Elemental be together?

"Senhor? Senhorita? We have arrived."

Chapter Fourteen

The Tivoli Oriente hotel, with a view of the Tagus River, or Rio Tajo as the locals called it, had all the amenities he needed…and Griff was sick of all of it. Lisbon was thick with neutral to malevolent paranormals, which was unusual. Perhaps something in the age of the city attracted them. Small gnomes moved among the tourists and locals alike, removing items of value from the people. One gnome looked up at him as he walked through the streets and then snarled and hurried off. Other beings pressed into his mind, ones with more power and impure intentions, but as long as neither bothered the other, they would leave each other alone. Griff couldn't find any hint of Amai-te-rangi, nor any of the other weather powers he suspected were part of this. He reached out but found no signatures. That was troubling on its own.

Clea appeared calm, but something roiled her mind, an agitation that had nothing to do with their predicament. His wings stirred, lifting up and brushing the white fabric of his cotton shirt. He was angry, and he didn't know why.

All the careful probing he had tried had come up against Clea's blank wall shield. Whatever was on her mind, she wasn't telling him. She had started out so open, and as they spent time together she had shut down bit by bit.

She was retreating from him, and it made him want to kick something. Savage red spots of rage danced in front of his eyes.

Griffin stripped off his shirt and dumped it on the floor. "I'll be back," he said. Clea followed his progress to the balcony where he threw open the door, unfurled his wings, and was gone. He dropped for several stories before leveling out, and then soared up into the sky, past Clea's startled face. His wings beat powerfully as he dashed straight through a fluffy cloud pattern and headed upwards. There were a handful of helicopters around, taking people to their destinations, but Griff ignored their propellers. Birds flew past, and he dipped a wing to them. He felt the touch of a hawk shifter and sent a faint call to the bird. A response echoed back a moment later. He flew higher still, through the troposphere. Planes buzzed around him, banking for their landing at Portela Airport or taking off from the same place. He ignored them, too.

He soared through the troposphere, thinking to fly the twelve miles of it until he was in the stratosphere. It was getting colder but his exertions kept him warm. Part of him wanted to keep flying up, going all the way up to the mesosphere, thirty miles up. In the past, he had flown up there and watched small rocks and other debris burn up as they descended toward earth, too small to survive their contact with earth's atmosphere. He could go up there and watch it now, take satisfaction in space objects meeting their fiery end.

Griffin slowed when he was eight miles up, in the upper limits of the troposphere. He came to a relative stop, his wings beating to keep him in position.

"You're far from home." A voice echoed in his mind.

Griff knew before he turned what he would see. Masud, the male half of the dual earth Sphynx Elemental, was there but not there.

"Masud," he said, "I have no home. You show up in the strangest places." He paused a moment and then swiveled around. The powerful Elemental was hovering, but Griff could see through his body. Projection. It was a neat trick.

"Your thoughts are transparent halfway across the globe." Sphynx didn't sound disgusted, but Griff sensed impatience in the elder Elemental.

"Don't you have Challenge?" Griff had to raise his voice for it to carry. It would have been easier to communicate telepathically, but he didn't want anyone peering into his soul at the moment.

Griffin saw shadowed pain in Sphynx's eyes but the earth Elemental's shields revealed nothing.

"Shani is visiting Ondine in Morocco while I am here. You have a Challenge to attend to, Griffin." Sphynx's words were simple but with an edge that sank into

Griff's mind.

"Non hai capito," he persisted, knowing he sounded like a child.

"Perhaps I do understand. Perhaps I do not." Griff could feel the concern in his counterpart. It calmed Griff in a way he hadn't expected. The fact that Sphynx had come here, even in spirit form, to talk to Griff impressed on him how close they were to danger.

"I'm being selfish," Griff admitted. "I am aware of what I need to do."

"Good." Sphynx was now in front of him, although Griff hadn't moved. "Time is growing short. The goddess is part of this, just as Phoenix's Ifrit and Ondine's shark are essential to their Challenges. Things are different this time."

"Good or bad different?" Griff's wings stood out straight, going rigid. He lost focus for a moment and dropped before flapping his wings and regaining his position.

Thin, cold air whipped around them. The bright lights of Lisbon shone like beacons below them. Griff felt the pulse of the city, humans and paranormals alike, beating, unaware or uncaring of the Challenge that loomed for the two Elementals above them.

"I don't know." It was rare for Sphynx, for either of the duo, to admit they were ignorant of something. Griff blinked. Cold seeped into his skin as he remained in one place. His wings started to ache along the tendons, a sign they were tiring. Masud was right to remind him of his duty. He was allowing confusion and uncertainty to cloud his vision.

"Grazie, Sphynx." Griff almost held out his hand before he remembered that, physically, the other man wasn't there.

"You are our Griffin. Without you we fail."

It was said with a brisk coolness, and Griff nodded. None of them had ever been close to the Sphynx pair. They were a self-contained unit and the defacto leader of the Elementals, if only by dint of their immense age. But they had never been friends with the other Elementals in times of peace.

He wanted to ask why Masud had come, but Griff clamped the thought down before it could escape his shields. He was a warrior. He had work to do.

"Griffin?"

Griff turned back. The light-skinned Egyptian was still hovering, but he appeared fainter now. Sphynx gave Griff a smile and raised his arms, a simple gesture, but the way he did it made it feel like part of a ritual.

"Be careful. We need you."

* * * * *

Clea decided she wouldn't say anything when Griff came back. When he arrived on the balcony, shirtless, his skin standing out in goosebumps from the cold, she made no comment. She raised an eyebrow to him when he went to the stocked bar and poured a shot of scotch from the decanter waiting there.

"It chases away the chill."

He downed the shot and poured another. Griff snagged a second glass and poured her a shot as well. Holding it out to her, he motioned her over.

She took the glass. His mind was clouded, although she caught an impression of a timeless, sleek being, who may have been human once but hadn't been that way for a long time. Not a god, but close to it. There was only one person that could be. She'd only met Shani but there was no doubt in her mind Griff had seen Masud.

"Did you have a nice flight?" she asked. "How was Sphynx?"

The second shot followed the first, and Griff tossed the glass on the bar where it slid across the polished marble.

"He told me to get my priorities straight. I have Challenge to face."

Clea let relief show on her face. Powerful emotions twisted and danced across her mind, settling in her soul.

She paused, and then drained her own shot, placing the glass back on the bar with more care.

"We have this Challenge, Griffin. You and me." She grasped his hands. His wings moved and covered her shoulders in feathers. They slid over her body like his arms were embracing her. "It's like events conspired to set this up so that I only had one place to go. I had to help in this Challenge. You needed a goddess."

Clea flushed, realizing how arrogant that sounded. She clenched her fists against the desire to reach down their mind link and see into his thoughts.

His wings swept over her arms and back in slow movements, making her pulse dance.

"Elementals work alone." There was no inflection behind the words.

"Not this time." She reached over and traced his cheekbones, his forehead, and the curve of his smile. A shall shudder went through Griff. "You're stuck with me." Pure emotion swept through Clea, and she pushed it to the back of her mind, where Griff couldn't see it. "If you fail, they all fail. I will not let you fail."

Clea had never felt this way before. Her heart had never been touched. All her lovers, even those she'd felt real affection for, had mattered to her, but not the way Griffin did.

Now there was Griffin, the Elemental she'd dismissed as a playboy. It had taken two and a half centuries, but finally Clea understood the difference.

She loved Griffin. She loved this Elemental more than she had ever loved anyone in her life, even Patrik. But Elementals worked alone. They also lived alone, except for Sphynx. Griff kept himself apart, in his isolated house in Iceland. Win or lose, he'd go back to that place, or one like it, and remain in his solitary existence. In turn, she would go to the Tuatha Dé Danann and learn their customs. She had no illusion that Griffin would stay with her. They had been thrown together by necessity and revenge. He liked her, but that was as far as it went.

Clea had a moment of self-pity for a love not returned and then she shook herself mentally. She was a goddess, for the love of Matka Ziemia. She was a powerful woman and she had a job to do. She had gifts that she needed to explore, gifts that could help tip the balance of this Challenge. Clea remembered the devastation after World War II, the failure of the Elementals and the destruction the Demonos wreaked. She remembered Patrik, although the pain was less. This time was different. This time it involved her. This time she would make a difference.

"Come on." She reached up and stroked the feathers that were still caressing her arms. "Let's check out some weather anomalies."

* * * * *

The weather pattern continued to gain force. It began its journey westward, picking up speed and beginning to organize. It wouldn't be long now. Under normal circumstances, the tropical depression would fizzle out, but there was an unnatural force pushing it that made it continue to strengthen. Sea temperatures rose, adding to its power. Soon it would be the promised tropical storm and after that, a hurricane. It was being tracked now. The meteorologists didn't expect anything out of this storm but a bit of wind and some rain but on the chance it could become a threat, they were monitoring it. They were not too concerned about this particular storm, however.

That was the human way of thinking.

* * * * *

"Look at this." Clea pointed to the screen.

Griffin floated over, using a combination of his wings and his air mastery to appear as if he were levitating. He crossed his arms as if he were what humans would call a genie, complete with a turban on his head.

She grinned.

"Phoenix's new amante is part Ifrit," he said as if out of nowhere. "They were the basis of the djinn, or genie, stories."

It was a strange transition, but Clea made no comment, waiting for him to continue. Griff shot the image of the woman he had met in San Francisco into Clea's mind. She absorbed the picture of a tall, pretty female. She didn't look like she could hold an Elemental. Clea flushed at her rude thoughts. This part-Ifrit

American was holding onto her Elemental as well as Clea was holding hers, if what Clea had learned from Griff's brief visit to America was the truth.

"She doesn't look like any of the Ifrit I've met." They were tall and broad, resembling the pictures humans had of legends of Sinbad and other Middle Eastern tales. Clea hadn't encountered many, as the Ifrit kept to themselves, and she had never had an urge to seek them out. They had a red cast to their skin and a sharp bone structure. They looked menacing and liked it that way. They didn't look like this woman.

He nodded. "I know. There's something else going on, but we haven't put the pieces together yet." He paused again and Clea sensed confusion, and uncertainty, in Griff. He continued to hover. "It's interesting, isn't it, that all of the Elementals have companions this time?"

She cocked her head, the thing she wanted to show Griff on the computer put aside. "Is it?" she asked.

He landed, his bare feet making no sound on the carpet.

"Aleric has Rachel," Griff said, and it took Clea a minute to realize that Aleric was the birth name for the fire Elemental. "You saw the man who emerged from the sea for Ondine. And here you are."

"Sphynx?" Clea hoped that he didn't notice she was stalling to give herself time to sort through what he might mean, if he were making anything other than idle conversation.

"They are *un coppia*, a pair. They always have been."

The prophecy echoed in her head. *Earth is always there.* "I know you work alone, but you're telling me you've never had helpers?" *Air will glide with air.* They were together, as Phoenix and his woman were. As the man had made it clear he was with Ondine. She had not realized when she plucked the saying out of Griffin's mind how true it would be this time. She frowned. What did it mean?

He shook his head. Griff was behind her, close enough to touch but still a fraction away. His mind whispered across their link, something wordless and timeless, more emotion than words.

"We have the occasional partner," he said. "But you said it when we first met. My playboy reputation was earned. We've never had confidantes at the time of Challenge before. We've rarely had help. I don't allow people in." There was an image there, something, and Clea followed it. In his mind was an ethereal, human-looking yet different being, accompanied by a name. Einar, the one who had told them to go to Luxembourg. He was a Huldufólk, an Icelandic legendary being. He had been Griff's friend for the last fifty years, since Griff arrived in Iceland. Einar was a good friend, as otherworldly beings go, but he and Griff were always separated by their differences. She saw other friends, other presences with whom Griff had crossed paths. None lasted long, outside of the Elementals. The emotion welled up in her. For the first time, she understood that Griffin was lonely.

There was a hole in him, carved there by grief he hadn't expressed since the death of their old Hippocampus. It was deep in him, an unspoken pain. Ten years was yesterday to their kind. He missed the man, and Ondine hadn't filled the void.

"What did you want to show me?" Griff sprawled across the king-sized bed, letting his wings flutter down to the duvet.

He made no comment on her intrusion into his pain, but it slid away, deeper into his mind, like water flowing down a river. Air will glide with air.

They work alone, she told herself, keeping the thought away from Griff. She would change that as much as she could in the time they had, but it wouldn't last. He didn't know he would take her heart with him, and it was better that way. Maybe Elementals had to be alone. Maybe in order to try and save humans they had to keep apart from the world. It seemed unfair, but life was rarely fair.

"I'm following several websites you might find interesting." She turned the sleek computer to face Griff. "There's a lot of chatter and groups of people who think unexplained weather phenomenon is a conspiracy covered up by the government."

His mouth twitched up. "They have a point."

She inclined her head in concession. "Here." She pulled up one of the tabs of bookmarks she had open along the top of the browser window. "Look at this."

Griff's gaze was on her as Clea opened the tabs. She had sorted through several sites, each less interesting than the other. The basic weather websites, the ones that reported weather in bland text with boring drawings, she had already checked and put aside. There had been little out of the ordinary initially. Then she had caught a few strange anomalies that made her look closer. The links were hard to find and often led nowhere, but she'd dug up some interesting stuff in the time he'd been gone.

Languages didn't deter her as she translated them in her mind. After she found one anomaly, the others became easier to ferret out. The weather anomalies were getting more frequent. The local Portuguese news had talked about the strange storm that came out of nowhere. They mentioned how a pod of creatures seemed to help the stranded boat, and that the weather cleared abruptly, but they did not find anything remarkable about the incident. Griff's fight with Amai had gone unseen.

* * * * *

Griff watched as she pointed the weather patterns out, clicking through to show him what she had discovered. Her ability to track down leads, guided only by instinct, was remarkable. She was an intelligent, capable goddess who deserved the best out of life. He wanted to kiss her and trace the pattern of her beguiling freckles until he moved lower to trace similar patterns on her body.

"Look at this." She pointed to a website that didn't appear to have any sort of official capacity. The text was in bright letters but the tone was dark.

"This looks like an end-of-the-world website," Griff said. Something tickled the back of his brain, and he stirred from his lounging position. "There are dozens of these, especially in America. Most dismiss them."

She nodded. "I know, and you're right. There's more."

He leaned closer and then started. He recognized the picture of the man on the blog she had just pulled up. It was that man from Luxembourg who had tried to kill Clea. The man was raving about weather patterns and the end of the world and people who could not be killed.

"He couldn't know you healed," Griff said. "That wouldn't be something humans would see."

"Keep going."

Pietro had been let go by the police as there was no evidence to hold him. He had a bright red mark on his cheek held together with stitches. The human should be lucky that he escaped at all. Death would have been deserved. Nobody hurt his woman.

Griff scanned the blog and then took the mouse, clicking around the website. "This organization is not taken seriously, which is to our advantage. But…humans helping paranormals? Pietro may have more depth to him than I gave the weasel credit for." Griff's mind turned over the possibilities. He needed to focus. "It would be conceivable if they didn't understand what they were doing. They could be assisting the paranormals who are helping Amai. There are many who would welcome a shift in the power dynamic."

She pointed to the pictures. "Some of these people? Humans?"

He nodded. "Maybe more than we know. Pietro spoke of others, but I dismissed him at the time. I thought that humans couldn't have an impact on our Challenge. That was a mistake." He paused. "There are other weather paranormals who are helping Amai. There have to be. Many don't like humans. They take away our usable space."

He felt her think about the Slavic pantheon, their land that took the form of an old, uninteresting city off the beaten path in the Czech Republic. Being invisible to humans when using paranormal abilities had its uses, but also did make their type hard to understand. Mortals had power, and if they ever knew what paranormals were, they could make things very difficult. "What do we do now? We have to win Challenge."

She was so fierce, such a warrior. Not in his five hundred years as an Elemental had Griffin wanted to be with one woman like he wanted to be with Clea. She stirred something in him, a primal emotion he hadn't experienced in a very long time. As a mortal he had thought himself in love, and a few times as Griffin he'd named what he felt as "love", but it had never been like this. There had never been a woman like Clea. Maybe there never would be again.

And it was hopeless, doomed by his mistake in World War II and her need to avenge a brother she thought Amai had killed.

He should tell her the truth.

He could not tell her.

"We can stop it," he said. "This is my Challenge. We haven't been able to determine what we are looking for. Amai has been taunting me with it, sending small tests our way. He is eager for me to discover the truth. There is a trap he's preparing that we need to find." He eyed the laptop and its websites as if it were a snake.

She rose, the need for reassurance high in her mind. She wanted to know that her help would tip the balance. She wanted to know that she would have her vengeance on Amai. Griff had no such assurances. Emotion stirred within her. He tried to grasp it and pull it forward, but Clea slid it away, shutting it off like a panel closed between the driver and passengers of a limousine.

"We'll find it, Clea," he said, and held out his arms. He spread his wings across the bed and with the tip of one, beckoned to her. "Today may be our last day of luxury before my Challenge. Let's make the most of it."

Their lovemaking was fierce and hot. Griff took her with no argument, suckling and caressing Clea until she moaned and begged for him, grabbing at his shoulders as her mind pleaded with his to fulfill her. He held off, teasing her body. He licked her breasts and bit her nipples. Clea twisted and cried out, but he kept her on the edge, not allowing her to plummet into fulfillment, even though his body ached. He wanted to brand her, to put his claim on her so that no matter what happened next, their time together would be seared in her memory.

Her eyes were glazed, and there was naked need on her face when she turned it up to him. His wings fanned out, covering the ceiling and bracketing her body until all that was visible to her was him. Using his feathers, he stroked her body, and Clea shuddered. Griff thought his cock was going to burst, he was so hard.

A primal part of him was urging him to take her, just take her and mark her. Bite her, own her.

"Do you want me?" he asked, poised over her entrance. Clea gasped and twisted, her hands clutching at the expensive covers. "Tell me you want me." He barred his mind, making her say the words. "Tell me you need me. Beg me."

Clea's eyes were unfocusing. "Please. Please."

"Tell me." He grazed her lower lips with his cock, running it across her lips and touching her clit with his small opening. He wanted to pound in her, take her. Still he waited. He could see need, want, and more, that elusive something she was keeping from him etched on her face. His griffin howled at him to throw himself against her barrier and discover her secrets. "Tell me."

"Oh Griffin, yes. Please. I want you. I need you. I must have you. Please take me. I am yours. Only yours."

"Sì." Satisfied, Griffin guided his body into hers. The way was slick, the passage easy. She gripped him as if in a vise, sweet torment along his hard length. He shuddered, need engulfing him.

"Look at me." Griff opened their connection and her desire surged through their mind link, a need so furious it swept over him like a tidal wave. He reflected it back, his own pounding desire holding him. Their minds connected and each felt the other's hunger. The white-hot burn of passion soared through him. "Keep looking at me, don't close your eyes. Stay open to me. Come for me, my Clea. I am losing control."

She cried out, clutching at the covers, and then reached for him. Her hands gripped his wings with furious strength. Still she kept her eyes open, and her mouth went wide in an O of ecstasy. Griff felt her orgasm pounding across their link and he let go, his thrusts wild. Her climax caught him and he shouted, passion searing across body, mind, and spirit, their mutual fulfillment multiplying until they appeared to be flying while still joined.

Chapter Fifteen

Neit jolted awake, not knowing what woke him. Around him were all three of his Morrigan wives in restless slumber. He reached out but could sense nothing around them that would have caused all of them to wake at once. There did not appear to be any danger lurking in their small village, and all appeared calm.

* * * * *

Cormac woke into full alert, leaping to his feet, searching for whatever it was that awakened him. It was quiet in the early hours of the day not yet dawned. He couldn't hear anything out of the ordinary. Yet something had woken him. Concentrating, Cormac reached out mentally for the disturbance but could not find anything around him.

* * * * *

Dodola came to her senses, thinking someone was shaking her, but she was alone in the bed. Perun had taken his evening entertainment elsewhere, and her temporary bed companion had long been banished back to his own quarters. There was nothing strange about the morning. In her mind was her Tuatha Dé Danann son Cormac, awake and confused. Her pantheon slumbered on, but Dodola knew there would be no further rest for her tonight.

* * * * *

"'Tis time for readiness," Badb said.

All four of them showed the effects of a swift toilette. As a war goddess, the Morrigan didn't care for feminine things, and they were dressed in sensible garb, with leather armor strewn around them. Neit too had on similar attire, and a length of chain mail rested near him. It was heavy, but the weight was no matter.

"I am after getting the Treasures and being ready." This was Nemain speaking.

Neit glanced at his three wives, whose faces betrayed their glee. There had been few wars that involved them in recent centuries; most of the bloody conflict had been of human making and they had stayed clear of it.

"It's time to retrieve them," he said. "I'm only after the spear and the sword. The rest will not be useful in this battle."

Macha nodded. "We're helping Clea, so we are."

He studied his wife. The choice to take Cormac and leave Clea to her mother's pantheon had been mutual. Neit always believed his wives didn't want another female in their midst.

"Why are you about helping her?" he asked, echoing his thoughts. "She is my kin, no relation to you at all."

Macha made a flicking motion with her hand. "She be Tuatha Dé Danann. She has your blood. We are not about turning our back on our own."

Neit nodded, although he was surprised. In all the centuries that they had been together, the Morrigan still astounded him.

"Aye. 'Tis time to begin."

* * * * *

Clea examined each one of her features. Nothing had changed dramatically. She still had the same heart-shaped face, her eyes were still green, and none of her bone structure had shifted. Although nothing had moved, it was all subtly different. It was as if she had been touched up for a glamour magazine. Her cheekbones were a little more prominent, her nose smaller and her eyes were perfectly set apart. She seemed lit from within, a radiance she hadn't possessed before. It had come on over the past few days without her knowing it. Her features hadn't changed much, but power shone from within her, making her seem different without altering the basics. She wasn't sure she liked the change. It had always been a point of pride for her to remain average. Clea turned this way and that, debating what to do.

"You are bella." Griff's tone held admiration, and she could see down their link that he was speaking the truth. "You always were, but there's something different about you. I saw it before but put it down to a trick of the light, and my growing appreciation of you. Thank you for keeping your freckles. You would have been incomplete without them."

His hand reached for her shoulder but then he let it drop. She felt uncertainty in him, a feeling that she had never expected in the Griffin she had thought she'd known. That man hadn't existed any more than she had. They'd both been illusions, constructs. Now they were real.

Maybe the shift in her looks wasn't bad after all. Clea met his gaze in the mirror. Whatever happened next, her future came down to this moment.

She turned to him and saw all the uncertainty, the fear that he was shielding from her mind in his expression. Clea smiled.

"I'm a goddess, but I'm still someone with emotions. Thank you for saying it and thank you for not caring about my looks. I have always been just another minor goddess. I never mattered, or thought I didn't. Now I know the truth." She could tell by his blank expression that he didn't understand. She eased her mind open to him, lowering the shields she had built to keep this hidden. He did the same, letting down his defenses one brick at a time. Still he held back, and that decided it for her.

Clea stepped into the harsh glare of the bathroom light and let down every defense, allowing him to see all the way into her. Every thought, every emotion, every deed was laid before Griffin. She was as naked and defenseless as the day she was born. Clea trembled. He explored her open mind, his touch reverent. She held her breath and waited.

After what seemed like an eternity, she looked at him. There was wonder in Griffin's eyes, their blue as clear as a brilliant sky.

"I love you, Griffin. I've never known what it was to feel a part of something, or someone. My pantheon didn't want me. All these years I've wandered without knowing what I was searching for. Now I know. I am a goddess and a member of two pantheons, whether one of them wants me or not. I always thought I wasn't good enough, and now I know that's untrue. I am a goddess, but I am also a woman, and I love you."

"Oh, Clea," he said, stepping in. His wings went around her body, stroking her. He cupped her face and smiled. She could feel terror, fear, and the pride at her words. That he hadn't said them back didn't matter. It wasn't the receiving of love that was important, although of course she wanted that, it was the giving.

"Clea, when all of this is over, we'll talk. I can't…I won't be able to make any promises before then. I am honored and humbled. You are a goddess. I'm an Elemental, but I was once human. You can't know what it means to me." He ran his thumbs along her higher cheekbones, his expression dazzled.

She smiled and his face lit up in return.

"I do know. We are alike, you and I, in many ways."

* * * * *

Griff shuddered, keeping his thoughts away from Clea. He should tell her now. He should tell her at this moment and not let this linger. The knowledge that he had killed her brother would wipe away her admiration. She would find out soon enough. Then he would be alone again. He could keep it from her for a little longer. He would keep her love for this brief moment. He hadn't said he loved her back, so there wouldn't be that to deal with when the inevitable came. He would take this shining moment of love before he went back to his lonely life and station.

* * * * *

Clea woke up from a deep sleep of swords and wind and flaming spears into…nothing. It was dark and quiet, the world still. Faint traffic noise and the lights of the city gleamed even at this late hour. Somewhere below her, life was going on in all its myriad ways. She eased out of the bed, careful not to wake Griffin. He was sprawled out, naked, his wings draped in slumber half across the bed and half across him. He would always need a king-sized bed to feel at ease, and then she shook her head at the foolishness of that thought. There were no doubt plenty of times when Griff had not been comfortable.

She knew little about his early days, his time prior to being an Elemental. Curiosity gripped her, but she doubted it would be satisfied. She wanted to know everything there was to know about Griff, but there wouldn't be time.

What had woken her? The night was still, especially this high up. There were no parties that would have disturbed her, and she couldn't hear anything out of the ordinary.

Then, outside their balcony window, a basket descended. It hovered in front of their room for a moment and then continued down, the ropes coming into view and also sinking. She stayed where she was, watching, unsure of what to do. Amai appeared, beckoning to her and then descending out of sight.

Griff still slept. She reached out a hand to wake him, and then stilled it. This was something she needed to do. Shielding her mind from his so her agitation didn't rouse him, Clea found jeans and a shirt among the items packed for her. The jeans were well crafted and fit her like they were made for her. The cream-colored shirt was form fitting, skimming her body, its drape making it clear it was well made and expensive.

She opened the balcony door. A rush of air and faint ambient sounds greeted her. She glanced down but there was no basket or ropes. She did see a large figure beckoning her. He was moving one hand in an impatient gesture and pointing to the reception area of the hotel with the other.

What did Amai-te-rangi want with her? It was obvious that it was her he wanted to talk to, otherwise he wouldn't be so stealthy with the basket. Clea glanced at a still-slumbering Griffin. It would have been much more satisfying to stay there and tease him awake. She wanted to slide over his cock, take him into her mouth and run her tongue and hands over his length, suck on him until he was panting and gasping for her. She wanted his hands in her hair, urging her to take all of him. She wanted him to pour his essence into her. Before this was over, she would be on her knees doing that.

Instead, Clea found her slip-on shoes, as expensive as the deceptively simple clothes she wore, grabbed her hotel card key, and exited the room.

Amai was waiting for her in the bar and to her surprise, he looked well put together. His head and body were gleaming and he smelled of musk. His jeans and blue shirt were clean and acceptable, a far cry from the loincloth he had sported before.

The bar was done in dark wood and had the plush, luxurious feel of high-priced drinks and quick service. There were only one or two other patrons in the bar at this hour. One of them appeared as if he'd had a rough night. His clothes were disheveled and his hair lank. He had a whiskey glass clutched in one hand.

Reputable clothing or not, Amai was too big and too menacing to look easy in this ritzy place. His aspect spoke of the outdoors, of weather-beaten times and hard work. It was what he had been before becoming a Demonos—a Pacific Islander mythological being for people whose lives were cut short by harsh conditions and treacherous oceans. It was believable that he would snatch people up in a basket and carry them away, eating them if necessary. Life was short for the people who had believed in this strange being many centuries ago.

The bartender eyed the two of them in surprise but said nothing. Their outer appearance didn't matter if the denomination of their money was high enough, or their plastic black.

"Senhorita? May I get you a drink?" The bartender spoke in Portuguese, which she automatically translated.

"Wine for the wahine and a piña colada."

She arched an eyebrow at Amai.

"I'll have a vodka tonic," she corrected, and gestured to the top shelf. "Make it Ciroc."

"Very good, senhorita."

The bartender was smooth, nothing showing on his face. Underneath the mask of cool politeness Clea tasted the disbelief that the gorgeous woman would be with such a brute. He did not appear sophisticated enough for such a fine lady. Perhaps the man had money, although he didn't look it. The lady would be much better off with someone else, someone like him. He could...

Clea shut off her connection with the man, strengthening her shields. She took a shot at Amai's thoughts but discovered that he was well shielded, almost impenetrable. No surprise. He may look ridiculous with the basket, but he was a strong and powerful Demonos.

Amai pulled out Euros, enough to cover the tab only, and slapped them on the bar. The bartender made no outward sign that the harsh sound affected him, but Clea sensed a deep rolling anger before she mentally backed away from his thoughts.

I'd have her bent over this bar so fast...

Clea gave the man a sharp look, and he flushed.

"We'll take our drinks over there." She pointed to a small table set off in a cubbyhole. The bartender shrugged. Amai glanced over at the table and nodded in agreement.

"Where did you park the basket? Valets take care of it?" She took a sip of her drink. Amai's eyes were dark and unreadable. His sheer bulk made her shiver.

"I was once a powerful atua," he said, his face seeming to glow. "I terrified children and adults alike. My worshipers were devout. Then these primitive islanders created this legend of Amai-te-rangi, the demon who snatches people up in his basket and carries them away. One day I had a basket and it's been part of me ever since. Humans are not powerless. Maybe I will be shed of it when the legend fades out of memory, or there are no more mortals." He moved the umbrella aside and took a long swallow of the piña colada. The sight of the foam and the pineapple on the tall glass seemed incongruous with his bulk, but she made no comment.

She sipped her own drink. The expensive vodka tingled against the back of her throat. There was something in his words, a lie in there, but she couldn't find it in the myriad truths he had tossed at her. She translated atua as something more complex than demon, a concept that seemed to transcend the idea of gods or demons to something understandable by the primitive race he came from.

"Is that why you became the air Demonos?" she asked.

He drank a large portion of his pale drink, his throat working. His fingers made marks on the condensation. Amai made a satisfied sigh and set the glass down again.

"What atua wouldn't want to be a Demonos? What atua could refuse?" he said, smacking his lips.

"The legends say you like to eat people," she said, knowing she was treading on dangerous ground. "Did you lose the need for human flesh?"

Anger, hot, dark, and savage, streaked across his face and in her mind. The jab of his fury was like a sword lancing into her. Clea almost cried out at the shock of the sudden, quick ire, but suppressed it. Quickly regaining her composure, she turned what she hoped was a bland expression his way.

"Legends, bah," he spat. "Lies. Those islanders were too thin to be good meals. I like lamb."

It was such an odd conversation that Clea was having trouble figuring out what she was doing there. It had been foolish to slip out and meet Amai at the bar. She should have woken Griff. She would have, but for the warning that told her not to.

"Why did you want to meet me?" she asked, appearing to take a sip of her drink but in reality just holding the glass to her lips. She checked on Griff down their mental link and verified that he was still sleeping. The agitation in his mind made her wonder if he was sensing this conversation.

"You look different," Amai said, studying her. When Clea offered no reply, Amai went on. "You're clever, for a wahine."

Clea said nothing, keeping her face impassive. Amai would have to do better to get a rise from her.

"Our lives would be easier without humans," he said. "You're smart but your own pantheon doesn't respect you." Clea tried to contain her flush at these words. It made sense that Amai would have her investigated, but she squirmed at the idea. "Like me, you have been pushed aside by everyone. Once I was worshipped, now I am forgotten. We are very much alike. We have no place in this world." He chugged the rest of his drink, and his Adam's apple worked.

The bartender's gaze was on her again, fear mixed with lust. Amai had said she was better looking, but she hadn't changed her looks. It was something else. Had she changed that much in the short time since she struggled up Griff's mountain? Something had fallen away inside her when she'd acknowledged the truth. She was no longer bound by the feelings of the Slavic pantheon. That was part of it, but there was more.

"You've never been worshipped. Imagine what life would be like when paranormals ruled. You could be revered in a different world. Your pantheon could take the place as top dogs instead of the Greeks, Romans, or Egyptians."

She toyed with the rim of her glass. Except for them and the man still sitting at the bar, the room was empty. The unkempt man had engaged the bartender in conversation, or rather a monologue, and the bartender listened with barely concealed contempt at the drunken ramblings. Once in a while he glanced over at Clea and Amai with more than professional courtesy.

"All a bunch of cheaters," drifted over from the drunk man. "Rob you blind."

The bartender nodded but also shrugged as if to say, "What can you do?"

"Top pantheon?" She pretended to mull the idea over. "What about you? What do you have in mind for Amai-te-rangi?"

His eyes gleamed in the dim light, a spark of red in them.

"I have ideas," he said. "There are demons who need replacing."

"And you're the guy?"

Amai leaned over. "I'm a Demonos. I deserve more. We win and I can make my own rules. Humans are a menace. They need to be removed from the earth.

Join us, wahine. Griffin will leave as soon as this is over. The Elementals, they're 'friends,' and they always go back to each other."

Clea flinched at the implication that the Elementals were lovers. She'd thought it more than once before she'd met Griff. Living as long as they did, it would be logical that their ideas of sexuality would be fluid, as it was to the pantheons. Griff had dashed off to check on his friend, leaving Clea behind. It would make sense…if she hadn't felt the passion inside Griff. He may not love her, but he wasn't indifferent to her.

"What can you offer me? What would joining the Demonos get me?"

He grinned and sat back. Signaling the bartender for another drink, Amai picked at his teeth with the small point of the umbrella.

"Challenge is here. I can defeat Griffin, with your help. Then they have to fight the common Challenge and we can take them all down. We will rid this planet of the plague of humanity. You will have the world to play in. You can even have the Elemental if that's what you want."

He hadn't answered her question. The bartender came over with Amai's second drink and shot Clea a glance before retreating.

"Amai, has it occurred to you that humans are necessary?"

Amai paused in the act of putting his glass to his lips. "Teka." Untrue, she heard in translation.

She laughed, a tinkling, bell-like sound. "We do, Amai. Look around you. We didn't make any of this. We didn't make machines, they did. All the advances are nothing the paranormal world would have done. They destroy, but they are also amazing. We need them more than they need us."

He scoffed. "They trap us."

She nodded. "I don't understand why things are the way they are, but people bring good to this world. Without them we would have different lives. We need them to survive. What good is being a god, or an atua, if nobody is there to remember us?"

Amai moved his hand and Clea saw a flicker of rope as if the basket was within him.

"I gave you too much credit," he said with a condescending tone. "That Elemental has you fooled. Join the Demonos and you would have power and recognition. Stay with him and you're another kairau."

Clea flushed at the reminder of the word he used to connote whore.

"He will leave you when all this is over, and you will be alone. You're not part of his world."

She hoped he didn't see that his words penetrated. "Never call me a slut again," she said, her voice deadly quiet. Amai gave her a sharp look. "This isn't about Griffin. We need humans. If there are no mortals, are we gods?" He snorted. "Is that how you got the weather talents to help you?"

Clea smiled inwardly when Amai's face darkened.

"You would know the truth, wahine?" He smirked, set down his glass, and motioned to someone outside the room.

Perun stepped through the doorway with an aggressive stride. His gaze was fixed on Clea, his look contemptuous.

* * * * *

Perun was a short man, but he filled the entrance, his broad bulk covering the polished mahogany. This man had exiled her from their home under pain of death. He wanted her dead. He had damped down her thunder. Hate beat within him. She should run. She had been running, but he was here anyway. The exits. She needed to get to the exits. She found the nearest one and shifted her gaze back to Amai, trying to appear calm while measuring the distance between their table and the red and white sign that said Saída and exit underneath that. If she could get there she could use her air power to escape. Maybe.

"This was no coincidence." Clea felt like an idiot for not thinking of it sooner. Perun had tried to burn out her thunder powers. He wanted her dead for a reason that went beyond his natural hatred of her. The rest had just been pretense. He was one of the weather talents helping Amai with Challenge. Of course he was.

Just like the Romanian weather creature Griff encountered on the plane. There were others.

Perun advanced into the room. Something in his manner made the humans stand up and take notice. The bartender began wiping down the clean bar and the sole patron shifted to a seat on the far end.

"You're helping him." Clea pointed a shaking finger to Amai.

Perun, his locks of blond hair tied back in a ponytail, gave her a sharp nod. "As you should be." His gaze darted around the room. "But you're too stupid for that. Relax. I am not going to try to harm you at the moment. I have information you need."

Clea blinked. Perun gave her a disgusted look as if she were beneath his notice. She was used to that too. But there was something else, an anger, something deep seated that made her study him closer. Saída, the sign called to her. She took a deep breath. The flight instinct was strong inside her, but Clea kept her expression neutral, hoping her shields were holding.

Amai had a satisfied expression on his face. He sat back, taking a sip of his piña colada.

Perun slung a chair around and landed in it. He had chosen not to be good looking, and she had never understood why until now. His aura was one of leashed menace, a fireplug of a man who could snap at any moment. The ugliness carried with it a certain grim authority.

Everything seemed off kilter. She was missing something. She pressed, but Perun's shields were good. Reaching out for the Elemental, she discovered Griffin was still sleeping restlessly.

The bartender glanced up but Perun glared at him. He went back to polishing the bar.

"Does it not make sense, holka?"

Child. He had always considered her to be inferior. She shook her head. "I don't understand." She should be running, fleeing back to the room, but she stayed her flight. Whether she could get to saída before Perun struck was debatable. For the moment, he wasn't attacking.

"I didn't think you were stupid, Clea," Perun said with a shake of his head. "A bastard, a levoboček, useless, but not a fool."

Her talent buzzed under her skin, and Clea reached for it. Thunder rumbled within her and air buoyed her. She may be no match for Perun, but she wasn't helpless.

"Just say whatever it is you want to say and leave," she snapped "We have work to do."

"It's a shock," Perun said, tapping his head with his fingers, "that you can sleep with the Elemental." Clea ignored the gesture signifying that she was stupid.

Clea checked her shields. They were holding, but Perun had known her for a long time. He knew how to read her, even if he didn't bother acknowledging her existence.

"Why does that surprise you?" she asked after a quick glance at Amai, who had still said nothing. "I would do anything to get vengeance for the man Amai destroyed." The image of Patrik filled her vision and she projected it to Perun, who nodded.

"Yes," he said. "Your bratr. You loved him. So did I. He was one of my favorites. His mother, ah, what a beauty. It was one of the reasons I tolerated your visits. He looked forward to them so much. Patrik. My son. That's the surprise," he continued and Clea stared at him. The buzzing under her skin started again, but this time it was a crawling, unpleasant feeling as if bugs were about to erupt from her pores.

"Thunder god," Amai cut in, his iron-shavings-mixed-with-whiskey voice booming. He rocked forward on his seat, threatening to snap the small legs. "Say it. Remove doubt from this wahine. Say it."

Perun nodded, although he cast an angry look Amai's way, as if the Demonos had spoiled his revelation.

"It surprises me," Perun said, and his tone was venomous. "Since the Elemental killed your bratr."

* * * * *

Things fell into place with a snap. There was no doubting the ring of truth in Perun's voice. His face was wreathed in smug self-satisfaction, his expression hard with malice.

She glanced from one to another. Sorrow and loss warred in her, spilling out over her shields and outward.

"No." She swallowed in a throat gone dry. "No," she repeated.

"Holka," Perun chided. "I do not lie."

She nodded, her gaze darting around the room. In the room high above them, Griffin jerked awake. "I…what happened?"

Amai handed her her drink, and Clea took a long swallow. It did nothing to ease the lump in her throat. Tears threatened, but she blinked them back. It wasn't possible…but it was all too right.

Perun made a harsh noise, sorrow in his eyes.

"My beloved son thought he was like the gods. He paid for that mistake with his life. Your Elemental created a storm to stop Amai, but it sucked the humans up instead, including Patrik. He dropped from the clouds back down to earth. The fall was too great. No demigod could survive that. The humans around him perished as well. Amai did not kill him. The Elemental did. The fault was his." He gave Clea a hard look. "Your brother was killed by the man whose bed you now share, and not Amai-te-rangi. Do not blame your mother. I forbad her to tell anyone the truth. Your Elemental has owed the pantheon a debt this entire time, to his shame."

Amai squeezed his hand shut as if choking the life out of an imaginary opponent. "I would have done what was necessary, but I did not take his life." He leaned forward and the chair rocked again. "That was your Elemental."

"Silly dítě." Perun's tone was mocking. "We tell the truth."

Clea slanted her gaze to the door and nodded.

"Yes. I know that."

Perun smiled, showing slightly yellow teeth.

"Then you'll join us." It was a statement, not a question. "With you added to our talents, we can defeat him." He sent a bolt of energy searing across her shields. Clea deflected it as if it were nothing. He frowned. "Your thunder cannot compete with mine. It never could. Your cursed father gave you strength, but not enough."

His arrogant confidence would have made Clea smile if she hadn't been sick at heart. She had been so committed to avenging Patrik it had never occurred to her that anyone other than the Demonos could have been responsible. It made too much sickening sense. She had been blind, and a fool, not to see the reality before.

"How?"

"It was un accidente."

As one, the entire bar's attention went to the door. Griffin stood there, magnificent in a white shirt and slacks, his wings taking up the doorway. She took a quick look into the bartender's mind and looked at the room through his eyes. To him Griff was just a good-looking man with a long braid, powerfully built and commanding. He, the bartender, could never compete. It was typical.

"Elemental," Amai acknowledged. "We were just having a korero, a conversation."

"I heard." Griff's gaze was on Clea.

"Perun." She flicked her gaze to Perun before sliding her attention back to Griffin. "My thunder is returning, no thanks to you." She paused. "Your truth doesn't change anything. I'm still with the Elemental."

Perun's start told her that he hadn't expected her response. Until she'd spoken the words aloud, she hadn't been sure of what she would do either. This time with Griff had taught her something. She couldn't stay on the sidelines anymore. To lose Challenge meant that much would be lost. Too much. She had come this far and she would help as she had said she would. If nothing else, she owed that to the brother she had sought to avenge. Patrik believed in helping humans, and she would honor that.

Relief and surprise warred over Griff's expression. Clea held up her hand to forestall whatever he was about to say. "I'm still going to try to save humanity." Now she allowed her mind to open to Griff's. "Things are different, but that hasn't changed. I'm doing it for Patrik." No wonder he hadn't told her he loved her, if he had ever had those feelings. There had never been a doubt what would happen when she learned the truth.

Pain, swift and sure, zinged across her nerve endings until she wanted to double over. Maybe things would have been different if Griff had told her. There was no way to know now.

She straightened. She was a goddess. She had just been betrayed and lied to by the first man she had thought she could love in a century, but she was still part of the Slavic pantheon, and the Tuatha Dé Danann. She would overcome this.

Amai paused a moment, as if giving Clea one final opportunity to go with them. Clea focused on a spot along the wall where a landscape painting hung. The bartender's gaze went first to Griff and then Clea, his lust still apparent on his face. If this had been earlier, Clea would have planted the notion that the bartender should be happy with the round-faced woman she saw in his mind, but Clea had no stomach left for romance.

Perun got up as if unconcerned, but a wisp of fear and anger crawled out from under his shields. He wanted to strike at Clea, try to kill her, but the Elemental's presence stayed his hand.

Amai turned to go. Clea couldn't see to the street but had no doubt that his basket would be waiting.

"I should have killed you when I walked in," Perun snarled. At a gesture from Amai, Perun rose and stared down at her, hatred gleaming in his eyes. "You will pay soon. You are a bigger fool than I thought." Perun turned on his heel to follow Amai out.

"Perhaps," she said in his mind. "But I doubt it." She purposely left it unclear whether she meant that she would not pay soon or that she was a fool. Clea wasn't sure she knew either.

The bartender and remaining patron breathed a sigh of relief when the duo left. Clea would have as well, if her life hadn't collapsed into a million shattering fragments.

The Elemental she had loved stood in the doorway watching her. He hadn't so much as glanced at Amai when he left, as if his legendary Demonos enemy meant nothing. She wished that that were true, that she could be everything to Griffin, but there was no time for regrets. Too late now. Her fate was before her and it was time for action.

She didn't look at Griff. "We need to check the weather sites again. We missed something."

"Clea, we must speak about Patrik," he began and she held up her hand again.

"No need," she said, and her voice was calm, toneless. "I know the truth now. I only wish you had told me."

* * * * *

No. This would not happen this way.

Griffin walked forward, never lifting his gaze from Clea. Her expression didn't change. Reaching into her mind, he felt a smooth wall blocking him from her thoughts. There was no way around or through. He didn't bother trying. He had expected nothing else.

She had told him she loved him and he had remained silent. Griff had come to know Clea over the last days. His silence was far more egregious a sin than the actual death of her brother.

"Perun told me what happened to Patrik," she said and there was so much pain behind the casual tone Griff wanted to cry out.

He nodded. "You were shielding, but Perun wasn't. He wanted me to hear. Clea, it was an accident. I didn't know they were there. There was so much chaos. I created the storm thinking that it was only gods down there and they could survive it. I miscalculated. Humans died that day as well as Patrik. My doing; my fault. I have to live with that." He paused. "I'm sorry. I should have told you."

She nodded. "Yes, you should have. I had to hear it from a man who hates me. If Perun had his way I would be dead. Just because I am useful to them right now doesn't change that fact. If I had gone with them, he would probably kill me, or try to, after Challenge was over. He's pretty sure you can't win."

Griffin wanted to reach out to her, but there was no mistaking her rigid posture. Nothing about his touch would be welcome right now.

"I don't think I can win without you."

Too late, Elemental. Too late. The mocking voice was his own.

The bartender was still at the bar, polishing the brass, trying not to look interested in the couple.

"As you said, it was an accident. When I thought it was malice, that Amaite-rangi had done it on purpose, it fueled my need for vengeance." Her voice broke. "You kept it from me." He saw the glint of tears, but Clea blinked them away before he could be sure. Sorrow leaked from behind her shields, but he could feel nothing else. Their mind link was gone, severed, her end in tatters. "I would have forgiven you but you didn't trust me with the truth. You didn't believe in me enough to tell me. I told you I loved you and you said nothing. I understand now."

"Clea." Griffin reached out for her. She backed away, putting herself out of wing reach. He would have used them too, if he had thought it would make a difference.

"No, Griffin. No. We finish this and then I am gone. I will help you, not because of who you are, but because of what you are. We have a job to do. After that, this is over."

Despair flowed through Griff. Win or lose his Challenge, he had lost. Until this moment he hadn't realized how much he had to lose.

Chapter Sixteen

"There it is," Griff said, pointing.

It had been in front of them the whole time, buried in boring text on the NOAA website. There were so many anomalies it had been almost impossible to pin the correct one down, but the moment he saw it he knew he was right. All his weather senses screamed.

"A tropical depression in the ocean off the coast of Africa?" she asked, doubt in her voice. "They are saying it won't last. It's the wrong time of year. It should dissipate shortly."

He clicked through the site, following the projected path. He read that it wasn't acting like a storm should. His Elemental senses surged at the sight of the storm. This was what they had been waiting for. Amai and the weather powers were doing this. This was Amai's handiwork—there was no doubt about it.

Clea traced the line on her screen. Her eyes widened. He could tell she understood what was happening. This was his moment. Challenge was here.

"If this doesn't break up like it's supposed to…" She trailed off. Her finger was resting over the city. A large hurricane should not be able to strengthen and reach Europe, but this was no natural weather phenomenon.

"It will strengthen into a category-five hurricane within a day, perhaps hours." Griffin spoke with absolute authority. His wings rose above him. "It will continue on this path, strengthening even more out over the ocean, and strike along the European coast."

"Why haven't we felt it? Shouldn't we know about a storm like this? You're the air Elemental."

He nodded, his mind elsewhere. "The Vântoase hid from me on the plane. They have been blocking our knowledge of their activities. If I had any doubt that other weather talents were involved, they are gone."

The hurricane could hit Portugal, destroy parts of France, and take out cities along the entire coastline. Although he would normally think it unlikely that a storm would reach that far, London would even be at risk, ripping apart buildings that had stood for centuries, and killing thousands. There was no protection against a large hurricane—even the best of mankind's inventions only muted the after-effects.

There were places like Indonesia, where a tsunami had killed hundreds of thousands and would do so again. That had been a natural disaster, a reminder of the power of Mother Nature, but it had been every bit as deadly as a Challenge. This hurricane would wreak far more destruction than the tsunami in Indonesia had if he didn't stop it. This was his moment.

"Is Ondine in danger?"

He reached out. The Elemental responded immediately. They were getting rain in Morocco, but Ondine didn't expect trouble. The storm would just get them wet. Sea creatures didn't care about a little water. The tempest seemed to be keeping away from their area. Griff had no doubt that Amai was showing respect for his fellow Demonos by not letting his storm interfere with the water Challenge. The finesse showed great power, more than Amai had had the last time they met.

"Isn't category-five the largest hurricane?" Clea asked. He noted that she didn't dispute his assertion and was grateful she'd accepted it.

He slanted her a look. "Sì, but there is the theory of something called a 'hypercane.' It would please Amai's vanity to create a grandissimo one. The category isn't going to matter as much as the wind speed and intensity. If it hits land in a populated area at full strength, it will be devastating. Even a lower category hurricane could do much harm." He paused. "Amai will allow for nothing less than his best. We should expect a hypercane." He paused, his face in harsh lines. "Dodola and the pantheon should be safe, but the Tuatha could be at risk in Ireland. It all depends on where the hurricane comes onshore."

He was surprised when Clea glared at him. "My people are capable of taking care of themselves. They will not hide behind closed doors when lives are threatened. That's not how we're made."

She was lovely, an avenging goddess, and a brilliant partner in his Challenge. She was the most incredible woman he had ever seen.

He had thrown her trust in him away.

"Clea, when this is all over..." he said, but she waved it off. There was no more talk of love. He had expected it, but he missed it more than he could have imagined. He had lied to her, if only by omission, and any love she felt for him was gone. The fact that she remained to help him with his Challenge was the small comfort he had. He had gambled with telling her, and he had lost.

"Can we stop it before it reaches land?"

He studied the storm, the possible trajectories its path could take, and traced all of them with his index finger. "That, dea, is what we are here to do."

* * * * *

A flashing red light caught the attention of one of the weather monitors. The man reached over to turn it off, expecting a false alarm, but then halted his forward progress.

He sent a text message to his boss and then studied the radar again. No question the storm was bigger. In less than a day, the tempest had gone from a tropical depression to a category-two hurricane and it was building fast. They were going to need to send planes out soon.

"This is impossible," his higher-up declared moments later as he studied the printouts. "It's the wrong time of year. This shouldn't be able to build like this. This should be fading."

The other man nodded. "I know, but it's a hurricane, Mike, and the computers tell us it's getting stronger. Look at its path." He pulled down the data from the satellite. "Look at it. If this keeps growing like this in the North Atlantic, it could gain strength and head out to sea or…"

The other man finished the thought. "Europe. Put out the alarm."

* * * * *

Griff and Clea used their combined talents to seek out the anomaly. Together, they reached past the wind to the heart of the storm. Now that they knew it was there, it couldn't hide from them. It didn't take them long to confirm with their weather gifts what they'd already seen on the NOAA radar. Within hours it would be a category-five hurricane or hypercane, and it was heading right for Europe. All the laws of nature and physics declared that it was impossible, but there was no denying the truth. It would be landing by or before daybreak. They followed its path together. It was going to be in this vicinity and could strike Lisbon.

"It's going to hit Europe. It could land anywhere. My god, Griff, it could take out so many cities with weather talents helping. And with Amai-te-Rangi at its core, it might not even slow when it hits land. Millions could die."

"We will make our stand here," Griff said. "We must get to it before it lands. Clea, you need to go. Get somewhere safe. Use your air power and go inland. Far away."

"Why?"

"You'll be safe. This building could poof—" he made an exploding gesture with his hands, "—if that monstro hits Lisbon. Amai will likely send it here to punish us."

"No. I'm helping you and that's all there is to it." Her voice was mulish, but it didn't matter. Patrik or no Patrik, she still had a job to do. There was just nothing left to believe in after it was over. That part of their tale, her silly hope that she had found a man to love, was over.

"Daughter, we are here. We are after helping."

"Who was that?" Griff's voice was wary.

Clea smiled in triumph. She didn't recognize the voice, but the feeling was familiar. "Hollywood has old movies called Westerns. I think that they would say the cavalry has arrived. My family is here. Cormac said he would come, but I did not expect the rest." She recognized her mother and her Tuatha Dé Danann brother, but the others were new. She tasted the familiarity of her father and also a three-part woman/women, with linked but separate minds. The Morrigan had come with her father. Badb, Macha, and Nemain. They had a ruthlessness to their mental touch that made her shiver. War goddess. Perfect timing.

As if on cue, the computer blared a warning. Weather alert, the crawl said along the bottom. Hurricane watch. It was expected to miss this area but hurricanes could be capricious about their path.

It had begun.

Griff's face darkened with an emotion like anger. Clea ignored him, reaching for the other minds.

"They're at the hotel," she said with satisfaction. "They are waiting for me."

* * * * *

The gods gathered on the hotel roof of the Tivoli Oriente looked at Griff and Clea as they emerged from the stairs. Macha was the only deity that he recognized besides Dodola. Griff was surprised that the vain Slavic goddess had come to help.

"Sometimes we have to choose sides."

Dodola nodded to him, regal in full goddess mode. She kissed her daughter and introduced her son to Griff. The man, Clea's brother, was big and red haired in contrast to his slight sister, their resemblance subtle in the lines of their cheeks and shape of the eyes, but unmistakable.

Around them the wind was already swirling, buffeting them on the defenseless rooftop. From the roof of the fourteen-story hotel they could see the river, and the Atlantic Ocean in the distance. The hurricane was far off, but they could feel it, like a malevolent spirit, churning toward land with a speed it shouldn't have had.

Below them, in the city, panic was in the air and many gods were prayed to. The suddenness of the storm and the unpredictable nature of its path meant everyone along the European coastline was bracing for it. The roads were thick with cars, red brake lights showing as people fled inland, away from the storm.

Clea was deep in conversation with one of the Morrigan—Nemain, he decided. She was showing Clea something that glinted off the moonlight with deadly sharpness. A sword, but not just a sword. They wouldn't bring a regular sword to battle. This was one of their legendary Treasures, the Sword of Light. He had never seen their Treasures and had thought of them as mythology.

Cormac, Clea's brother, was tapping his shoulder to get his attention.

"What is this?" Griff asked, eyeing Cormac, who was holding something similar. It was a spear that glowed as if flames danced within it. Griff's eyes narrowed when he took in her brother. If Cormac thought he could waltz in here and save the day, he was mistaken.

The man chuckled. "We are not in the way of fighting you, Elemental," he said. "We brought things that will be useful, so we did." He tossed the spear to Griffin and Griff caught it with one hand.

"Che cosa è questo?" Griff turned the spear over, feeling its heft and seeing a line of fire dancing along it. The fire didn't seem to burn with heat; it was a cold flame. The blade was perfectly balanced, and there were runes etched into the metal. He reached for a memory and found it. "This is one of the Tuathan Treasures. The Spear of Lugh." Clea's brother nodded. Griff raised an eyebrow. "I'm flattered."

The man's expression darkened. "'Tis not for you, Elemental. We are in the way of bringing them for my sister."

Neit joined them, Dodola with him. "'Tis your Challenge this is." He followed Griff's gaze to Clea. "The blood of the Tuatha runs in my daughter's veins, so it does. Our Treasures are hers. If she be sharing them, that be her business."

Air will glide with air. He had forfeited his ability to fulfill that part of the proverb.

Clea was hefting the sword and testing its range with the Morrigan watching.

The fact that they brought two of their four Treasures, the greatest source of their strength, told Griff how the Tuatha felt about their recovered child. He wished they had more time to learn about these weapons and how they could best be used in battle.

Wind blew, swirling debris on top of the roof. Thick, heavy rain began falling. The city was lit up in brilliant neon and fluorescent, people scurrying around the streets, their movements erratic as they tried to figure out how to get to safety. There were other paranormals who were fleeing as well, moving to higher ground, or other safer places. He felt the touch of sea creatures in the ocean around them. Their mental signature was unfamiliar. These were not the beings who had traveled with Ondine, but perhaps she had more friends. They appeared to be lingering, safe below hundreds of feet of water.

In the distance out in the ocean, the hurricane roared, churning toward Europe. There was fury in it, as if it were alive. In a way it was. It had been created from wind and sea and the power of weather paranormals. Soon it would dash its fury on the land, destroying everything in its wake, if Griff didn't stop it by beating Amai-te-rangi.

It was time. Griff pulled off his shirt and unfurled his wings, feeling their comfortable, familiar strength flow out behind him. Griff hefted the spear and then took a strap that Neit held out to him. It secured the spear along his body, giving him freedom of movement. The fire flickered and danced with an unknown power. Fire was Phoenix's domain, but today it was his as well.

Clea approached, fervor written on her face. With the sword in her hands, she looked like the magnificent goddess she was. The Tuatha Dé Danann gods and Dodola gathered in a semicircle around them, like an old Druidic gathering. Perun's betrayal had to sadden Dodola, but she showed no sign.

Griff studied the elder Tuathan god and inclined his head toward Neit, slanting his gaze toward Clea.

"Take care of her," Griff said to Neit. He ran his hand along the length of the spear. Clea stood motionless but with an air of expectancy. It was time. He needed to go. Griff strode to her but Clea backed away. His wings picked up the wind, and he nodded.

"Be safe," he said.

She raised the spear. "And you." Clea looked around at everyone but Griff. "For Patrik," she said, her voice ringing.

Cormac nodded. "Aye. For Patrik." The others chimed in and Griff also raised his arm, his wing following the motion.

"Yes, Clea. For Patrik."

Her emotions were shielded where he could not reach. Griff stepped back. After one final look at Clea, he turned and summoned his strength. With one powerful leap, he was in the air, soaring toward the sky where Amai awaited.

* * * * *

Up this high, he could see the hurricane that was designed to destroy cities. It was huge and menacing, glinting white in the moonlight. He rose higher until he could see more of it. It covered a massive section of the Atlantic and was moving fast. Wind and rain tore at Griff, but he paid it little attention.

Far off was movement from the same direction as the hurricane. Amai, his old enemy and Demonos challenger was here. All Griff's senses danced on a surge of adrenaline. The spear danced with cold flame, unaffected by the pelting rain. He touched the Tuathan Treasure, and its energy flowed through him.

Somewhere around them were other paranormals, the ones aiding Amai. He felt Perun and the Vântoase and others, ones unfamiliar to him, all on the ground near the city and pushing on the wind and the storm, enabling its progress.

"Elemental," he heard. "I am coming."

Amai soared in, flying with no visible means of support. His basket was not with him but Griff had no time to wonder where it could be. Amai had painted markings on his face and body that rain did not wash off. He let out a war cry and plummeted toward Griff. Griff dodged him, flying to one side. Amai dashed past and jerked to a stop. He turned, pivoted, and headed toward Griff.

Thunder boomed and lightning crackled, illuminating the sky, deafening him with the sound. Behind them, the hurricane in the Atlantic churned in the sea, its destination unclear. Clea and her family were down below, watching him. They stood but did not act.

He could not—he would not—let them down. If he failed in everything else, she had to be safe.

Griff focused. Amai charged, using the power of the hurricane to travel. He roared and went for Griff again. This time he connected, landing a punch to Griff's solar plexus. Griff grunted, his breath going out of him. Their rain-slicked bodies were too slippery to hold, and Amai lost his grip, falling below Griffin.

Griff turned, using his wings to pivot. The wind beat at them, and he sleeked his wings along his back, relying on air currents to stay aloft. Griff summoned a small whirlwind and hurled it at Amai. It sailed past the Demonos, narrowly missing his torso. Amai countered with a wind shear, trying to knock Griff off balance. Only his folded wings saved him from plummeting.

Amai soared up, bursting through a cloud. He sent a hapless bird hurtling toward the Elemental, a hawk that hadn't gotten away from the storm fast enough. Griff moved aside and the creature continued its plummet down. He spared a brief air current to steady the path and straighten the bird. The rest was up to the hawk.

Thunder boomed again, and lightning lit up the sky in vivid yellow. Perun's mental signature flared in that blast. An unfamiliar power gathered to meet Perun's thunder. Neit, Griff hoped.

Through his shredded but still present mind link with Clea, Griff saw Amai's basket moving laterally across the roof of the hotel as if daring the gods. It slowed, dancing on the hemp ropes that dangled toward the ground, held up by something unseen. Clea looked at the basket and then grasped a rope as if testing it. What was she doing? "Clea. No."

Griff had no more time to think. Amai roared, raising his hands to the sky and then directing them toward the air Elemental. Thunder rumbled, followed by lightning, so near that it made his hair sizzle. The impact of the lightning knocked him back. Electricity sizzled around him. It struck him again, and Griff staggered. Smoke curled from him and the burst sent a frizz through his mind. Lightning hit him a third time, and his wings would have caught fire if not for the rain. His skin was hot, as if it were molten. He struggled to keep consciousness but felt it slipping away.

* * * * *

Clea stood still as the battle raged. Amai's basket bounced in front of her like a mischievous child that wanted attention. The ropes were damp with rain when she touched one. Dodola made a small noise as if guessing Clea's intention. The basket started to move, and Clea had no more time to decide. It began to gain speed, heading off toward where Amai and Griff were fighting over the Tagus River. It flew toward the edge of the roof, and Clea ran alongside. With a burst of air power she propelled herself into the basket, rolling with the motion. Inside was the crumpled figure of the human Pietro, his mouth wide in shock. He still held the gun, his fingers curled around it like he'd been shooting it at the time of his death. In the end, it appeared, Amai had discarded the human when he had been of no more use to the Demonos.

He showed no signs of being eaten, and Clea chalked one up for legends. The basket continued moving, aiming on a lateral upward motion toward where Amai and Griffin fought.

Streaks of lightning and the boom of thunder were all around her. She could make out Griff grappling with Amai. His wings beat against the furious winds forming the leading edge of the massive storm.

Clea felt the Morrigan, Cormac, and Neit focused against the weather powers aiding the storm. The hurricane was just visible in the distance, a vast whirling body of churning gray clouds. It would blow through in a matter of hours, skirting the coast to wreak more havoc as it gained power from the water. Already rain and winds were sweeping throughout the European coastline. Using human eyes as her guide, she saw the street signs clank in the storm, flags being torn from their moorings and fluttering away. All along the coastline, boats rocked wildly in the bucking waves. In London, the Thames storm barrier was up, but that would not deter this unnatural storm.

Thunder boomed again, and there was an answering blast closer by. Neit, by the familiar and yet unfamiliar power signature. It was similar to hers but more masculine. Her brother was lending aid to their father's power, his own a potent force as well.

"Clea. Get out of that basket." Griff.

"Too late." She stepped over the form of Pietro. The basket continued its journey up, gaining speed, heading for its master in the sky. Amai lunged at Griff and the Elemental peeled away from the Demonos. There was a boom of thunder and then lightning lit the sky, showering everything in brilliant light. It hissed again, and to her horror, it hit Griffin, sending him staggering back. Amai's laughter could be heard even through the howling gale. Her mother's power surged, and the rain deflected away from Clea. Something fought against her, a weather power with the touch of the Vântoase Griffin had mentioned. The rain droplets shifted, going lateral before falling away from Clea.

Clea and the basket were high above the ground, but that didn't concern her. Even if she had to jump she would only be slowed down for a moment while her limbs mended. She pulled the sword from its strap along her back and leg. It came free with a snick in a satisfying sound. Lightning flashed again, striking Griff, and he faltered. It ignited the sword, glinting off the piece as if shining a beacon.

Amai turned from Griff. The storm continued charging toward the European coastline, ready to attack with two-hundred-mile-an-hour winds and rain, blowing buildings apart. She tested the edge of the blade; it was sharp and deadly. Clea gripped it two handed and raised it up over her head, her attention fixed on the hemp in front of her.

Amai's chagrin was palpable, and he broke off with Griffin, leaving the Elemental staggering.

"Ehē!" No!" she heard in her mind, and even as the word reached her, she acted.

Clea aimed at the first rope and sliced through it. The hemp parted, the individual strands separating from their former mates. Without pausing, she severed the second, and the basket lurched. Pietro crashed into her legs, almost sending her off balance. Summoning her air talent, she levitated her body enough to clear the remains of the human.

More lightning struck a staggering Griffin, and his back arched. The assault went on and on, lighting up the sky and Griff until it was as bright as day. It was ball lightning, made thousands of times more powerful by Amai and the weather talent aiding him. Clea stopped her hacking at the basket ropes to focus on the storm and Griff. His pain streaked through her. She reached for her still-weakened thunder. Regardless of her strength, her first target would be Perun. Maybe the combined strength of the Tuatha Dé Danann could destroy Perun forever. Even a god could not regenerate from ash.

Neit, Cormac, and the Morrigan focused on the ball lightning raining down on Griffin. Neit deflected several blows but more got through. The streaks of deadly electricity were everywhere, lighting up the sky with their bolts, all aimed at Griffin. Cormac helped his father, aiding Neit's strength with his own thunder and lightning.

"Clea." Griff's voice was weak. "Do not worry about me. Let the Tuatha Dé Danann handle the storm. The basket. Finish it."

The Morrigan were battling the other weather talents, ones whose names Clea did not know. The war goddess dispatched each of them easily, as if they were nothing to the combined strength of the triad.

Dodola and Neit continued to pound on their unseen targets in the distance. Clea focused on the basket, listing to one side on its two remaining supports. She touched the bottom and skidded down, momentarily losing her focus on the third rope. Amai began moving toward her. Clea felt strength adding to hers, a mental signature that could only be her brother's.

"'Tis now it should be done, deirfiúr."

Aiming the sword, she drew back and with one powerful stroke, sliced through the first rope and then the last. The basket dropped, Pietro's body rolling in it. A quick glance at the battle scene showed Griff hanging motionless in the air.

"Nooooooooooooooooo," came a voice from above her. She stayed where she was when the basket fell, the wind steadying her, her ability keeping her upright. Holding the sword aloft, she descended to the ground slowly, a smile of victory on her face. If humans could see her at all there might be stories later about the woman descending from the sky, but they would be chalked up to hysteria. The basket hit the sand of the river beach and Clea leaped out. It smacked against a rock and crashed open, its wood panels breaking from the impact. Some clattered to the river, where creatures snatched the pieces of the basket from the water and carried them away.

"Griff?"

Far off, the Elemental moved slowly. Fire danced through him and around him. Clea realized that it was coming from the spear at his side. As if hearing her voice, Griff straightened. She could feel the electricity still smoking within him. The lightning had seemed to add to the power of the spear, and it glowed with cold flame.

Perun created another burst of thunder, but Neit shot his own toward the sound and it immediately subsided as if the two were canceling each other out. Rain moved away, doubling in strength over what Clea thought was the suburb of Cascais. Clea had little doubt that was where the weather talents were. Her mother would know for sure.

"All along, his basket was part of his power. I didn't know."

"Finish this, Griff."

Amai was being buffeted by the storm, appearing dazed, diminished, and smaller. The Morrigan's collective mind touched hers. They were amused. It had been foolish of Amai to use lightning against one who carried the spear. Lightning could harm the man, but not the spear, and it had given it more strength.

Griff lurched as a wind shear slammed into him. Amai raised his head. Agony, desperation, and loss shot through the Demonos. Clea didn't know what she had just done, but it was far more powerful than she had anticipated.

Griff took the spear and gripped it one-handed. He aimed at the swirling edge of the winds in the distance. Clea, Cormac, and the rest of the Tuatha Dé Danann focused on the spot where Griff was focusing the spear. Below her, she sensed her mother was targeting the water. How appropriate that a goddess of rain would take on the sea.

The others, the weather talents helping Amai, pushed back, their gathered powers preparing to strike.

Griffin hurled the Tuatha Dé Danann weapon at the winds, shouting "Savoia" as he flung the spear. Fire streaked along the sky, outlining the spear's path. She heaved the sword at the storm at the same time. It glinted as it soared through the air and joined its counterpart. The weapons struck the leading edge of the wind and then vanished.

She waited. And waited.

The spear and sword appeared to have done nothing, and the hurricane had sucked them into its maw, swallowing them like it would devour everything in its path. It continued to blow its fury, churning white death toward Europe. Soon the worst of the winds would hit and then it would be carnage.

We failed, she thought, and sagged. The hurricane would continue to gain strength before it moved onto land to destroy whatever cities lay in its path. Then it would continue north, to annihilate London. That would be the final blow, and it would mean Griffin had lost his Challenge.

Then, something changed, a shift in the wind so small at first she couldn't be sure she'd felt it. Clea held her breath, turning toward the leading winds of the monster storm. Griffin was upright but unmoving. Amai-te-rangi, too, was still in the air but appeared stunned by the loss of his basket. As if turned inside out, the squalls lost some of their fury. All around her water splashed out of the sky and back into the sea. The winds lost strength like a popped balloon. Inside her, a shout bubbled up and she let it come, screaming her relief. There was a streak of fire and now a shine of metal as both spear and sword moved in a counterclockwise direction, appearing briefly before speeding on their way around the storm in a blur of motion. The triple mind of the Morrigan aided the Tuathan Treasures on their path. The weather talents on Amai's side tried to fight this new power, but they had no answer for the ancient weapons, and the Morrigan batted their attempts aside with ease. Wind flowed under Griff, bolstering his wings, but that was all he could manage in his barely conscious state.

Amai shifted his focus from Griffin and angled down toward where his basket lay shattered on the sand. Clea raised her arms, prepared for attack, but he only shot her a malevolent look and turned to the remains of wood scattered around the beach. Pieces of the basket rose and flew to him. She dodged one as it tried to clip her. The pieces surged to Amai, the rope ends trailing behind the shattered parts. The water bubbled as if more pieces were trying to get to him, but the parts of his basket that had gone beneath the waves did not emerge.

Thick rain pelted down, and thunder still rolled in the sky. The winds continued to dissipate, losing the whirling formation. Far in the distance, Clea felt the eye collapse as the storm scaled back to category five and then category one. In a matter of minutes, it was nothing more than a tropical depression. It was impossible for a hurricane to lose force that quickly, just as it had been impossible for it to gain strength that fast. Humans would be studying this storm for years trying to figure out both how it formed and how it vanished. It would be a mystery, and scientists would be checking their instruments for failure for a long time.

Amai and the pieces of his basket soared into the sky, rope trailing, and he disappeared into the clouds. She could no longer sense his mind but had no illusions that he had been destroyed. He would be back to fight Griffin again.

The weather talents began scattering, leaving Cascais as quickly as possible. Whether they would aid Amai again was a question for tomorrow.

There would be heavy rain and wind across the Atlantic coast of Europe. The cities would be damaged, but they were used to weather. She felt the relief in the human signatures huddled in the cities, the knowledge that they had been spared. They would never know the truth, but it was satisfying to feel their gratitude just the same. Closer, in Lisbon, people began emerging from the buildings cautiously.

Several turned their heads to the sky as if tasting the air. Prayers in Portuguese echoed around them.

In the distance she saw Neit, Cormac, and Dodola rushing toward her, unmindful of the rain-slicked street as they dashed to meet her on the riverbank. It was several blocks from the hotel roof to the beach, but they sprinted the entire way.

She turned her attention to Griff, his hurt surging through her, agony filling her mind. Griffin tried to use his wings, faltered, and then with a sickening lurch, tumbled from the sky.

"Griffin!" Clea cried. Heart in her mouth, she watched as he shot straight down and hit the water of the Tagus with a force that would have killed a mortal. She sought his mind signature. It was there, but it was weak and thready.

"Daughter." Neit reached her and took her elbow when she would have plunged into the river after the air Elemental. He shared a glance with Dodola, who stepped up to take Clea's other arm, her expression sympathetic. "Look."

Strange mental signatures were in the water around where Griff had fallen. They were neither wholly human nor were they fish. They reminded her of the creatures that had been near Ondine in their encounter.

"Let the water beings have the way of this," Neit said. As they watched, dolphins crested the surface and then slid under the motionless Griff. With the Elemental on their backs the dolphins swam down the Tagus River until they rounded a bend and disappeared from her sight. After a confused moment, Clea realized they must be towing Griff to the deeper waters of the Atlantic Ocean. When she lost them, an unfamiliar dolphin mind touched hers almost diffidently, granting her access to its underwater vision. Clea watched through the creature's eyes as they retreated into the sea until a shape dominating the ocean loomed in front of them. There the creatures loaded Griff onto the back of a large white whale so vast it couldn't be anything other than a paranormal entity. She touched the mind, and a name echoed through her consciousness. Bahamut.

The other shapeshifters clustered around the whale, who shifted to allow them to slide Griffin onto his massive back. The great beast acknowledged her mentally, its signature strange and wholly unlike anything she had ever encountered. Even though they couldn't see each other, Clea waved a hand at the behemoth, recognizing the name now. The giant mythological whale had come to Griff's aid. Legend had it that Bahamut should bear a bull, mountain, and angel, but as with most other myths, Bahamut's was mostly fiction. What the massive whale's purpose here was she did not know, but at the moment the only thing that mattered was that Bahamut was helping the man she loved. Had loved.

"Thank you," she said. She owed Griff that much, but beyond that there was nothing to say. The pod turned and started away. The island nation that was Bahamut's destination shone in her mind. It was natural they would take him back to Iceland. That was his home. The whale would see to him. Griff had won his Challenge and she had avenged Patrik, although it had not turned out the way she had expected. Her part in his life was over. Even if her dead brother hadn't stood between them, their life together would still be at an end. Twenty-four hours ago, she would have gone to him. Now betrayal and secrets stayed her hand. Wind plastered her hair to her skull and debris swirled around her. It was too late. She was not the person she had been when she professed her love. She withdrew from the others and turned her attention to her family.

"I am after finishing Perun, on your say so," Neit said as if recognizing her as the leader of this conflict. It was a new thought. Dodola gave him a sharp look. Clea put her head on her father's shoulder.

"No, Father, but thank you. Perun will have his own punishment. The Tuatha Dé Danann should not be trying to destroy others without provocation. He lost. That is enough."

"Aye." Neit slipped his arm around her. "The Morrigan will not be in the way of liking it, but aye."

Clea and her family had helped Griffin with his Challenge. She was no longer needed. Their paths now diverged. He would go back to the life he had before his Challenge. She had a new one of her own to start. Clea nodded at Neit and slipped her hand into Cormac's.

"Let's go home," she said.

Chapter Seventeen

"Where am I?" Even as he asked it, Griff knew the answer. Iceland. The soft familiarity of his own bed, the high-beamed ceilings and the drift of snow outside the windows told him that. Gingerly, he raised himself up and felt no pain. There did not appear to be any serious after-effects of the lightning that had coursed through his body, more than mortals and many paranormals could stand, and almost too much even for the air Elemental. Griff reached out, gripped the side of the bed, and hauled himself to his feet. He was naked except for a small pair of shorts. His wings moved slower than he would like. They would take a little time to get up to top condition again.

Einar was hovering a foot off the ground by the bed. He appeared as concerned as the placid otherworldly being could look. Gratitude flooded Griff. His friend had not let him down.

"Welcome back," Einar said.

Griff swallowed. He was thirsty and hungry. He thought he'd been out for a few hours, but if he was home then it had to be longer. He was home, and they had done it. They had defeated Amai, for the time being. It was over, unless there was a final battle. He had completed his part for the Elementals. He had faced his Challenge and won.

Where was Clea?

"Bahamut, the whale that is not a whale brought you back to Iceland," Einar said. "We carried you home. Were your sleep-demon dreams interesting? You shouted as you healed."

The Huldufólk had helped him? Griff stared at Einar. He hadn't expected that of the legendary Icelandic creatures. Apparently even now he had something to learn about the nature of the beings. He wouldn't take Einar for granted again. Love and friendship had sustained him, even though he had destroyed any chance for happiness by lying to Clea.

"Grazie, Einar. I'm glad to be home." He hoped his voice showed his sincerity, but just in case, Griff reinforced it with his mind. Einar grinned and bobbed his head. The Huldufólk seemed pleased.

"My dreams? They were curioso," Griff said. His feet were bare. His wings were a darker yellow than normal and his balance seemed off, as if he was experiencing the human sensation known as vertigo. It would take some time to recover, but winning his Challenge should give him that time. Without Clea and her family, he would have failed. Without Clea, Amai would have won and great sweeps of Europe would have been destroyed. The loss would have been devastating, but more than that, it would have meant that final Challenge was assured.

"Why did you send us to Luxembourg?"

Einar gave Griff a sharp glance as if that was not the question he had expected. He sank nearer to the ground but didn't land.

"You had become too isolated," Einar said without inflection. "It was time to get you out of Iceland and focused on your Challenge." He gave Griff a long stare. "Even if it meant losing you as a friend."

Griff considered this for a moment. It was true that if Einar had not sent them on the quest to Luxembourg he may not have left Iceland. He imagined he'd been doing fine with his life, but he had been wrong. Clea had filled a part of him he hadn't known was empty, and he had thrown it away.

"Thank you," he said simply. "You did not lose a friend. I am returned."

Einar said nothing.

"Where is Clea?"

Einar studied his feet floating in front of him. Griff scanned the mind link and didn't feel Clea's touch. She had declared her love, and he hadn't responded. She and her family had come to his aid, and he had won his Challenge. But once that was done, there had been no reason for her to stay with him. He had lied to her, and it was over.

Her bravery and intelligence at figuring out that the basket was part of Amai's power humbled him. She had jumped inside the basket without fear and taken action.

Amai had been wounded but not vanquished. Griff had seen his counterpart vanish into the sky, but he was sure to reappear for the next encounter. Without his basket, Griff didn't think his old foe would be quite the same. He didn't know how long it would take to repair the thing, but if there was a final Challenge, Amai might not be as effective. It was the best Griff could hope for.

The lightning had struck him hard, propelled by air and weather talents. Knowing others had helped Amai didn't stop Griffin from being dismayed he had been taken out so easily. He would need to be better prepared next time. He would need to find out who else had helped Amai. His enemies were greater than he had imagined; Perun, the head of the Slavic pantheon was among them.

Einar told him Europe would survive this storm that was now just a storm. There had been no way to escape the rain and wind across much of Europe. The weather forecasters were trying to figure out how the hurricane had dissipated almost in an instant. They would never discover the truth, but they would come up with a plausible theory that humans would believe. Hurricane Impossible would be explained, in the way humans did when something paranormal surfaced. They came up with a concept that fit human minds, and the mortals, with their ability to see and then dismiss what they did not understand, would be satisfied. Griff didn't care.

He had won his Challenge, and lost everything.

He had told Clea they would talk afterwards, which meant Patrik, and now that meant nothing. She no longer needed an Elemental who could not tell her the truth. She had left him, and that was appropriate. In the end, he was only an Elemental and she was a goddess. Despite all that, she loved him, and he had held his tongue, telling his stupid self that there would be time afterward. But there had not been. There never would be now.

Clea was gone.

Einar gave him a look that was almost human on his perfect face.

"I feel the defeat in you, Elemental. I do not pretend to understand your ways, or the ways of the gods, but I am disappointed. Are you giving up so easily?"

The unexpected rebuke made a flash of anger sear through him. Griff staggered as legs still wobbly from the fight threatened to give out. Spreading his wings, he managed to keep his balance.

"I won my battle," he said, his voice edged with steel.

"It is not Challenge I speak of." Einar made a gesture upward that encompassed the sky. "Although there is perhaps a piece of Challenge in all things, including your goddess."

Griff had never been able to read Einar's mind, and today was no exception.

"I killed her brother. I lied to her. She only stayed at the end to help with Challenge and defeat the Demonos. It was her sense of honor, and not her love for me, that kept her there. My lies killed her love."

Einar's full belly laugh made Griffin's wings shoot up. There was a touch of something impossibly old in that laugh.

"You are not the Elemental I thought you were if you would let that stop you. Do you not fight for what you want, Griffin? You would just let her walk away? No, Elemental, I cannot believe that of you. You are not so weak. You are powerful, and you go for what you want. Anything less is a failure. Your failure."

* * * * *

Ireland was not that different from her Czech Republic roots. Clea liked the quaint village where her Tuathan relatives lived. Power rumbled under the surface, but the face it presented to the world was one of quiet living, pleasant and unhurried. Just like the town she lived in as a member of the Slavic pantheon, the Tuatha Dé Danann home was overlooked by humans, forgotten as if it turned sideways and vanished when they weren't looking.

The Tuathan Treasures had come back to them after the battle and had gone to the Morrigan. They had been hidden away, protected by Badb, Macha, and Nemain. Clea had liked the feeling of that sword in her hand. She would ask about training in its use soon. It would be necessary to know how to wield the weapons of her heritage, as well as the other Tuathan gifts that lived with their pantheon. They had served their purpose in the Challenge. Their part in the Elementals' battle was done, but she was not done with them.

She had a lot to learn about her brother Cormac and her Tuathan side. She wasn't sure how she felt about the three Morrigan goddesses. Her father was a ruler in a different way than Perun was. Less domineering, but still the clear leader, with an open hand and generous nature. The idea that for the first time in her long life she had a real father still stunned her at times. The Morrigan were kin as well. She would have to embrace them and learn their gifts. She had lost a brother in the last Challenge and gained a family in this one.

Perun had been on the losing side of Challenge, and was not taking it well. She was no longer in danger from him. Her mother had opted to stay with her god, to Clea's surprise. Then again, Dodola was what she was. In the end she had come through when Clea needed her. What Dodola would do next, with a leader who had chosen to side with the Demonos, was anyone's guess.

Clea glanced around her, enjoying the scenery. It had been a long time since she'd made one place home. A sense of rightness filled her at the knowledge that she was welcome here. It wasn't the Czech Republic, and it wasn't with Griff, but this was as much home as she had ever found. She would stay and enjoy this place for a while. No amount of being a goddess could change what a man did. Love didn't couch itself in gods and mortals. It was beyond paranormal, and just as inscrutable.

She wandered because she had never found a place she could call home. Now she would have the chance to find out if Ireland was right. It might be that she liked roving for itself, the ability to discover new places. The world was big and there was much to see.

Clea smiled at her brother. He had chosen to look like a hero warrior, and his square chin and features suited that role. She could imagine him on a hilltop surveying his wins. The resemblance between them and their father would always be the same shade of hair. Neither would ever change that.

She let out a small sigh at the sharp pain that lanced through her at the thought of her brief lover. Dodola would have had no way of knowing what would happen when she sent Clea to Griff. Clea had been the difference between the Elemental win and loss.

Cormac touched her mind, and she widened her smile, displaying emotion she did not feel. The Tuatha Dé Danann were without the political maneuvering she was used to. Theirs was the powers of the land and the sky, and she would embrace those talents in herself as well.

"I'm fine, brother," she said, glancing at him. They had on jeans and simple wool sweaters, a nod to the chill that was in the air. This part of Ireland was cool most mornings. She had spent time in colder climates in recent years, and was used to the chillier weather. Sort of.

"Aye, I know." He cuffed her on the arm. "I am just checking, so I am."

It had been hard to let Griff go with the whale. There would have been ways to get him back to Iceland via human means, but the humans may have raised questions that none of the people couriering him would want to answer. His Challenge was done, he had won, and her journey with him was at an end. This way there was no need for protracted goodbyes, no long explanations, just a clean break and a step forward into her new life. Even if the memory of her brother hadn't stood between them, it would have still been time to go.

Cormac and Clea entered a clearing with a small stone bench at the back of the dell. It was a wide field, often used for gatherings and tournaments. It would be a good place to practice her fighting skills. The few tourists that came their way picnicked there, despite the lack of amenities. There were spots of brown where blankets had been spread. There must have been a recent picnic then, because the brown never lingered. Anu always took care of the grass. Nearby a small stream burbled, rushing toward its destination of River Boyne, once known as Bubindas, where Boann reigned.

She sighed out a breath of regret. She had been too angry to listen before when Griffin had tried to explain. There had been no deception in Griff's telling of the tale, just sadness and regret. He'd done wrong keeping it from her, but she had held onto her anger too long. She'd had a few days to consider the events in Portugal, once the action had calmed down. Being here in Ireland, with her family around her, made her realize how much her grudge had defined her. Even if it had been Amai-te-rangi who had caused Patrik's death, she would need to let go of what happened. Much worse had happened to the Tuatha Dé Danann over the years and yet they lived and loved, not letting old hates mar who they were. She would take a cue from them and move into her new life, putting aside old concerns. Patrik had gotten himself in the middle of the war. Sometimes their kind died. Life was rarely fair.

There was a darkening of the sky as something blocked the sun.

On instinct she looked up. A figure blotted out the light, a form once familiar and beloved. Clea pointed with a shaking hand and Cormac followed her gaze.

Looking every bit an avenging angel, Griffin flew down to them. It was his wings that had obscured the sun, his powerful frame keeping the yellow rays glinting through his feathers at bay.

Clea gasped, blinking. A flicker of hope danced along her nerves, setting her skin on fire.

Together Cormac and Clea watched Griffin descend. He angled his flight so that his feet were aligned with the earth. Landing on the ground without even a thud, Griffin was moving toward them even before he was fully on the soil.

He had on a shirt that matched his eyes. His hair was tossed from the wind; strands from the long braid coming out along the plait. His clothes clung to him in places where the wind had buffeted them. Clea remained still, rooted to the spot in the clearing, as if she were an incipient tree goddess.

Cormac moved in front of her, blocking her view of the Elemental.

"Griffin." Cormac's tone was icy cold, dripping with menace.

She stepped out from behind Cormac, ignoring his warning look. Her brother should know better. He had been raised with the Morrigan, who cowered behind no man. Nobody could fight her battles but her.

"I am in the way of protecting you, deirfiúr."

"I know."

"Clea." Griff's voice was rough and unsteady. "Cormac."

"Griffin," she returned. He still showed some after-effects of the powerful strike of ball lightning that had taken him out. It had been several days, but his wings were a sallow ochre, off their normal vibrant butter yellow. His mind and body still read as weary, and she doubted he was in any shape to fly. As she watched, he folded his wings behind his back until they almost disappeared in the bulk of his body. The hooks at the top and his tail feathers at the bottom peeked out, but that was all.

He was here. Her heart leaped, stuttering in her chest as it began pounding. She kept her thoughts sealed away behind her highest walls. She purposely refused to know what had happened after Bahamut had taken him out of sight. She had hoped that she wouldn't see him for a decade or longer, and when they next met again, he would be only a memory.

"Griff," she said, and was annoyed to find her voice was breathy. "Should you be flying?"

"Cormac." Griff clearly spoke man to man. Elemental to god. Supernatural being to supernatural being. Lover to brother? Her mind whirled. "I need a few minutes with your sister."

Clea couldn't take her gaze off Griffin. They would have seen each other again. Their paths would have crossed at some point, but that time should have been far off. Not yet. Not while her love still beat against her body and mind, a living thing that could not be controlled.

"It's home I'll be. I am after a word with Neit and Badb." Cormac glanced at Griffin. Clea felt Cormac send Griff an image of a bird being mauled by a tiger. She smiled and touched his arm.

The gods in question were old and wise, and Clea doubted they would run to the rescue of a new daughter. They knew the ways of the world better than that. They knew about love, and passion. The Tuatha Dé Danann gods had love, an enduring affection that had stood the test of time. A love she wanted for herself.

"Do that," Griff said, his tone dismissive. He never stopped looking at Clea. He examined her from head to toe before meeting her eyes again. There was a look in the clear blue of his, something powerful and deep. Clea blinked again, her emotions clouded.

"I'll be back shortly, Cormac," she said. "Thank you."

Her brother grunted and raised a hand. He gave Clea one final look and loped off toward the edge of the clearing.

Clea watched him go before turning back to Griffin. She could feel her brother's agitation in his mind, his uncertainty that he was doing the right thing. Part of him wanted to turn back, pluck Clea away from Griffin, and carry her off.

"He's protective," she said. "It's nice."

Griff frowned. She felt him trying to break into their threadbare mind link but refused to let him in. Whatever his reasons for coming, she wanted him to say the words. She had no defense against him if she let him inside. Some things had changed.

"Does he think you need protecting from me?" The eagle that was part of his namesake flickered over his face, beak and feathers advancing and retreating before resolving into his features once again.

"Do I?" Clea crossed her arms.

Griff's frown deepened, his wings fluttering before subsiding across his back again. Even as shielded as she was, Clea tasted his anger at Cormac's interference. There was emotion dancing along his shields, something stronger than she'd ever felt in him before.

"Clea, about Patrik," he said, spreading his hands helplessly, "sono desolato. I was wrong. I should have told you. It was an accident, but that is no excuse. I've been sorry for it every day since it happened."

Clea remained silent for long moments before opening her mouth to speak. "I know, Griffin. I held onto my anger, but it was the loss of him that went deep. I didn't have anyone besides him, and when he died I was so alone. But he chose to try to defend humans and it was a worthy cause. The truth is…" she stopped, cleared her throat. "The truth is that I stayed away from my pantheon, and I wasn't there to help him. My rage is in part self-directed."

His blue gaze bored into hers. "Clea, will you forgive me?" His voice was deep, with an unfamiliar tone.

She was silent for long moments and as she continued to remain quiet, his body language changed from straight and proud to a subtle slump. His feathers drooped and his wings dragged further on the ground.

"I do forgive you, Griff. It wasn't your fault. It was an accident." Clea relaxed her shields a little.

"Grazie," he said, a formal statement. "That means more to me than you will ever know. I would not have succeeded in my Challenge without you. You and your family are responsible for this victory. I owe you more than I can hope to repay."

She uncrossed her arms. "Is that what you came here to do? To thank me? For your stupid Challenge?" Her fury was instantaneous. She launched at him, closing the distance between them to stand in front of him. Her fists balled, and she wanted to hit him, he was so dense. "Do you think I gave a damn about your Challenge? I mean, of course I do. I want to save the humans too, and not because of Patrik. We need them. But I wasn't there for your dumb battle. I stayed, you stupid idiot, for you. You know that. I told you why and it didn't matter. You had nothing to say to me."

She couldn't look at him. Clea turned away, but not before one wing reached out and grazed her shoulder.

She was a goddess. She would not let this defeat her. She was a member of the Tuatha Dé Danann, and of her Slavic pantheon, and she would rise to this occasion. The old uncertain Clea was gone. The new Clea had centuries of tradition behind her.

His wing was still touching her shoulder and it stayed there as she rotated back to look him in the eye. She would hear him out and then dismiss him. It was just a moment in her life, and she would be past it.

"If that's why you came, then here you go. You're welcome. From both my pantheons, you are welcome. You are, of course, in our debt, but that is nothing new to you. There are many ways the Tuatha Dé Danann can use the gratitude of an Elemental."

He opened his mouth to speak, shut it, and then opened it again.

"That isn't why I came," he said. "Grazie di cuore was all I could think of. I flew the entire way here trying to think of a good opening line."

"That was the best you could do?" she scoffed. "You've done better."

"I know." Emotion stirred behind his eyes and in the recesses of his mind.

Clea lowered her shields a little bit more. They were standing so close they could touch, but the only contact was his wing resting on her shoulder. She didn't move to shake it off nor did she advance closer to him.

"Why are you here?" Hope beat a slow pattern in her heart. He continued to probe, reaching for the link that had been such an integral part of them during their race to defeat the Challenge. Still she refused to let him in.

"I've been alive for five hundred years," he said. "I've had hundreds of lovers." Clea winced at the not-subtle reminder of his playboy lifestyle. There were so many ways that he had been unavailable for her, or any woman. "I've been happy with my life, with the way it was structured. Then you came into it and turned it upside down."

She blinked. The hope became a tattoo against her brain, soaring with possibilities. "Go on," she said when he stopped talking.

He pushed a hand through his hair. His other wing came up to rest on her other shoulder and she let it. The warm down of his feathers tickled her skin like a caress.

"You said you loved me. Is that still true?"

Hope fled, replaced with red-hot anger. She wanted to shove his wings off but let them stay. She didn't move. "Unfair, Elemental. I laid my cards out once, and you had nothing to say. I would be an idiot to show them a second time." He probed again, but she batted it away.

He nodded with no surprise on his face. "Sì, it was. I'm sorry. You are beautiful and warm. There will be dozens of men lined up for your hand. You will have your pick of gods. I am just one poor Elemental, a man chosen to fill a role. I don't know how long I will be around. We can be killed. It was Hippocampus last time, but next time it may be me. I would have died in that Challenge if not for you. Amai had me beat, but you saved the day. You deserve better than me. You deserve an immortal god who can guarantee you eternity."

She lowered her shields some more and he was there, probing for a path into her thoughts.

"What I deserve and what I want should be the same thing." He tilted his head like the griffin he was named for in a gesture of noncomprehension. When he still didn't speak, she took both hands and pushed him. He staggered back, his wings breaking free of her body before he regained his balance.

"Damn you, Griffin, say whatever you came here to say. If you love me, then say so. If you don't, then I can handle it. You gave us your thanks and I acknowledged them. Stop playing." Air will glide with air. Her skin felt hot as sensation rushed over her. Not daring to believe, Clea met his gaze, knowing her heart was in her eyes.

He took her in his arms, his wings surrounding her. His skin and feathers were warm from the sun. She wanted to lay her body over his, take him into her. The grass under her feet sprang up higher, as if it was responding to the emotions of the two people standing on it.

"Let me in." He was no longer probing, he was pushing and soaring down their path trying to break his way back in. His mind pummeled at her shields, demanding she give her secrets to him.

She opened their mind link.

Her mind filled with images of the radiant sun, of perfect clouds, of the Earth below him, curving off into the horizon. A field full of flowers and the cool perfection of a glacier. The stars winking through the thin atmosphere when he was high up, beautiful in their cold radiance. A bird building a nest and two horses running together.

"I didn't know," Griff said. "I thought it was over, that you would never forgive me. You said you loved me but that was at an end because of Patrik. I didn't believe the saying, but air does glide with air. I don't want to be alone anymore. Not since you came into my life. Iceland isn't home; no place on earth is. You are my home."

"I love you." The words erupted in her mind, pure and clean, a wash of emotion behind them. They sang through her, clearing away the doubt, the uncertainty, the pain.

"I love you. Ti amo," he repeated out loud, his fingers lingering over her face. "I love who you were and I love who you are. If you still love me, I will do my best to make you the happiest goddess this world has ever seen."

He paused. Clea's lip trembled with the effort not to cry. It was so sweet, this moment, so perfect that she wanted to bottle it. But life couldn't be contained. However long or short, it was to be lived and embraced. Now was their beginning. It would live on only in memory, but she savored it as emotion danced on her tongue. The trees whispered beyond the clearing. The minds of her ancestors, strange and earthen, sang in the leaves.

"I love you," she said and felt relief sag through him. "I didn't know it then but I think I have from the moment you picked me off your mountain in Iceland."

His arms went around her then, and he pulled her so close she was buried in cloth and feathers, passion singing along her nerve endings. In the two hundred and fifty years she'd been on the earth, she had never been so alive.

"I don't know if the others succeeded. If one did not, I will have a last Challenge to face," he said. "When it's done, I will come back for you."

She lifted her head off his powerful chest. "Lorenzo Griffin Traverso, you are not serious. If you think you are facing your final Challenge without me by your side, you are wrong. We're in this together."

"I love you too much to risk you." His voice was flat.

"Don't be medieval. I'm a goddess, not a doll that can be broken. I am not Patrik. You need me. If you love me, then we do it as partners. You and me."

Emotion zinged down their mind link and she let him in all the way. Body and soul she opened to Griffin and felt his love fill her until she thought she would burst.

He studied her for a long time. "What if something happened? I could not bear losing you."

"Goddesses are hard to kill." Unlike their brothers. The pain of Patrik dying would always be there, but she could cherish his memory. "We are one." She waited, her heart thudding.

"Yes," he agreed. "Together. Oh Clea, I didn't know how much I wanted a woman in my life until you showed up on my doorstep." He pressed kisses on her face, licking each small freckle he could until his lips took hers in a kiss of claiming, of belonging.

They heard the sound of footsteps and the mind signatures of Cormac and Neit coming toward them. Displeasure rang in the atmosphere around them. It seemed she was doomed to be surrounded by alpha males in her life. So much for letting her handle it.

"Your father approaches," Griffin said with a smile. "I'll fight him if I have to, but you're coming with me." He caressed her face, his thumb rubbing over her lips. "I won't let you go. Your place is by my side."

"Why don't we stay here for a while? I need to learn more about the Tuathan Treasures if I'm going to be a proper member of this pantheon. It's nice here. I want to know more about this side of my family. I need to understand my heritage," she said. "We can go back to Iceland later."

He nodded. "That is a good plan. Wherever you are is home. I'll stay. We'll learn together, if the Morrigan will let us."

The us in that statement was questionable but would be faced another day. Clea kissed him and his relief and love were in his touch and the soft feel of his lips. He loved her. All that had happened, all that had gone before them, faded away in that reality. They loved each other. Everything else was an afterthought.

Clea smiled up at Griffin's beloved face. This journey had just started. Griff's love, the unbelievable, amazing truth of his love, echoed inside her.

"Let's go," she said.

Hand in hand, they turned to face their destiny together.

About the Author

Claire has written on and off for most of her life, starting with fan fiction when she was very young. She writes across a wide range of genres, and does not consider any of it off limits or out of reach. If a story calls to her, she will write it. She currently lives in Los Angeles and spends her free time writing novels and short stories, as well as doing animal rescue and enjoying the sunshine. Claire's website is www.clairedavon.com.

Interested in being on Claire's mailing list? Signing up is easy! Just go to: http://clairedavon.com/mailing-list/ and you will have access to news, as well as giveaways and special bonus content only available to her subscribers!

Look for these titles by Claire Davon

Now Available:

Elementals' Challenge
Fire Danger

Shifter Wars
No Ordinary Fairy

If you loved this book, then you're sure to love the third book in the series as well! Keep reading for an excerpt of Ondine's story.

WATER FALL
Elementals' Challenge, Book 3

To face the rising wave, she must trust him with her back.

Even without the fish leaping out of the water, Lara would have known the shifter was coming. His mental signature blazed across her consciousness like a comet.

Lara scanned the waves lapping around the marina but saw nothing. That was no surprise. The shark was too smart for that. She could look under the surface if she wanted to, but there was no need. He would show himself soon enough.

"You are looking in the wrong place, Ondine," a strong baritone voice said from behind her. "Has your tenure as the Elemental taught you nothing?"

She slammed her shields down before any sound—or emotion—could slip out. "Sullivan," she said, schooling her face into blank lines before turning. She looked up, way up, into his mocha colored face where taupe eyes shone.

If only he weren't so damned sexy.

The chatter of the marina where her boat was slipped dimmed and vanished. Her high wall removed her ability to hear others but right now she didn't care. The hazard this shifter presented outweighed the inconvenience.

"Ondine."

"You show up in odd places." She congratulated herself on her neutral tone, her true emotions safe behind a mental defense. "I don't recall issuing you an invitation to my waters."

The shifter, in his human form, was three feet away. Clad in board shorts and a t-shirt that proclaimed "Hispaniola, one land, many colors" with an outline of the island that held both Haiti and the Dominican Republic, Sullivan would have appeared relaxed if not for the way his eyes darted from the marina to the water and back to Lara, never staying in one place for long. Standing 6'5", with mocha colored skin and shoulder length dreadlocks, he had a swimmer's build, as if in homage to his other form. While he wasn't strictly good looking—his face was too roughhewn for that—she saw other women on the dock giving him speculative glances as if drawn by his aura. Not that it was any concern of hers.

"An invitation was not necessary."

"Is that so? Do you intrude on all the Elementals like this?"

She was no longer the oceanographer turned youngest Elemental, mortal become paranormal, human to…something else. It had been ten years since she became the water Elemental. Lara drew her brows together, shooting Sullivan a disdainful look. She couldn't afford to look weak in front of the hunter who had been accused of killing her predecessor. A hunter who had always been deadly to her peace of mind, and body.

He bowed as if conceding the point. "My apologies, Elemental. You are correct. I apologize."

"Apology accepted," she said and a look of relief crossed Sullivan's face, one that was at odds with his brash entrance.

"Thank you," Sullivan said. "I need a word."

Sullivan being here meant one thing. Challenge. For better or worse, the time for her to do her part to defend the world against her water Demonos counterpart was on them. She'd sensed a subtle shift in the earth over the last few weeks, like the way pets felt earthquakes. She wanted to believe she was imagining things, but Sullivan's appearance removed that doubt. Lara had been preparing her yacht for ocean travel because of the feeling inside her. Now she knew she hadn't been wrong in thinking the time was coming. It was part of the innate senses that made up her station. The question was: how did Sullivan? She was told early on that Challenge was reserved for Elementals and Demonos.

"I know why you want to talk. Challenge is here," she said, lifting her chin.

"This is not a discussion we should have in public," he said, taking a few steps toward her on the dock. Before he could get too close Lara crossed her arms and sent a warning shot across his senses. Sullivan stopped so fast his feet slapped against the wet wood.

"It is not wise for Elementals to be alone with you, shark king. We die."

As if her words had struck a nerve, the skin on his arms changed to grey hide for a moment before facing back to mocha skin. He said nothing, but his eyes narrowed to slits, and his nostrils flared.

She looked out over the Rehoboth Bay marina, noting that the fish were still agitated by the presence of the predator. They swam in tight circles, some jumping out of the water as if to escape a lurking hunter. Reaching out she felt unfamiliar mind signatures, as well as the more soothing minds of the dolphin pod that made their home near her waters. The dolphins she knew. The others she did not.

"You brought company?"

His smile was as tight as the dreads laying in ropes over his neck.

"I rarely travel without my shiver."

"Unlike me. I travel alone."

"You are the Elemental."

Their handful of brief meetings had left a searing impression on her soul. It was something she kept hidden from the shark who was the only suspect in the killing of her predecessor. It was foolishness to remember the ways the giant man looked naked and buried inside her. It was a comfort that Sullivan didn't know.

"You have my word that I have honorable motives, Ondine. This is important. We must talk."

Ondine. Her Elemental name. She had been able to live in a bubble these last ten years, but that peace was shattered.

"Not here," she said, looking around the dock. Seagulls crowded the planks, searching for morsels left behind by the pleasure craft, undeterred by the scent of shark. Many boats were out on the water, taking advantage of a sunny day. In her time in Dewey Beach, Delaware, Lara had not encouraged her neighbors at her condo or in the boat clubs and most kept their distance. If any were curious about the huge man engaging her in conversation, they didn't show it. This beach town had appealed to her for more than one reason. It had a wild side, with all manner of bachelor parties and a party vibe. If she wanted to pretend to be the twenty-five she still looked, it was the perfect place. What permanent neighbors lived at her complex learned long ago she wasn't interested in friendship. As time went by and she didn't age, it was safer that way.

"That is wise, Elemental. Ondine," Sullivan said, and she knew he was using her Elemental name on purpose, to remind her of her station. A station she hadn't asked for. A station she couldn't resign from.

"Sullivan," she countered, meeting his eyes without flinching.

"Come. We have much to discuss. Challenge is coming. Do you have a restaurant you recommend?"

"Let's stay local. We'll grab a bite here."

Rehoboth Bay Marina Ventures had many restaurants within easy walking distance. Lara chose Que Pasa, a place known for its margaritas and fabulous views. The early dinner crowd would keep intimate conversation to a minimum.

They said little as they made their way to the local restaurant. Lara was aware of Sullivan's presence next to her, a giant of a man who turned more than one head in appreciation. Hers would be turned as well, if she didn't know what he was.

Heat poured off him mixed with a briny, musky scent that reminded her of the Caribbean. It worked with his tall, brawny frame. There was no mistaking his island heritage with his dusky skin and dreads; it was almost a cliché. In his tan t-shirt and board shorts he could have been a surfer catching a wave. But the steely look in his eyes told onlookers that he'd as soon kill you with that board as ride it.

Rumor said that she was the water Elemental as a result of his actions. Ten years ago she knew nothing about Challenges and Elementals or the world that overlay the human world, until the day her mind was filled with the dying cries of something not human. Then dozens of other thoughts started screaming inside her head to be replaced by another, more soothing mind that told her what she needed to know. After a time she believed it. There was a world that she had never known that she was now part of. A world that she was responsible for defending.

Challenge was here. The last time there had been a Challenge the result had been an Elemental loss and World War II. Millions of lives had been taken by the Demonos, their enemies. After that horrific defeat, Challenge wasn't supposed to happen again for another century or so, yet here it was. She had been assuming she had another twenty or thirty years; instead she had no time, if the signs were true.

The restaurant was more packed than she liked but the hostess gave her a friendly look and managed to find them an uncrowded spot in the back. A structure in front of them blocked the view of the ocean and therefore these tables weren't prime spots for the tourists who blanketed the area.

"Can you drink?" Sullivan asked, looking over the selection of margaritas.

She tapped her finger on the menu. "I can drink. I can't get drunk."

Sullivan's grin had a hint of shark in his mouthful of revealed teeth. "Good."

After they had placed their order Lara studied Sullivan from under her lashes. In some ways it was a relief to see him. So many nights she had allowed herself to remember his well-built form and craggy face and wish that he was just Sullivan and she was just Lara and they had met as humans did. Only in the privacy of her own mind did she allow herself to remember that unwise night six years ago. It was a night that had never been repeated; it had been foolish beyond measure in the first place. He was a shark and she was the Elemental. It was ridiculous. Even if he hadn't killed Hippocampus, the idea was absurd. Shifters and Elementals didn't mix.

As if sensing her thoughts, Sullivan lifted his gaze from the menu and met her eyes. A frisson of fear—and something else—went up her spine.

There was a scar over his left eye, bisecting his eyebrow, giving him even more of a dangerous look. He looked like what he was. Killer. King.

"I don't understand the reason for your visit, Sullivan. Challenge is my responsibility. Why are you here?" Lara asked after appetizers were ordered. The sun was beginning to set behind them, reflecting off the ocean in vivid reds and oranges. Even in their out of the way table with themed umbrella, the view was impressive, both near and far.

He licked the salt off his margarita glass and the sight of his tongue shot through Lara's core. Her stomach did a funny flip and she had to look away to the lapping waves several feet beyond them.

Lapping. Tongue.

He took a long draught of the margarita, his Adam's apple working, before setting the glass down and meeting her gaze with his piercing topaz brown eyes.

"You can't face Challenge alone," he said. "I am here to help."

* * * * *

Sullivan straightened, looking at the woman who had been human, and now not. This new Elemental, the one who preferred to be called her human name of Lara, instead of her Elemental name, had caused ripples through the paranormal community when she became the water Elemental. He had been one of them who thought she was too human and too young. Then he spent some time with her. He shook his head to rid himself of those memories. They could only distract him.

The stirring of his cock told him how he could be willingly diverted.

"Help?" Ondine asked. "With Challenge? I don't think so. That's my job, or so I've been told. Elementals work alone. Even if we didn't, I wouldn't turn to you. I don't need help from the shark king."

Sullivan sprawled on the wooden slat chair, his bulk spilling over the too-small seat. He was being intimidating on purpose. He knew what the supernatural community thought. He was the shark king, the one suspected of killing the last Elemental. He could not allow that to get in the way. If the new Elemental could be scared off by a mere shark, she had no chance against her Demonos counterpart. The Iku-Turso, which looked like an octopus but was the size of a blue whale, made him look like a minnow.

He took a sip of the margarita and looked around the restaurant. It was filling up with tourists and rowdy partiers from the local area. Sullivan frowned. It would have been better to do this in private but he knew within seconds she would not allow him on board. He'd force his way if he had to but he needed her cooperation, not her animosity.

"Nonetheless, that is why I am here. I was there during World War II. Not all that died were human. Thousands of shapeshifters in Europe were butchered with the humans. I didn't lose any direct kin but many sharks numbered along the dead. The Elementals' failure to win Challenge paved the way for the deaths. It cannot happen again."

She looked surprised when he mentioned World War II and then grew quiet.

"I didn't realize…" she began and then stopped. "That wasn't me. I wasn't a part of that."

"No," he agreed. "That was Hippocampus, but he is gone and you are Elemental. It is your task now. You haven't been wise with your time. I hear it in the ocean. You fritter this new life away in Dewey Beach instead of preparing for Challenge. You are not ready so I am here. It would be unwise to refuse my help. You need me."

Being charged with killing the previous water Elemental had not bothered him until he met the new one. Then he wished he would see something besides condemnation in her pale green eyes. Then he had. It haunted him.

None of his thoughts showed on his face when he gazed at Ondine. A burn began low in his gut that had nothing to do with the liquor he'd swallowed. Damn it. Being attracted to the young Elemental was the last thing he wanted, yet she had been seared across his soul from the time of their first encounter, until their separation six years ago. He hadn't wanted to leave her then and within moments of being in her presence again he knew nothing had changed. It was one of the reasons he had kept his distance all these years.

"You think I need help with Challenge?"

"I know you do. You've been an Elemental for a paltry ten years and even by human standards are still young. The others count their age in centuries, not decades. They have been through several Challenges and know what to expect. Before Hippocampus was murdered the Elementals had been stable for five hundred years, the last change occurring when the current Griffin became the air Elemental. Your Demonos foe is formidable, and there is no chance you are ready for the Iku-Turso. The ancient sea creature has proven on more than one occasion how deadly she is. Ondine, you cannot do this alone."

Lara averted her gaze. For some reason the other Elementals had not called her out when she did nothing but idle on the East Coast. Perhaps they thought another Challenge was decades off. Now it was here, too soon, and she was unprepared. The Elementals could not lose Challenge again. He would see to it. The world was at stake, and he would be damned if he would let it go down without a fight.

"Whether I can or not, you aren't who I would go to for assistance."

His lips turned up in a tight smile full of teeth and peril. "I wasn't offering you a choice."